COULD'VE BEEN

SAVANNAH GARDINER

STERNCASTLE PUBLISHING
Newport, Oregon

Find more books, buy sweet merch, and support indie publishing:
www.sterncastlepublishing.org/shop

Published by:
Sterncastle Publishing
644 SW Coast Highway #203, Newport, OR 97365
sterncastlepublishing.org
community@sterncastlepublishing.org

Library of Congress Control Number:2024943722

ISBN: 978-1-960120-14-4 (Paperback)
978-1-960120-13-7 (Ebook)

Contents

ONE

The streets hold a level of nostalgia I don't expect. Nowfilled with strip malls and commercial buildings, memories of my youth stillflood the sidewalks. Memories of laughter and joy, but also heartbreak andsorrow.

Friendships are made and broken in unsuspecting places. Noone expects to meet lifelong friends in a school parking lot, and they don'tplan on that parking lot being the spot where they speak to someone for thelast time.

A small group of teenagers stride towards the grocery store.Their infectious joy makes me smile. One of the boys hoists a girl into afireman carry, eliciting a happy shriek from her. She playfully slaps his backand arm, to which he tosses his head back, laughing.

Do they know how fast this can all come to a screechinghalt? Do they realize one of their friends might betray them? Teenagers are sonaïve.

I spot a coffee shop on the other side of the median, justbehind them. It must be new … or maybe I just didn't pay enough attentionwhen I visited last Christmas. "Brewtiful Day" is written in large,looping letters with a sun rising behind the words. Once the light turns green,I make a U-turn despite the sign telling me not to and enter the parking area alittle harder than expected. Whoops. No flashing red and blue lights in myrearview. Not sure why I expected any. The cops are probably in the KampingWorld parking lot, circling the campers and talking to each other through openwindows.

With only five or six cars, it's a lot slower than theStarbucks across the street. Though I enjoy a Frappuccino as much as any basicbitch, I made a promise to myself to try new things. It's not my adventurousspirit making me step outside my comfort zone, it's necessity. But if I candrink the sludge from a campaign office, I can drink anything.

My paint-splattered yellow Converse hit the pavement when Iget out of the car, and just my luck … I step on sticky gum melting in thesun.

Fuck. What am I doing here? Ripped jeans, yesterday'smascara, and a disaster of a top knot accurately portray my mood. I'm a mess.Renovations aren't exactly going smoothly at the new house.

I should just go home and make myself coffee, except thatwould require me to figure out which box the Keurig is in. I wish this could bequick. In and out. No small talk, no making eye contact with anyone.

Walking through the doors, I look around, not really surewhat I'm expecting to see. Every coffee shop is basically the same. Wobblyblack tables, wooden chairs, and some indie versions of normal songs quietlyplaying in the background. A few people wait in line, but they must be gettingit to go since they're all standing with eyes glued to their phones and keys intheir hands, ready to bolt at the sound of their name.

I used to be that person. Always anxious to move on to thenext task of the day. As though moving quickly could somehow guarantee successand happiness. I want to warn them to slow the fuck down. That running yourselfragged is not the key to a fulfilling life. Thinking better of the idea, I holdmy tongue, not wanting to be the messy <u>and</u> crazy lady.

I made the choice to not be one of those people anymore, sotoday I'm going to sit and work on my laptop. Now I feel like a hipster whobrags about how much they love working from the local coffee shop. I am not ahipster nor am I cool. I just don't have reliable WIFI in the house yet.

Jenn and Dre have offered their house and WIFI, but I'mstill avoiding them, which is stupid since they're the only friends I stillhave in this town. Of all the ways I've evolved over the years, pride is stillmy downfall. I refuse to be pitied by them, the woman who returned with hertail between her legs. The girl who left with the promise of never lookingback, landing right back where it all began. Small towns are like undertows,they will drag you down with them until you quit fighting and just die.

Spotting a small round table at the center of the room, Itake a seat and pull my laptop out of my bag. I'll look busy, even if I'm onlyscrolling Facebook. The screen lights up and notifications ping one afteranother. All eyes move to me as I scramble to silence the never-ending dings.

One hundred and fifty-six unread emails in my office inbox.Fuck. I've spent the last two weeks using my lack of internet as an excuse, andnow I'm insanely behind. Joanne's email says she's looking for the analysiscomparing ten years of poll numbers regarding property tax in the state ofWyoming. I still have three days, but she always wants everything long beforethe deadline, which is not something I'm capable of. I'm more along the linesof an e-mail it to you ten minutes before the deadline. I thrive on thelast-minute stress.

"Liv?"

The hesitant voice has me lifting my eyes to the counter,expecting the barista to be holding my iced coffee. No unclaimed cup and thebarista is nowhere to be seen.

"Oh my God, Olivia?"

This time I pay attention to where the voice comes from andlook to the table next to the window.

His voice straightens my spine. A voice that evokes tearsthat have long since dried. I can't quite make out all the features on his facewith the sun glaring behind him. I don't need to, though. I could havedescribed him down to the cowlick in his eyebrow.

He stands. Jake. <u>My Jake.</u> I haven't seen himsince graduation, and we haven't talked in even longer. But once upon a time,he was mine.

"Hey you." It's instinctual, left over from a lostlife. Is this greeting still etched in his mind the way it is in mine?Flustered, I stumble out of my chair, stretching to look up into hisface.

No longer a grungy skater boy wearing thrift shop finds,he's in a tailored suit. And judging from the fabric, it looks like a prettyexpensive suit. He's traded in a shaggy mop for a shorter style that doesn'thide his eyes. They're still as blue as I remember, now framed with just a hintof lines that aren't quite wrinkles yet. He looks exactly the same—well, if Ilook past the hair, the clothes, and the acne-free skin which now sports aperfectly full, trimmed beard.

I'm in awe and have to force my hand down because I can'tjust go around touching people's faces.

He holds his arms open wide for a hug. What the hell?Considering how we left things, a hug is out of the question. It's even more

inappropriate than my thinking about touching his beard. Hiseyes draw together, bringing the inside corners of his eyebrows up and in sothey're nearly touching. I've seen this look before, when he's bracing himselffor something unpleasant. This definitely adds to my apprehension, butmaybe a hug will remind us of why we were friends in the first place. Fifteenyears is a long time to hold a grudge. Maybe it will help usforget why we are no longer friends. I move in towards the offer of his embrace, pushing aside the dread churning in my gut.

With only inches between us, the barista loudly calls, "Liv?"

Thank God. I hold up a finger to Jake and sidestep towards the counter to retrieve my drink.

A wave of relief rolls through me. Hugging Jake would be the least genuine move on both our parts. We said things we can't take back, no matter how much time has passed.

The last time we spoke, Jake and Ben were standing near the front of Jake's Jeep, concern visible long before I could make out the words in their hushed voices.

"Hey, what's wrong?" I moved to complete the triangle, looking up into both of their faces, attempting to read what they weren't saying.

"Liv, you should probably get a ride home with someone else," Ben suggested.

Turning to gesture to the now barren parking lot, I returned his stare with one of my own. "Oh? And who would you suggest?"

"Maybe someone you're <u>not</u> willing to sell out like a fucking rat." Jake spat as he threw the accusation, knocking me back.

"I'm so confused. What happened?" My breathing was ragged and panicked. I was missing something big.

"I <u>told</u> you I didn't want to get CPS involved," Jake shouted, moving closer so I had to strain my neck to keep eye contact.

"I <u>know</u> you don't. I still think we should but—"

"There is no <u>we,</u> Liv. This has nothing to do with you. It never did."

The years of friendship seemed suddenly in question as his anger began to boil over.

"Seeing you limp, tending to the cuts and bruises, holding you as you cry. None of that has <u>anything</u> to do with me? I didn't know it all meant so little to you, Jake. What the hell?"

"It meant <u>everything</u> to me, Liv!" His shout bounces between the few remaining cars. "That's why I don't understand why you would go behind my back, instead of talking to me."

"Behind your back? I've never once said <u>anything</u> behind your back that I wouldn't say to your face, Jake Larson. I'll just walk home and let you figure your shit out."

The way we left things that day, I really don't know what the hell is going through his head right now, but you don't just jump right back in like nothing happened. Assuming the worst in me was a complete doublecross, and I never bothered to wait for his apology. A hug can't erasethat.

Turning back from the counter, coffee in hand, I look Jakeup and down as he makes himself comfortable at <u>my</u> table. Sliding mylaptop away to make a space for his cup. Asshole. Despite the lingering angerand annoyance, I still feel that little spark for him.

The lanky, awkward boy has certainly grown into himself. Hehas an air of confidence and rigidity as he fiddles with the cardboard sleeveof his cup, sliding it down and back up to its snug position in the middle.He's nervous. Maybe as nervous as I am.

I sit down across from him with a warm smile. Setting myplastic cup to the side, I close my laptop, not wanting to seem rude ordistracted. Since he's not making any effort to start a conversation heinitiated in the first place, I say in my sweetest voice, "It's goodto see you. It's been an eternity."

It <u>is</u> good to see him.

He attempts to match my smile but is unsuccessful. Instead,I get a crooked smile that reaches the scar just below his left eye, causing itto

dimple. He always told people it was the result of a fishinghook mishap, but I know the truth. His dad gave it to him. It wouldn't havescarred as badly if he'd listened to me and gone to the hospital for stitches.The super glue worked, but the scar is worse than it had to be. Even though ithas faded since the last time I saw it.

Though this isn't the wide, infectious grin I loved, I'mhappy to take whatever smile he's willing to offer me.

"What are you doing here? I heard you were living inlike Florida or Georgia."

"D.C." Does he really not know where I've been forthe last decade or is he just trying to make it seem as though he doesn't careenough to be accurate? "I actually just moved back to town. I've been backlike three weeks now, but I'm finally getting unpacked enough to venture out ofthe house. At least for coffee." I hold up my cup in a mock cheers beforetaking a sip. Jake doesn't respond, he just nods his head. Nervousness bubblesin my stomach, maybe it's getting him too. Apparently, I'll have to keep talkinguntil he loosens up, but I'm not sure this new Jake is capable of that. He'sthe one who approached <u>me</u>, not the other way around, so it gives mea glimmer of hope.

Jake sits in complete silence, staring at me with an oddglint in his eyes. I've never seen this look on him before. It's unsettling. Ihave no choice but to continue blabbing like an idiot, unable to sit in thesilence.

"It's crazy seeing you. I haven't seen anyone from highschool, except Andie and Jenn, in like years."

He nods but says nothing. Clenching my jaw, I fight the urgeto call him out and ask why he came over here if he has absolutely no interestin actually trying to be friendly. He could have pretended not to recognize me,just like he pretended I didn't exist after things went south between us.Anything is preferable to this weighted silence. We're adults now, and he'smaking me feel like an angry teen again.

"What are you up to these days? You look good!" Itry to get some sort of response from him, but I'm quickly losing faith in hisability to carry on a civilized discussion. It was one thing when I thought hewas coming over to bury the hatchet or catch up. But this is ridiculous, it'slike talking to a wall.

Enough of this. I need to find a way <u>out</u> of thispathetic excuse of a conversation. Just as I place my hand on the chair tosteady myself to stand, Jake breaks his silence.

"I come here almost every morning. My office is righton the other side of the parking lot." He gestures vaguely in thedirection of the strip of businesses spanning a solid block. A block that hadonce been a pasture filled with cows and one token llama. "I can honestlysay that I never expected to run into you, and here of all places." Whilehe doesn't say the exact words, I can tell my return isn't exactly a welcomeone. He's acting like he has some sort of claim on this town.

I want to yell and say it's a free country and I can gowherever I want. I don't yell it, but I really want to. I just sit quietly, andI feel like this is growth, because not long ago I would have done it without asecond thought.

As badly as I want him to leave the past where it is, Isuppose we're bound to see each other around town. Quashing the bad bloodbetween us would make life in Coburg significantly easier if we could simplysmile and wave, keeping a respectable distance from each other for the rest offorever.

"I just wanted to let you know that I'm—" I wantto apologize for how things ended, but I can't find the words when I look athim from across the table. My hands wrap around my iced coffee. Thecondensation on the cup makes my hands feel less clammy.

"I know." Jake looks down at his steaming cup,refusing to meet my eyes. "I know," he repeats even morequietly.

We hurt each other and never looked back to see how ouractions affected the other or ourselves.

Jake reaches across the table and touches my hand in areassuring gesture. Smiling at the olive branch, I gasp when I feel the shockjolt through my body. Jake's eyes search mine as his hand makes contact withmine.

Fear and bewilderment fill my gaze as the electricity movesbetween us, realizing too late that this isn't electricity.

Two

I'm sitting upright but I feel like Alice, plummeting down the rabbit hole. The windows of the coffee shop blur and fill with a blinding light. My eyes remain fixed on Jake. All those years he was my metaphorical anchor, and now his eyes are the only thing <u>not</u> spinning. He doesn't look as scared as I feel, he's cool as a cucumber.

His eyes hold mine as we spin out of the coffee shop and into a memory that plays out starkly different from what had actually taken place eighteen years before, when I'd held Jake's hands in my own and ended things, asking for time, time to heal, time adjust. The memory of the actual event fades as I become immersed as an observer in this new memory of an alternate reality.

Standing at the bottom of the stairs of our high school's front door, my hands hold Jake's tightly. I wasted our entire lunch date worrying about this conversation, and now I'm rushed to do it before my courage completely disappears. The hallway clears as everyone makes their way to their fifth-period classes. I'm going to be late to geometry—the fourth time this semester—which means I'll land in detention later. Great. At least that will give me uninterrupted study time.

Jake pulls me into his chest, his mouth slightly open and moving towards mine making me flinch. I pull back to meet his eager eyes, desperate to do this without ruining the friendship we've spent a lifetime building.

"Can we slow down, Jake? I just feel ..." The last word struggles to leave my mouth. "Smothered." It's blunt and probably a little mean, but I know that anything less to the point and he won't quite get it. It wasn't even anything Jake was doing that made me feel smothered. I agreed to be his girlfriend before I was ready to be <u>anyone's</u> girlfriend. Before I healed.

"I'm sorry. I had no idea..." understanding crosses his face "...well, I guess I had a bit of an idea after last night, but I ... yeah. Of course. We can take this as slow as you need." I practically ran away when he'd kissed me the night before and cried for an hour in the shower afterward. Kissing Jake should have been exciting, not triggering, and there is no way to explain that to Jake without telling him <u>everything</u> that happened, and I can't do that. Saying it all out loud would mean admitting to myself that it actually happened. That I was so weak that I let someone hurt me. That I am still letting it keep me from being happy.

"I think if we just slow down a little, I can catch up to where you already are." This is the benefit of dating my best friend. I can talk to him in a way I can't talk to anyone else. He doesn't take things personally. It helps that he's been in love with me for years, so asking him to slow down is something he'll do to try and make this work. He wants this to work more than I've wanted anything. I've never felt the same intensity about Jake, I still don't know that I do, but there is an inherent safety in being with Jake.

"I want you to feel safe. We can go as slow as you need. Okay?" He repeats, nodding reassuringly at me, and I can't help but smile even as the tears prick at my eyes.

I've been terrified for days that this conversation would result in losing my best friend. The person who holds my most treasured secrets of adolescence.

The knot in my stomach releases into a wave of serotonin, relaxing every muscle from my center out to the tips of my fingers. My finger-crushing grip on Jake's hands loosens, and I watch as the color returns under his nails. Jake leans down and kisses me softly on the forehead. Not as my boyfriend, but as my best friend. For the first time since I met Jake four years ago, I feel excited at the possibility of something more with him.

Then everything becomes blindingly bright, the memory bursting into thousands of fractals as they scatter, twisting and turning, piecing together a different memory entirely. I try to search for Jake, to anchor myself to something real. That wasn't how that day played out, and now it seems, we're moving through memories that aren't even based on real events. This is the path we would have gone down if, in that pivotal moment, I'd stayed with Jake rather than breaking up with him as I'd done.

Winter has passed leaving us on a stifling summer day in my backyard. Jake, Ben, and I sit around the table situated on the cobblestone patio my dad paid Jake and Ben to build for my mom earlier that spring. Three giant bags of Doritos and an open pack of Oreos sit on the table. The Igloo cooler filled with ice and soda cans rests on the ground between Jake and me. My mom thinks summers are meant to be spent outdoors. Scratch that. They are meant for me to spend outdoors. My mom stays parked in front of her sewing matching with the oscillating fan pointing directly at her.

It's our first summer with a vehicle, and I still can't quite figure out why we are hanging out in my backyard instead of driving to he beach or the lake or exploring some off-road trail, getting stuck, and spending all day trying to un-stuck us. Jake takes a sip from his Mountain Dew.

"What's the point of anti-skip, if it's still going to skip?" Ben's made this argument countless times, upset that no matter how much he spends on a Discman when he taps the top of it, the music jumps. I got him a Walkman, only kind of joking, for his birthday after the idiot tried to go for a run with his Discman and ended up throwing it in the path of a cement truck.

I hold my hands up, surrendering. "Get an iPod." A ridiculous suggestion. None of us have four hundred bucks to splurge on one, even with Ben's summer job at his uncle's construction company. He's saving up for a car so he can quit sharing one with his mom.

"Those are a fad Liv. I like having a binder of my music I can physically hold. Give it a year, and that white brick will be forgotten." Always resistant to change, Ben brushes off my suggestion. His bike is practically falling apart because even changing tires makes him feel like he's betraying the old tires that took him so far. He's probably going to buy a car without automatic windows because his mom's car doesn't have them and getting them would be crazy. He's crazy.

I roll my eyes and throw a Dorito across the round green wrought iron table at him. The chip bounces off his forehead, sliding down the side of his nose and into the neck of his T-shirt. Lifting the bottom of his shirt up to his chin, he plucks the chip off of his ab muscles and pops it into his mouth with a wink and a smile. I'm not sure when he got ab muscles, but he has a lot of them. Jake does too. My body must have missed that memo. I have pretty decent calf muscles, but no one seems to think those are as attractive as ab muscles. I get it, but also, they just won the muscle lottery and still think they deserve them. I think I deserve abs as much as they do, but oh well.

"So my parents canceled our trip back to California for the fourth. What's the plan?" I'm tired of Ben's technology and money ranting, and it's the first time that I've ever been given the go-ahead to hang out with friends for the Fourth of July. No more sparklers and baby cousins for me.

But a look passes between them. I take a sip from my can of Mountain Dew, giving them a second to figure out who's going to tell me something. Their shared look is obvious, but the silent conversation they're having is lost on me. "What?"

Moments like these remind me I'm the third wheel to a duo that was established in the early years of their life, long before I moved to town.

"Nothing, it's just ... usually Jake and I spend the fourth fishing at the lake," Ben says without breaking eye contact with Jake.

"I've never been fishing." The words are out of my mouth before I even really hear what he said to me. God, always putting my foot in my mouth. Now I have to figure out a way to not feel like a dumbass. Ben was clear. I am <u>not</u> invited. Best to just backtrack and turn them down before they have a chance to turn <u>me</u> down. "Maybe you guys could take me some time. Not on the fourth, obviously, but sometime before school starts back up."

Maybe, if I take my book and move to the hammock, it will take any leftover pressure to invite me away. The hammock is <u>our</u> spot. Our place in the world which no one knows about. I mean yeah, Ben knows about it, and obviously my parents. It's a hammock, not an underground clubhouse. But no one uses it but Jake and I. It's been our place since long before we were ever a thing. Sitting unsuspecting in the corner of the yard, just past the hydrangea bushes, and under the shade of the large cedar.

I can still hear the murmur of their voices as they continue their conversation. They're arguing about who has to come over to talk to me. Shit. Why can't they just leave my awkward self-invite alone? Now I have to act like I didn't want to go anyway. I mean, I'm bummed that I have to figure out some other plan for the holiday. I <u>don't</u> want to get stuck being the only person under forty at the barbecue my parents offered to drag me to.

As I slide onto the edge of the hammock, I catch Jake's eye before falling back into the embrace of the fabric. I don't know why it took me so long to realize how perfect he is for me. Side to side I sway, mentally berating myself for allowing our friendship to cloud my view of him. Six months ago his touch or kiss as anything more than friends was gross to imagine. Now, even with him only being across the yard, I need it to be him who crosses the distance to come talk to me. I need him to be close enough to touch. I don't know why I brought my book with me. I have absolutely no intention of reading.

He reads my mind. Jake pulls the book from my hand and gently tosses it onto the ground. He climbs into the hammock, His weight forces us both in towards the center, and now we're facing each other. Hips to hips, chest to chest, and practically nose to nose.

I'm more than a foot shorter than him, and most of that height difference is in our legs, so lying down is the only way this is possible.

My heart races as he tilts his head and moves in for a kiss. If I'd known how exhilarating kissing Jake was, I would have done it years ago.

"I'm sorry I didn't tell you about the fourth before. I just thought you already knew." Jake's apology is unnecessary.

"I was going to be gone anyway. It's totally fine, don't sweat it!" I'm not about to be <u>that</u> girl who insists her boyfriend ditches his best friend, his <u>other</u> best friend. I'll take the snub without any indication I'm disappointed.

"We've gone up there every year since we were in second grade. Ben's dad used to take us up there ..."

"And now you guys continue the tradition on your own." We don't have to say <u>why</u> they have to continue it on their own. We don't need to drudge up the terrible reality that Ben's dad can't take them because he's dead. "Go and have fun! Seriously, it's not a big deal. Andie was already planning on a big backyard BBQ. Her dad got a ton of fireworks from the reservation, so it's gonna be big! It's <u>you</u> who's going to miss out." I have no idea if Andie is throwing a party, she probably is, because she always does, even if she doesn't, I'm not going to tell him that. I don't know why I add the last part. Now he's going to get ideas.

Moving his hand through my hair, he pulls my face to his. Eyes closed, I feel the sparks as he kisses my mouth, the tip of my nose, forehead, and cheeks all while repeating, "You're the best," between each kiss.

It's taken months for me to be in a place where I feel remotely comfortable with even the smallest acts of intimacy. There is no way Jake could have known how long my road to recovery would actually be when he agreed to pump the brakes and slow down. That would require him to know the extent of what happened with Aaron. My eyes are still closed, but I can feel him staring at me. I crack one eye and see his goofy grin.

"Unless you were planning to hmm-hmm on the fourth. Then Ben will be on his own." He thrusts his hips in case I somehow missed the meaning of hmm-hmm.

Sleeping with Jake will change our relationship forever. There will be no more going back to being friends if things don't work out. I can't risk losing my boyfriend <u>and</u> my best friend. Jake made it clear he had crossed that threshold months ago. Convinced that we will either be all or nothing. The decision of when to move to the next step is mine. It's a <u>lot</u> of pressure. And no matter how much he teases me, I know he'll wait as long as I need him to. Which, honestly, I don't think is going to be too much longer. I think I can be ready. I just need the moment to be right.

"No, Jake Larson, I was not planning to hmm-hmm." I push his shoulder with the heel of my hand.

"Worth a shot!" He laughs and kisses me again. This kiss is slower, more intimate, as if he's trying to convince me.

The fabric is pulled out from underneath and I'm falling. Laughter from Ben drowns out my scream as Jake and I fall onto the moss and dirt below. Ben attempts to escape, but Jake grabs his ankle with a grunt of amusement. He didn't land varsity receiver as a junior for nothing. Jake is fast.

The two are in an all-out brawl, hands grasping for a hold on the other. Arms and legs twisting around each other so I can't see where Jake ends and Ben begins. I step over them, feeling a chuckle rise in my chest.

The memory shatters just as the last one had, the laughter still audible as the daylight dwindles.

The reflection of the moon dances on the surface of the lake, giving it some extra pizazz on top of the larger-than-life gold orb it is mirroring. I've hinted for days that I want to go somewhere to see the supermoon. Jake showed up just before dinner, asking permission to take me out for a moonlit picnic, I knew it would be special, but I didn't expect _two_ supermoons. This is incredible. My parents agreed quickly, without any questions or interest in where we were going, or even when we'd be back. Sometimes it's kind of nice having parents who don't really seem to give a shit.

We'd shown up to the lake, outfitted with a large blanket, lanterns, and a basket filled with cheeses, meats, crackers, and fruit.

"Do you hear that?" I ask, moving my plate aside and lying back on the blanket.

"I just hear the water."

The water laps against the pebbles, softly shifting them so they click against each other with each breath of the water. We lie shoulder to shoulder, our fingers loosely intertwined. "Exactly. It's so peaceful."

"I could fall asleep to this." His eyes are closed. I don't need to look over to confirm, his voice is softer when his eyes are closed.

"Where would the fun in that be?" I move a finger across his own in what I hope will be a hint.

"Hmm?"

Swinging my leg over Jake, I straddle him. The nerves I've been feeling since we arrived are twisting into a terrified excitement. We're really going to do this. "I mean, we're all alone. We've got this romantic moonlit lake ... it would be a shame to waste it on sleep."

"Got any ideas?" Jake asks, catching on but not coming outright to say it. Always the gentleman.

"A few." I lower my face to his.

The memory leaves the intimacy of the lake, shifting instead to the bright lights on the sidelines of the football field.

Jake's Sheldon High football hoodie hangs down to my knees. He stands from the bench and grabs his helmet, turning to shoot me a wink. God what that wink does to me. I melt. After months of worrying about

what sleeping with Jake would do to our friendship, it's somehow brought us closer than we both thought possible. We sneak out after our parents are asleep and lie on the hammock, intertwined in each other's arms we talk about everything and nothing. The last two weeks have perhaps been the best two weeks of my life.

Normally, when something <u>huge</u> happens in my life, I tell Jake. But he already knows all about this. I was about to burst, so I confided in Jenn the second we were alone.

"Like did <u>it?</u>" Jenn's red hair twists in front of her face, trapping the secret she's just been given.

I press my lips between my teeth to stifle the smile from growing any wider, though my cheeks are warming enough to give me away.

"It's about time! I can't believe you guys didn't do <u>it </u>years ago. Ugh, those condoms they gave us are impossible to open though, right?"

"We weren't exactly planning on anything happening, so..." I foolishly thought by <u>bringing</u> condoms, it would seem less spontaneous and romantic. And Jake apparently quit carrying them months ago, resigned that I would keep him a virgin forever.

"Oh my god, you're pregnant." She says this loud enough that I can feel eyes moving to us.

"Shh, I'm not pregnant," I whisper, hoping Jenn will catch some of my discretion.

"You're pregnant." She repeats in a hushed tone.

"No, I'm going to take the morning-after pill."

"Liv! It's too late for that. It's called the <u>morning-after</u> pill for a reason."

"I'm not pregnant." I <u>meant</u> to take the morning-after pill sooner, but I just haven't found time to run to the store away from town, where everyone wouldn't watch my every purchase. I was also under the impression I could take it any time <u>before</u> my period. I thought "morning after" was just a name. Apparently, I'm wrong about that too.

"Okay ..." I don't miss the sarcastic tone in Jenn's voice.

Dre throws the ball downfield into Jake's unguarded arms. The bleachers erupt as Jake sprints towards the end zone, the other team realizing too late that they just made the mistake that is going to cost them the game.

"Run, Jake!" I scream, jumping up from the bleacher and forgetting Jenn and everything she's just said. If I think too long about it, I'll freak myself out. I'm <u>not</u> pregnant. We only did it the <u>one time</u> without a condom. Every time <u>since</u> has been protected.

Light pours from every direction as the night and cheers break into fragments.

I'm sitting on the edge of Jake's bed. His bedroom door is open. His parents don't allow closed doors when I'm around. As if a promiscuous teen is what they need to be worried about. As if we aren't terrified enough of his dad that we would risk having sex where he can catch us. Yeah, no thanks.

Jake's dad, Dave, was injured in a logging accident when Jake was little. He spends his disability checks on alcohol while Jake's mom, Chrissy, had to pick up a receptionist job at a dental office in town to make sure they can afford their bills. It's complete bullshit. I haven't seen Dave today, so he's probably already at the bar. At least I didn't have to deal with the smirk he gives me every time I show up. He gives me the fucking creeps.

Staring straight ahead, my eyes fix on the hole peeking out from behind the Green Day poster. Is that the one where his dad threw him through the wall, or is that a different one? I make it a point not to spend much time at Jake's house, but tonight it's unavoidable. He was home sick from school so his mom wouldn't let him leave, and I know she listens in on the kitchen phone when I call. I had to do this in person. I can't just hope that he shows up in my backyard after curfew.

Jake sits up against his headboard supported by pillows. He hasn't said anything, and it's starting to scare me.

"Are you sure?" His words are barely audible.

I bob my head as the lump in the back of my throat grows, causing the words to come out in a squeaked whisper. "Yeah, I've taken four tests already." Jenn and I drove all the way to Corvallis to buy the pregnancy tests to make sure no one saw us. There wasn't even a question; that second pink line was there nearly as fast as my pee hit the stick. "What are we gonna do, Jake?" I focus on my hands, nervously sliding the nails from one hand onto the other like a washboard.

"It's gonna be fine. We can handle this." Jake pushes himself away from the headboard and pulls me into his arms. The same arms that have held me so many times, reassuring me that everything would be okay. Only this time it isn't enough. I <u>know</u> it won't be okay. It can't be.

"We're seventeen. We can't have a baby."

A horrified gasp brings my attention to the door, where Jake's mom stands frozen in the doorframe.

The memory whirls and transforms into a room with mauve-colored walls. A calming abstract painting hangs directly across from my hospital bed. The soft glow from the last few minutes of sunlight filters through the blind slats, bathing the room in calm magic.

Jake sits hunched in the armchair next to the window, pushing his feet he rocks the chair, holding a bundle in his arms. I don't need to see the face to know. It's Scarlett. Perfect and tiny and new.

Softly, Jake sings a tune he's been humming for months. My mind supplies the up-coming rise and dips in the melody, now with words I've never heard.

"Sweet as a strawberry, soft as rose petals. A face that could launch a thousand vessels."

My eyes close, listening to the boy I've grown to love, singing to the tiny creature I already love more than life itself.

"A night that's starlit, has nothing on Scarlett." He finishes the song, continuing to hum the melody on a loop, lulling me into a sleepy daze.

I can feel the memory starting to break apart, and I try to hold on just a little longer to this one. It's perfect and warm, protecting us from the cold harsh world waiting. I catch Jake's eye and wonder as desperate to stay as I am. The struggle is futile as the room erupts in the glow of the sun. As quickly as it appeared, it's gone.

I enter the tiny gray house directly into the living room. At less than four hundred square feet there is no room for the pretense of hallways or foyers. Jake paces around the living room, Scarlett close against his chest as he sings his lullaby, bouncing her as he walks.

Setting down my backpack against the front door, I step lightly across the worn floorboards to greet them. Moving up onto the balls of my feet, calf muscles flexing, I reach my neck out in a silent question. Jake meets my rise with a bend of his own. It's a light kiss but holds the promise of impending passion.

"Hey you," he breathes.

Crossing the room to the bouncer next to the couch, he slowly lowers Scarlett down, managing to keep her asleep. This is a skill I don't have.

Following me into the kitchen, Jake grabs me from behind. Catching me off guard, I let out a squeal. A small sound from the bouncer reminds us that we're not alone, and if we don't keep quiet, we'll be joined by a grumpy baby. Smiling, we shush each other loudly, stifling giggles as we do so.

I reach into my jacket pocket, pulling out the crumpled bills from where I stashed them earlier. The space where a fridge is meant to be instead houses a mini fridge. There is an empty formula can on top where we put <u>all</u> our extra money, which isn't much. But after months of picking up odd jobs, we're so close to being able to get a full-size fridge, one where our milk doesn't have to lie horizontally.

My twelve-dollar contribution might put us over the threshold. We'll have to pour the can out on our bed later and count it. I'll suggest we find one for the amount we have saved, and Jake will say we should keep saving so we can afford one with an ice maker. It's always the same. As soon as we have enough for the bare minimum, Jake pushes us a little further.

Pulling out the stool on the left of our table-really, it's just a board bolted to the wall-I take a seat. My neck has the usual kink in it which seems to show up on the nights when Scarlett isn't sleeping. Reading my mind, Jake moves behind me and wraps his hands around my shoulders, gently kneading with his thumbs at the base of my neck, just a tiny bit harder than is comfortable.

"How was school?"

His thumb finds the knot and it takes everything in me to not squirm away from the pressure. I just need to breathe through it till it loosens. "It was pretty good. There was a pep rally during fourth period, so I skipped it and squeezed in some extra ACT prep. How was your day?"

I know he has no interest in going over the mundane details of stay-at-home father-hood. He wants to be at school with me; the pep rally was in honor of our football team making it to the playoffs. Jake's team made it to playoffs without him, and I know that stings.

Instead of dwelling on it, he spins the barstool so we face each other. Reaching down, he lifts me off my seat. My legs wrap around his waist—not <u>only</u> for stability. Jake carries me from the kitchen, stumbling through the doorway of our bedroom, where we collapse onto our old mattress on the floor in a tumble of flying clothes and heavy breathing.

The sun lowers, changing the light in the room from a bright beige to the gray of afternoon shadows. Rolling onto my side, I look at Jake. Chest rising and falling, I'd think he was asleep if his open eyes weren't staring intently at the ceiling light. My fingers brush over his smooth chest.

"Hey, you. What are you thinking about over there?" Something's churning in his mind. Knowing he can't get anything past me, he turns his face to meet mine. Tears threaten to spill over the edge of his eyes. "Woah, what's going on?" Jake's not a crier. He was conditioned his whole life living with an abusive dad to swallow any big emotions. Something has to be <u>really</u> wrong.

"I was just thinking about how lucky we are. How lucky I am, really. I have the two most beautiful girls in the world. Our house has nothing but love, I just—Well everything seems to be going right. Doesn't it?" He always sees the best in our situation. After all the shit with his dad and being a high school dropout, his ability to brush it off and continue to smile is admirable.

We won't survive if Jake can't continue to bring home extra food from the market where he works or if Jake's grandparents hadn't set us up in one of their rentals. Without any support from our parents, we have to rely on each other. And somewhere in that struggle, we found happiness. Content in our little one-bedroom with a mini-fridge.

"I mean, it seems to be going well right now. We just have a lot of work to do to <u>keep</u> it going so well." I answer with a heavy dose of realism, like a complete jackass. I can't help myself but to take a tender moment and turn it on its head. It's too late to take it back, but that doesn't stop the regret from pooling.

Jake rolls over to look at the alarm clock on the floor next to his side of the bed.

"I have to leave in about an hour. But I'll be back before midnight tonight, so I might catch you for Scar's midnight snack." His smile is soft.

I blink and the room is gone. The afternoon light turns to night. After two blissful memories, I know something worse is coming. I try to brace myself, but the anxiety I'm fighting turns to rage as the new surroundings solidify around us.

The regret hits me immediately the moment we arrive. I can't believe I agreed to this. Jake promises it will be the first and only dinner with his parents, an attempt to patch things up. But I see the disappointment on his face as the evening falls apart before it even begins.

I look across the table for backup. Jake avoids my eyes, focusing instead on helping Scarlett cut her food. Son of a bitch. Neither his age nor the years spent away from his dad have lessened the effect Dave has on Jake. He flinches at even the smallest of his dad's movements, and every flinch of Jake's makes me surer that if Dave gives me an excuse, I'll kill him. I don't mean that in a joking ha-ha way. I mean I've put some real thought into it, and I think I could not only do it, but get away with it.

The minute we entered the house, it all came back—every beating, every time Jake showed up at my house late in the night, bruised and terrified. I sit silently, willing Jake to stand up and challenge him. Instead Jake remains frozen as Dave makes comment after comment.

"You won't catch anyone from _my_ generation staying home and playing mom, letting their woman go out in the pants. And college? Pfft, no, more people in trade school is what this country needs. "This country," as if Dave has ever actually put in an ounce of effort for the goddam greater good of any group of people. It's nice to see that in the absence of his only son, he's taking in a heavy dose of opinions from the talking heads on TV. "Scarlett, wouldn't you rather your mom be a good mommy and be home with you instead of making your daddy be your mommy?"

"Excuse me?" I slam down my fork before taking my first bite. Jake may have grown accustomed to this abuse, but I won't stand for it. I have no issue stepping in to shut this down. He beat Jake mercilessly throughout our childhood, and now he's attempting to pass on his toxic ideologies to our daughter. No. Fuck this.

I clear the plates from under Jake and Scarlett, condemning us to another night of ramen as we leave behind the home-cooked meal that had our mouths watering the second we walked in.

Panicking, Chrissy tries to stop me. "Liv, please." She's working herself up into a frenzy. "I haven't seen my son in _years_. Please don't go." The words come out and it's clear that she blames me for Jake not being in their lives.

I ignore her, not even willing to make eye contact. I want to tell her she's a terrible mother, that she hasn't seen her son for years because _she_ kicked him out. That the little girl at her table is the same one she begged us to abort. That I would _never_ treat Scarlett the way she's treated Jake. But God, I can't. I know that our leaving puts her in a dangerous position with her abusive husband. I'll call the sheriff and have him check in on her after we leave.

"No. We're done here." I hold out Jake's jacket as he finishes helping Scarlett into her own. Jake carries Scarlett to the Jeep, unable to meet my gaze as he passes me. I step out onto the porch closing the door without so much as a goodbye, but I hear Dave huffing his way across the dining room to the front door. It's not hard to pick up my pace, imagining the look of fury as he realizes he's not getting the last word. I just need to make it to the car before he comes out.

I'm not quick enough, though. The door opens, bathing me in the yellow glow from inside their trailer. Dave's gonna wish he stayed inside because the adrenaline coursing through me will obliterate any filter I have. I face my opponent and stand my ground as he closes the space between us.

Dave stomps until he's practically standing on my feet." Who the hell do you think you are? We invite you into our home and you disrespect my wife? You disrespect _me_?"

My legs wobble with the smallest amount of fear, but it's immediately replaced by anger which straightens them with force. I grew up seeing the damage he was capable of and willing to inflict on those he was supposed to love and protect. He's a bully and has never had anyone stand up to him. If he touches me, I will have him arrested so fast. I know how desperate the sheriff has been for Jake and Chrissy to press charges. Dave flinches, taking a step back. I'm easy to read, so I'm sure he sees a hint of what's coming in my eyes. He can back up all he wants, hopefully there is a ledge I can push him off of.

"Dave. It is impossible to disrespect someone unworthy of an _ounce_ of respect," I spit, my heart racing as I unleash the words I've held back for years. "You invite _my_ family into your home and then you insult myself and your son in front of _our_ child? I should be home, taking care of our daughter? Where the fuck was that attitude when your wife had to go get a job because of the pathetic man that you are, wasting every goddam dollar you've ever had on booze." I could stop, but I don't want to. The Mortal Kombat "finish him" line plays in my mind as I take a step towards him. "Don't talk to me about what our family should look like when you fucking beat yours into submission. You come near any of us again, and I swear to God, Dave, I'll kill you."

I take a breath, feeling more powerful than ever. Dave stumbles back, eyes bulging as my words hit their target. I decide to leave before he regains his composure. I slam the car door as Jake throws the car into reverse, peeling out of the gravel driveway.

Safely in the car, I'm stunned Dave didn't raise his hand to me. I'm not sure if I ever believed he would actually hit me, but I expected him to make a move to at least try and intimidate me. Then it hits me. Jake was standing with one foot in the jeep while I was toe-to-toe with Dave, too far to do anything in my defense if it had come to it.

Scarlett snores from the backseat. Anger grows where the rush of power had just been.

"I know I should have said something," Jake admits, his eyes focusing on the windshield.

I know it's not fair to be angry, but this whole stupid night was his idea. He brought me there knowing what would happen. He knew what would happen. We both knew. Nothing has changed.

"I froze." He's ashamed. I need to say something to reassure him, but I'm still trying to slow my breathing. Jake chuckles, quietly at first, but then it grows louder.

"What could possibly be funny right now?" I swing my hand across the middle of the Jeep, swatting his shoulder with the back of my hand.

"Did you actually threaten to kill my dad?" He's laughing now. "I'm sorry, I'm just trying to figure out logistically how that would work."

Humor has always been his defense mechanism, so I'm not surprised this is the road he's taking. I'm not there yet.

"Do you think murder has to be a physical attack? How incredibly naïve of you." Anyone who knows anything knows that a woman determined to kill has any number of options.

"You're right. You just kicked his ass with only a few words."

"No help from you." The words are out, and I regret them. I stood up to Dave <u>because</u> I know it's not fair to ask Jake to do so. It's easier to take on someone else's attacker than your own. Was it really so long ago that Jake took on my own attacker?

"If I'd stepped in, it would have gotten really ugly, in front of Scarlett. Plus, you didn't need me. God, you were incredible. You're gonna have to get yourself a pantsuit."

He knows I long to feel powerful. He's moved from joking to flattery. I already know the next step in this dance.

"It's not going to work, Jake."

"Oh, it's working." It's too dark to see the wink, but it's there. "After winning a football game, I used to feel exactly what you're feeling right now. It's kind of a rush, isn't it?" He reaches over, resting his hand on my thigh with a squeeze.

"Jake." I protest, but my resolve is fading.

The memory splinters, reconstructing itself in the way a kaleidoscope does as it's turned.

Soft curls spill onto the shoulders of my graduation gown from underneath the cap. Eyes searching the crowd, I walk onto the lawn. I spot Jake with Scarlett on his shoulders as they gallop towards me.

Scarlett's chanting, "Mom, mom, mom!" as they make their way to me.

She looks more like Jake every day. Wavy brown hair, clear blue eyes, and ears that stick out just a little at the top. At almost six years old, Scarlett is the tallest kid in her kindergarten class. In just a few short years, Scarlett will tower over me in the same way Jake does.

Jake reaches up and grabs under Scarlett's arms helping her complete a front flip on her way to the ground.

Sweeping his arm around my waist, he pulls me close against his chest and kisses me, uninhibited by the knowledge that my family is likely watching. Being the center of attention is not something I enjoy. Especially when it comes to public displays of affection. Jake takes joy in making onlookers squirm; I'm just collateral damage.

"I couldn't have done any of it without Jake." This is my canned response to each extended family member who takes the time to commend me on accomplishing something they wrote off as an impossibility.

My response, while kind on the surface, is a bit of a "fuck you" to them for doubting me and reminding them that Jake and I did it all without any of their help. They feel pride in my accomplishment like they had anything to do with it. I want them to know that they are undeserving of this pride, since they've been noticeably absent for the struggle.

I was hesitant to invite any of our extended family members for this reason. Jake had pushed me though reminding me that it could be a lesson in humility for those who abandoned us.

Jake is only a few weeks away from completing his apprenticeship, moving him closer to becoming an electrician. It isn't exactly what he's always dreamed of being—it's more of a stumble into something with the potential for a stable income. We're keeping it a secret, though. He wants today to be all about my accomplishment as if his own isn't as praiseworthy.

Jake promised me that my life wasn't over when I got pregnant. He would do everything in his power to guarantee that we would defy the odds. We wouldn't end up in the trailer park next to his parents. I believed none of it, yet he's stayed true to his word, pushing us both to reach every goal we've set for ourselves.

Ben comes up from behind Jake and grabs Scarlett from his side, throwing her up into the air. "Uncle Ben!" Scarlett squeals with delight. Ben kisses the top of her head before setting her back down on the grass. Pulling me into a tight embrace, he speaks so quietly only I can hear.

"I'm so proud of you <u>and</u> Jake. You've proved every person who ever talked shit about you guys wrong. Way to go, Sis."

The hug between Ben and I transforms from day to night in another swirl of spots and lights. We are now standing under a canopy of bistro lights in a clearing surrounded by evergreens. The green and brown of the ground meet where the shadows of trees begin. Fragmented outlines of the bottoms of the trunks, seemingly unattached to the higher branches, overlap in a way that makes it impossible to discern from a distance where each belongs.

Ben lets go of me with a kiss on the cheek as soft as a breath. "You look absolutely beautiful."

My cheeks warm as I smile awkwardly. I feel silly, standing in a wedding dress. It's not huge and flowy. Just a simple tea-length A-line with a lace overlay that sits just under my collarbones. I found it online from a shop overseas, which makes it feel more like I'm playing dress-up. I've been with Jake so long that a wedding seems trivial. We don't need to promise each other about the life we'll build together. We've already built it. In my mind, we forfeited the right to a wedding thirteen years ago, when we went out of order: a baby, moving in together, and now our wedding. It's backward from how I'd imagined my life, but there's nothing I would change if given the chance.

This wedding costs more than the down payment we put on our house. We don't owe any of these people a wedding. But Jake wants this. I don't know if he wants it more for himself or because long ago he saw the scrapbook I'd made from a wedding magazine. Never mind that I was eleven and had just attended a rooftop wedding at a fancy San Francisco hotel. He saved money for more than a year before officially proposing so I wouldn't have an excuse to say no to anything more than a courthouse.

So while I feel silly standing in a wedding dress, it truly is <u>everything</u> I dreamed of as a girl.

Ben shifts his body to embrace Jake. Whispering something in Jake's ear, they both erupt in laughter. Ben pats Jake roughly on the back. I give them side-eye. How inappropriate must a comment be to cause this degree of laughter?

Ben takes Scarlett's hand and pulls her to the dance floor. She looks so grown in her green satin dress. Apparently, thirteen isn't too old to stand on Ben's feet while he lifts each foot, guiding her in a waltz. I was her age when I moved to Coburg. I was her age when I met Jake.

Jake steps closer, holding out his hand. "May I have this dance, Mrs. Larson?" My hand in his, he spins me into his chest and out again—the only move from our high school ballroom dance class we can still pull off.

He holds me close against his chest as we move on the dancefloor. Leaning down, his lips brush against my ear. "You are breathtaking."

"You're not so bad yourself." I pull back enough to appreciate his attire.

His gray suit gives him this old Hollywood vibe. His emeraldgreen bowtie now untied hangs slack around his neck.

As Harry Style's "Sweet Creature" begins to winddown, he holds me, unwilling to let go of this perfect moment.

My champagne is still bubbling as we return to our table. I nearly collapse. Heels are not my normal footwear. Blisters are starting to form on the inside arches of my feet.

"I just wanted to say a few things," Jake speaks loudly, clinking his fork to the side of his champagne glass. Ben steps up, handing Jake a microphone. "As most of you know, Liv and I met when we were thirteen, and we haven't exactly had the most conventional of relationships."

The crowd chuckles as they feel permission to openly judge us. Dicks. God, like they don't have their own judge-worthy secrets. We all know about your affair, Craig, we just aren't going to laugh about it to your face.

Jake turns to me, pulling my attention back to him. His voice lowers to the soft tone he uses when it's just us, the microphone still to his lips. "Liv, I've loved you since I first saw you on your first day of school wearing that red T-shirt and those pants that flared from your knees so much they covered your entire shoes. I could never have imagined this is where we would end up. Loving you and Scarlett is my greatest joy. You've given me the one thing I never had, a family, and for that, I can't thank you enough."

He's blurry through my tear-glossed eyes. The entire crowd under the tent sniffs, moved by his honest words. That'll teach them to judge us.

I smile, but it feels wonky with all the quivering. "I love you." The words don't come out, but Jake reads them. Leaning down, he presses his lips to mine and my heart nearly breaks as the memory is pulled away, fading as it leaves.

After spinning out, I land in the coffee shop, sitting across from Jake. Back in reality, only in addition to the memories I have from a very real life, I now have another set of memories of a life I've never lived. A beautiful life, a daughter, Jake. His eyes are wide, unblinking. He just experienced it all with me.

"Jake?" It's a hoarse whisper. "What the hell was that?"

Three

I take my hand out from under his and hold it. Did he know what he was doing when he touched me? Why would he do that?

"You saw that?" A look of panic and then excitement crosses his face. "Don't freak out, Liv. Just take a breath." He reaches out, urging me to give him my hand. Yeah, I have absolutely no intention of allowing him to touch me again, who knows what kind of bullshit he'd pull me into this time.

"Don't freak out?" I speak too loud and can immediately feel the stares from other patrons in the coffee shop. I want to tell them to mind their damn business, but if I were them, I'd totally be listening. Lowering my voice to a harsh whisper, I repeat my question. It seems like he knows a lot more than he's telling me. "What was that?"

"I don't know." He shakes his head defensively. "I have some theories, but I don't know for sure." He's looking at me and grinning.

Did he not just feel the complete rewrite of our _actual_ lives?

"The first time it happened, I threw up. You're not going to puke, are you?" His eyes search mine for an answer, unwilling to look away until I give him some kind of reassurance.

I shake my head. Of all the emotions rushing through me, I don't _think_ nausea is one of them. My mind races through what I just saw—not only saw but _lived_. I was _in_ the memories. We touched, kissed ... oh my God, I _slept_ with Jake. I cross my arms in front of my chest.

Then Jake's words "the first time" hit me. How many times has he gone through this? I'm sifting through memories, struggling to sort them into what is true and what isn't. The idea of doing this multiple times is something I have no interest in.

Only a moment ago Jake was a stranger. If asked about Jake and where he landed in life, I'm confident I could have honestly answered, "I have no idea." Even now, I still don't <u>really</u> know anything about him. I mean, I know intimate details about him, and judging from the look he's giving me, he knows more than a little about me as well. That's the thought that brings a wave of nausea. I will not puke in front of Jake. No. I shake my head again, reaffirming my decision not to be sick.

"Good. I'm not sure exactly what it is. I met up with an ex for lunch. When she hugged me, the same thing happened. Except it was dark, it was nothing like..." he waves his hand between us "...that. It happens with every ex, but none of <u>them</u> have ever seen it." The scar near his eye dimples as his cheeks lift into the broad smile that I had longed to see. His joy is off-putting, wrong. I was ambushed, assaulted by the experience, and he sits here all giddy.

"I can't do this." I need to get somewhere where I can breathe, where I can think.

Standing, I gather my laptop, keys, and phone in my hand. The hand he hadn't touched. I look down, trying desperately to steady my mouth so he won't see the flood of emotions I'm holding back.

Our eyes lock. I could stay. I could be here. It wouldn't be hard. I break the stare, knowing that if I don't leave now, I may not be able to. My heart skips as Jake reaches out, taking my hand in his. I brace for impact, but I'm still standing in the coffee shop. Nothing spins or swirls. It must only happen the first time.

"Liv, please. Don't go." His fingers wrap around my hand in desperation, his touch familiar and warm. I'm shaking. I <u>want</u> to stay, to fall into whatever this is. I <u>can't</u> and I don't know how to tell him why.

Snatching my hand back from him, I rush out the glass doors. I left my coffee, but I can't go back for it now.

I slide into the driver seat, and I'm barely keeping it together. Starting the ignition, I hope the AC blasting on my face will help keep the tears at bay. What am I supposed to do with this? I just lived a love story, <u>the</u> love story I spent years convincing myself would never have happened, that we had been doomed from the start. Jake ended our friendship. He <u>chose</u> something ... someone else.

The passenger door opens and Jake climbs in, setting my abandoned coffee in the cup holder and accepting the silence of the car. I'm terrified he's going to reach over and take my hand again, but also, I kind of <u>need</u> him to take it. To reassure and anchor me. He doesn't.

When I first saw him in that coffee shop, I talked incessantly, trying to fill the silence, unable to cope with the tension that had accompanied it. Now the silence feels comfortable. Only within the walls of my car can we relish in what we've been through and seen, refusing to admit that it's all an illusion.

Four songs pass quietly on the radio before either of us speak.

"That wasn't real." The words are so quiet I'm not sure he can even hear them. Staring out the windshield, both my hands rest on the steering wheel.

"Wasn't it? Because it sure as hell felt real. " Jake looks over at me, willing me to return his gaze. I have to admit it <u>had</u> felt real. So real that I don't know what to do with it all. The idea of simply returning to my normal life, trying to forget this ever happened is an impossibility. He knows it and so do I.

I give in and glance over at Jake, regretting it immediately. I can't think clearly. I see a man I love fiercely in a way I can't even fully comprehend. I turn away, fixing my eyes to the lights on the dash. The red seat belt light flashes.

On.

Off.

On.

Off.

I know I have to, but I don't know how to explain to Jake that I <u>can't</u> feel the same way he does. Why can't I lean into the warmth and comfort that this alternate reality showed us?

"I've wasted the last two years of my life tracking down my exes to find out what could have been. I just knew there had to be one out there that might have ended happily. The more I looked, the more I was disappointed." He pauses, fiddling with the glove box latch. "A couple months ago I decided I needed to be done. I couldn't look anymore. But <u>you</u> walked in. I didn't go looking for you. <u>You</u> came to <u>me</u>. It's fate Liv."

"You and I dated for less than a month." I don't mean to come across as a complete bitch, but it's true. And if I don't latch on to the anger I'm feeling, it's going to be so much harder to leave this whole thing behind.

"We both know my feelings for you started long before then, and they sure as hell didn't end just because you needed <u>time.</u>" He hits me with his own cheap shot, fueling my anger. I dig into it.

"Oh fuck you, Jake."

"No, I didn't mean anything by that."

"Oh, I think you did. Did you do this to get <u>even</u> with me?"

"No! I swear! I didn't expect to see what we just saw. And I swear to God, I didn't think you would see it too. None of the others have ever gone through it with me. I never would have done it if I'd known you'd see it all ... well, okay I probably would have still done it, but I would have at least warned you." I let out a small bark of a laugh trying to imagine what explanation could have possibly preceded what just happened. His voice is softer now. "I only thought I was tormenting myself. But I wouldn't take it back now. You <u>did</u> see it. You <u>know</u> how happy we can be. We had a <u>daughter,</u> Liv." His voice cracks, and it's a knife pressing straight into me.

Tears spring from my eyes. I know it would be easy to embrace what never happened. At least it <u>would</u> be easy if my life wasn't already set in ways that can't be altered. He reaches across the car and takes my hand from off of the steering wheel. I close my eyes, feeling the guilt stirring in my belly. I have to tell him. "Don't. Jake, I'm <u>married</u>." The grip around my hand weakens slightly. My voice is caught in my throat, and I clear it. "I need you to go, Jake. Please." I pull my hand out from under his and hold it protectively to myself.

Tears fall freely now. The strength to hold them back is gone. There is so much more I should tell him, but I can't do that without betraying Scott. This already feels like a step too far in that direction. Jake pushed his way into my life in an instant, and I'm not sure how to reconcile that with reality.

"What are you going to do?" He whispers so quietly it's just a breath.

The question is so loaded I'm unsure how to start unpacking it. My heart is cracking from the possibilities I'm pushing away.

"I'm gonna go <u>home</u>."

"And what? Pretend you aren't in love with me?" He's panicking, but pretending I'm not in love with Jake is exactly what I intend to do. It's the only thing I <u>can</u> do.

"I'm <u>not</u> in love with you." I growl the lie, hoping to convince myself as much as him. My cheeks and neck grow warmer as I allow the anger to return. "I don't even know you.

I may have, once upon a time, but this..." I wave between us mirroring his earlier gesture "...isn't a thing. I need you to get out of my car."

"You just felt what I felt. You remember everything I remember. You can't feel <u>nothing</u> for me after everything we've been through." He pauses almost like he's debating whether he should keep talking. Usually, the answer is to stop right then and there, but Jake barrels through that stop sign. "You wouldn't still be sitting here if things were <u>all</u> that great with your husband."

The fuck did he just say? I look across to the passenger seat where he sits, and he's smirking. My fists clench. God, I could kill him. Even if I <u>did</u> hit him, I don't have the power in my arm to do the damage I want to. He sees his mistake and moves to reach his hand towards my face in apology.

I recoil against the door and glare at him with every bit of fury I have stored inside.

"Get the <u>fuck</u> out of my car, Jake Larson." The measured tone I use hits him harder than my fists would have been able to. Breaths huff through my nose as I fight the urge to scream a repeat of my demand.

It's a power struggle as I hold his gaze. He opens his door in defeat and climbs out. Standing on the pavement, he bends down just enough to place his head back inside the car.

"It might not have been tangible, but you can't tell me that what I am feeling right now isn't real." He's softening again, trying to plead with me. He can't know how strong the pull of his words are. I look away, my resolve diminishing.

I put the car in drive, keeping my foot on the brake. Jake holds the door a moment longer before giving in and pushing it closed. Making his way away from the car, he crosses the parking lot towards the strip of businesses. I don't wait to see where he's going. I hit the lock button on the door and take my foot off the brake.

Four

"**M**om! I need your help. I can't figure out what I'm supposed to be doing!" Noah ambles into the kitchen, where I'm unpacking a box of things we should have thrown away instead of hauling them across the country. Batteries I'm not even sure are still good, burned discs that may or may not hold pictures or music, along with a number of half-empty bottles of lotions cover a layer of belongings I can't even yet see.

"Help with what?" I turn to see him holding out his game console to me. "Dude, I don't know how to play that." I've never had the coordination or dexterity to be considered adequate at video games. I find just as much joy in watching someone else play, serving as the back-seat driving sidekick on their quests.

He's still holding it, nostrils flared, eyebrows crinkled as he sets his foot down in what could almost be a stomp, pleading, "I can't do it by myself!" His voice transforms from a groan to a whine.

"Well, then how did you get as far as you are?" I turn back to the box, continuing to empty its contents. "How about you take a break from your game and go work on unpacking the box of books onto the bookshelf in your room. I'd <u>super</u> appreciate it."

I can practically <u>hear</u> the eye-roll.

His groan turns to a shout as he stomps away. "Fine, I guess I'll just have to do <u>everything</u> around here!"

The dramatics of this kid. I let a chuckle slip. "Oh no! Poor Noah has to unpack every box in the entire house while Mom does nothing." I stand, arching backwards, attempting to stretch the muscles threatening to spasm if I keep hunching. I buried myself in boxes, hoping that by touching every object of my <u>actual</u> life, I'll forget about my morning with

Jake. It might have been easier if I didn't find the box with my old yearbooks; those took me down a rabbit hole I really didn't need today. A glass of wine or maybe a whole bottle in front of the fire on the patio is tempting. I rest my eyes on the mountain of empty boxes I've spent the day emptying and stacking into the dining room, making it impossible to walk through to the door leading to the back porch

Our apartment in D.C. had offered a fire escape as a means for sitting out in the fresh air—if you could consider city air fresh. When we made the decision to move back to Oregon, I ordered the back patio furniture. My childhood was filled with outside dinners and lounging beneath the blanket of stars, listening to Dad relay stories from work. And then as I grew up, sitting out there night after night with Jake and sometimes Ben, talking about everything and nothing. I ordered the furniture hoping that Noah would grow up with similar memories. If I plan on getting a little bit drunk tonight, which I _fully_ intend on doing, I need to break down the boxes and clear a path.

The doorbell rings, and I leave the box of useless trinkets to retrieve the pizza. Did I go grocery shopping yesterday after meal planning? Yeah. Did running into Jake take every ounce of my mental energy, making it impossible to cook? Also yeah.

Setting the pizza on the counter, I walk into the bathroom to wash my hands. The bathroom floor is stripped, consisting of plywood and nothing else. The contractor promised it would be done weeks ago, but he's yet to touch it since the day he made it nearly inaccessible. I swear to God I'm one YouTube away from getting the supplies and doing it myself.

Scott's sitting on the counter next to the pizza boxes, when I return, hands clean. My heart leaps at the startling joy of seeing his easy smile. Everything just feels right, and maybe I don't need to get wasted if he keeps smiling like this. His tie is loose and hangs down his shirt.

He sniffs just over the box. "Liv, tell me there aren't pineapples on this." The earnest need in his eyes makes me roll my own eyes, accompanied by a small laugh. "Noah is going to turn out as weird as you if you keep letting him eat pineapple on pizza."

"He's going to turn out weird for a _number_ of reasons, plenty of which are your fault." Licking the buttery inside of a popcorn bag comes to mind, but I keep it to myself. I don't know that I've ever met anyone that's truly _normal_ and, really, do I want to?

Scott looks around at the pile of empty boxes thrown into the dining room and then at the still filled boxes sitting next to the couch. "Nooooo! Seriously, though, do they never end?" He throws his hands up to the sky.

I laugh, genuinely this time, reaching around him to grab a slice for Noah.

"I've been saying literally the exact same thing all day. How do we have this much stuff? We lived in an apartment!" I gesture at the remaining boxes. "It's like a clown car in here. More just keeps coming out of these boxes that remain impossibly full." I take in the disaster before glancing back at Scott. "Wanna keep me company? We can push through and maybe finish tonight." I just need him here. When he's here, I don't feel like I'm swirling through a tornado, unsure of where I've been and absolutely no clue where I may land.

"Let me go change real quick and then it's a date." He winks. And I don't think he notices, but I flinch. How did I never place the familiarity in this mannerism? Jake and Scott have the same wink. Is it the same or am I confusing the two memories now? I would have noticed that before. I'm sure of it. It's likely just my guilt getting to me.

I find stacks of books and knickknacks meant for the built-in shelving that surrounds the TV and fireplace in the living room.

The leaves on the artificial eucalyptus hang down covering the two shelves below it. I try to use the hidden spaces to place the internet router out of sight, hoping the plant won't interfere with the signal. After testing the strength on my phone from multiple corners of the house, I decide that the plant can stay. Crouching to dig through the box, I look for the perfect item to place on the shelf near the plant. The sparkle catches my eye, and I pull the silver frame from underneath the black frames.

Scott and I on the balcony of the Hay-Adams hotel. Orange, red, and yellow leaves framing the White House, and the Washington Monument behind us. Scott holds me in a dip, bent over me in a kiss. The train of my mermaid gown covers the ground, hiding Scott's legs and feet entirely. My back arm wraps around Scott's neck while the other hovers over my train, holding the bouquet of dahlias, hydrangeas, and wildflowers.

I run a finger over the couple in the picture. Two kids in their twenties with no idea how complex life can be. Setting the frame on the shelf to the right of the router, I find myself comparing my two weddings.

Traveling through the memories with Jake, our wedding in the forest seemed excessive. Compared to my actual wedding, it now seems quiet and quaint. The venue for Scott and I's wedding cost more than the entire event with Jake. Ugh, it's embarrassing how much fuss we put into a single day. The rush of emotion and complete bliss was the same in both. Neither the menu nor the flowers had made either of the days more or less than the other. A wedding is perfect because of <u>who</u> you are there with rather than where you are and how much you pay to get there. That's some wisdom that could have come in handy earlier in life.

The difference, I know, is the optimism I'd had standing next to Scott, reciting my vows. Naïve promises of forever and never loving anyone else. Promises made before any life was lived. Promises made before seeing Jake. Marrying Jake came _after_ we knew what marriage meant.

"Has it really been almost ten years?" Scott's breath tickles the hair on my neck, and goosebumps cover the back of my arms.

"Time flies." I push the memory of Jake back down.

I spin into Scott and we sway to music we can't hear. Scott is only a few inches taller than me, so when he holds me, his cheek brushes the top of my head.

I've never understood why women care so much about how tall a man is. Part of the reason I don't care might be that at five foot two, I've almost never come across a man who doesn't stand at least as tall as me. I love that I don't need to strain to kiss Scott. That when we hold hands, there's no pull on my shoulder. It's easy. Loving Scott has always been _easy_, without any of the drama or mess that accompanies Jake. But along with that mess is a whole lot of joy and history.

Everything would be simpler if I could forget what Jake and I saw and go back to Jake being a fleeting memory. Just a boy who broke me to the point that I ran, leaving the entire coast that reminded me of him. Instead, I'm comparing him to Scott, marring the memories of a life I've worked hard for.

Scott's whisper sends a chill through my spine. "Where are you right now?"

It's the question he poses when I'm everywhere except in the moment. What it would be like to not have a million thoughts running through my mind at all times? To accept the moment for what it is and nothing more.

"I'm with _you_. Just _you_." Eyes closed, I breathe deeply, hoping the smell of cologne on his shirt can solidify me here. So I can pretend the morning with Jake never happened. Instead, I smell coffee and conjure an image of Jake sitting across from me. I open my eyes and step back, leaving Scott where he stands, the last hint of daylight through the windows silhouetting him in an almost angelic light.

The toothbrush buzzes, indicating I should switch quadrants, and I almost don't because I'm thinking about today, about this last year, about _every_ choice I've ever made. How many happy relationships have I been responsible for ending too soon? Jake said all of the glimpses he'd seen were dark. Maybe my experience would have been the opposite.

Maybe every relationship I've ever been in could have ended just as happily as mine and Jake's or even mine and Scott's. Or maybe I've fucked up countless paths to happiness and just stumbled into Scott. Except that the definition of happily ever after is merely the decision of where to end the story.

"Hey." Rolling onto my side, I prop my head on my hand. "Do you ever think about how different everything would be if you had just made one different choice?" I place my hand on his chest, trying to feel the movement of his lungs filling and deflating.

"You know I do." Scott winces. He <u>knows</u> the pain he's responsible for. I <u>know</u> he would do anything to take it all back, and in this moment it feels cruel to talk about it. "But I think all we can do is accept what is and move on rather than dwelling on it."

Moving on seems like an oversimplification of something incredibly complex. I'm trying, but it requires every ounce of my energy to pretend as though it's as simple as just accepting life the way it is.

Scott turns his face to meet mine. "Fantasies aren't real, Liv." It's a direct contradiction of what Jake said, that something doesn't need to be tangible to be real.

"But you <u>feel</u> real." Sadness strangles my voice. I can feel Scott fading into the night. I try to hold on to him with my eyes, refusing to blink. If I can just keep my eyes open, he can't leave. He blurs into obscurity through the tears. The guilt I feel in response to feeling something for Jake mixes with the reality that there is nothing left to betray. Only a memory.

A creaking in the hallway steals my attention for the briefest of moments, and when my eyes return to the bed, Scott's gone. The doorknob rattles as Noah opens it and runs full speed to climb into bed where Scott had just been. Noah crawls into my arms, and I hold him—he only piece of Scott I have left.

"I miss Dad." It's clear from the rawness in his voice that he's been crying. I'm not the only one being haunted tonight.

"I know, buddy. Me too." The tears find their way out, dropping silently onto the top of Noah's head.

FIVE

The school drop off line is as close to hell as a person can get. No one seems to give a shit which lane is a no-stopping lane. The moms just use it as a place to gather and chat, not caring that some of us have shit to do.

"C'mon, Noah." I throw the car in park on the side of the road and get out. We'll walk. We stop at the bike rack, where I give him as much of a hug and a kiss.

"Livvy?" The nickname I would have been fine to never hear again. I turn to find a tall waspy brunette that I can't place. I put on a fake smile and raise my eyebrows.

"Yeah?" I mean I know I went to high school with her, but I've got nothing when it comes to a name.

"Nicole!" she supplies, and I realize why I didn't remember her name, because I've blocked her from my memory. She was part of Heather's group. We've never been friends, but hey maybe she's changed.

"Nicole. Of course. How are you?"

"I'm so good. I didn't realize you were back. You look..." she looks me up and down "...good."

And I know what she's doing. She's making me second-guess her words so I wonder if she's sincere or if she's mocking me. There is no straightforward here, it's all backhanded and fake. The only thing I'm second-guessing is why I returned to a town where people like Nicole are. Except there are people like Nicole everywhere, like landmines. Placed for the sole purpose of avoiding, or being blown to bits by their inevitable explosion.

"We should get together and catch up." But there is no catching up because we have no history.

"Of course!" I answer a little too enthusiastically. I don't want to seem too bitchy, but I also have zero intention of following through on that offer.

She waves a third or fourth time as I pass her in my car, still standing and chatting with the other perfect moms.

I rethink my plan the entire drive. I don't rethink the plan as much as I rethink myself. I can't live up to the woman in the vision we saw yesterday. She was strong and confident and I'm more unsure of myself now than I've been in a long time. Maybe I should just go home and forget it. Who am I kidding? I can't just leave things the way I did. And I don't think leaving Jake behind me is a realistic option either.

I walk into the coffee shop. A woman on a mission. Yesterday, I was caught off guard, but today I'm prepared. The barista greets me. I hold up my hand in a wave as I bypass the line and instead march to Jake's table, the same table by the window he'd sat in the morning before. He told me he comes here every day, so I took him at his word and was rewarded with not having to search all over town for him.

With his back to the entrance, there's no chance he saw me enter. An iPad bigger than I've ever seen sits in front of him, open to a document or news, I'm not sure. I sit down across from him and wait for his attention. He holds up a finger rather than looking up and meeting my gaze. I don't know if what he's reading is really that important, or if he just doesn't want to seem as desperate as he very obviously was yesterday.

He nods, indicating that he's nearing a point where he can stop. I wait as patiently as I can, which is maybe not so patient. My foot bounces on the bar between the two chair legs. I had built up the nerve necessary for this in the car, and it's dissipating with each second I have to sit here, waiting. Hurry the hell up already.

Setting down the iPad, his face lights up without a hint of surprise in his expression. Moving his hand, he slides an iced coffee across the table to me. He was expecting me and somehow seems optimistic about my being here. How he can be sure of anything after yesterday is beyond me. Everything I know is turned upside down. Yet here he sits, eager-eyed.

"I owe you an explanation. For how I acted yesterday." I'm trying to keep my tone indifferent. Allowing a single emotion to show is like allowing every emotion to break through the dam I've built.

Cold droplets roll over my fingers as they wrap around the cup.

"You don't owe me anything. I'm the one who needs to apolo—"

I press my lips tightly together and shake my head just enough so he knows to stop talking. I don't want to go around in circles apologizing for everything. He sits up a little straighter, waiting for me to continue.

There is no way to move forward from yesterday without being honest and upfront with Jake. Even if we <u>don't</u> move forward, I <u>want</u> to tell him. Being married, and widowed, is one thing. Having a kid ... something he thought <u>we</u> shared ... is another. I'm not really dreading it though, the part of me that used to confide in him is relieved at the opportunity.

"I have a son, Noah. He's the most <u>amazing</u> kid in the world. He's going to be eight in a few weeks." I look down at my hands and click my fingernails against each other. I want to tell him how Noah reminds me a little of him with the methodical way he thinks about the world, but I don't. "Noah and I moved into the big old house on Crane Street a few weeks ago. <u>Just</u> Noah and I." I can feel the question on his face without looking up. "My husband, Scott, passed away earlier this year."

The bridge of my nose burns as tears begin welling in my eyes. I can stop here. Jake won't ask any follow-up questions. I tighten my grip on the cool cup, the dripping condensation now feeling a bit like a forewarning. I need to get it all out and in the open.

"We were all supposed to spend New Year's Eve together. Scott had a bachelor party in Baltimore. We booked a fancy hotel that Noah and I were going to camp out in to watch the ball drop. Really we were just going to fall asleep with room service and some dumb cable movie on the TV. But Noah and I caught the flu, so last minute Scott had to go alone. He offered to stay home, to get egg drop soup from my favorite restaurant and nurse us back to health, but I insisted he go. He wasn't even out of the city limits." Tears fall, tiny droplets on the table, on my hands. I try some deep breathes hoping to collect myself but fat chance of that happening.

"The driver was the son of a senator and an opioid addict. We were part of the same extended social circle. His addiction wasn't a secret. We all knew he was on something when he hit Scott. But he's rich and has a powerful family. I was vocal, maybe too vocal for what was considered appropriate in Washington. I still don't really know how to shut up and drop something." I give a self-deprecating chuckle. "My boss tried to back me as long as possible, but it reached the point that there really wasn't another choice but for me to leave."

When Scott and my dad went in together and purchased the Crane House, the plan was to use it as a rental property. My dad gave us regular updates regarding the plan for renovations. After Scott died, it turned from updates to suggestions that Noah and I should move into the Crane House. At first, I was a firm no. But since I was unemployed and blacklisted from every political consulting firm in D.C., I reluctantly agreed to move back to the only place in the country I vowed never to return to other than for a holiday visit.

Jake reaches across the table, setting his hand on mine. The comfort is instantaneous. This is the Jake I grew up with. The best friend who knew when I needed to hear something, but also appreciated when simply being there was just as valuable.

Taking slower, deeper breaths, I squeeze Jake's fingertips and look up. His own eyes are trained on the table.

When he raises his chin to meet my gaze, I feel my heart leap. My feelings for him are not just those lingering from a childhood friendship. There is something real and new.

"I've spent _so_ many days and nights wondering what my life would be if _one_ choice had been made differently. If Scott had left only a few minutes before or after he did. If I hadn't pushed him so hard to go so we didn't have to pay for an empty hotel suite. I have gone over _every_ scenario in my head over and over, every single day for the last nine months." It's amazing how quickly time passes when each day feels like it will never end.

Jake's silence yesterday felt awkward and torturous. Yet as we sit across from each other while I pour my burdens onto him, his silence is now a show of respect.

"I'm not telling you any of this so you feel bad for me. I just want you to understand where I'm coming from. I've lived in the land of what-ifs and could-have-beens for the better part of a year. And when it comes down to it, it never changes where I am. I'm a thirty-three-year-old widow, living in a construction zone of a house, trying to navigate the waters of single parenting—and not super well. No amount of wishing is going to bring Scott back or change what's happened." The tears spill over again. I reach up to meet them with the back of my hand as they emerge.

"Liv, I'm sorry." His tone is low, intimate. Jake has never been far from tragedy or heartbreak. I nod in appreciation, sniffing.

We sit, his hand on mine, eyes locked.

It can't have missed him that all traces of the carefree girl of my past are gone. Is he going stand and walk away, realizing the baggage I come with? But then there is the possibility that he might feel a kinship having historically _been_ the one with the baggage.

The Jake I saw glimpses of yesterday was one that reminded me of the laughter and joy that shaped our teen years. I realize, with only one different decision, that laughter could have continued throughout our life together. But since yesterday when he called my name, there's only been sorrow and anguish. We aren't the same people that we saw fall in love.

Pulling my hand out from under his, I break the intimacy of hope.

Wiping away the last of the tears, I clasp my hands together.

"Now then ..." One last sniff and it's down to business. "I have questions."

"I'd expect you would." Jake smiles knowingly.

"When did this all start?"

"Couple years ago."

"How?"

"Hmm..." Jake takes a sip, contemplating his answer "...next question."

"No, that's a valid question and none of the other questions even make sense without that one."

"My theory sounds crazy." He purses his lips as his brows furrow.

"Crazier than seeing a life I threw away because rather than have an awkward conversation, I broke up with you instead?"

"Fair point." Jake studies my face as he decides how to explain best. "Gramma June died a couple years ago. I'm sure you remember I moved in with my grandparents junior year of high school." He leaves out the part where he thinks that I am responsible for that, but it's there underneath the words he says. "When Grampa Bill died, I moved her into my apartment because I was all she had left. My mom hadn't spoken to her in years after Gramma insisted she leave my dad."

I sit quietly, trying to follow how this bit of his history connects to the events from yesterday.

"Gramma pushed me for years to try and find my soulmate. She was a big believer in fate since her and Grampa had only met due to a series of missteps. She also believed my mom ignored <u>her</u> soul mate and instead married my dad. Gramma June always thought that was the reason my parents' relationship was so toxic. You know what they say about fate being a bitch ..."

"Do you mean karma?"

"Her too."

Jake chuckles. He speaks about his grandma with amusement and devotion. I never met his grandma, but the idea that he had at least one relative who showed him love and tenderness brings me peace. He deserved that kind of love. Everyone does.

"When she realized that she would die before seeing me married off, she insisted I must have missed my soul mate, and if I didn't retrace my steps and figure out who I was meant to be with, I would be doomed to the same unhappiness I had grown up with. I sat by her bed as she asked me to list the women in my life who I at some time or another had a relationship with. Once the list was complete, she told me it was time to get to work, to find each woman and see if there was still something there. She died that night." His mouth works trying to form a word before settling into a frown. I see pain cross his face, similar to the pain I'd displayed only moments before.

"So you think your grandma is what ... guiding you from the other side?" My mouth is sticky and dry. Lifting my cup, I take a pull from the straw. A small glob of caramel is followed by the ice-cold liquid.

"It's the only thing that makes sense."

"So how do you explain me being able to see it too?" The question sparks excitement in his eyes. Sitting up, Jake leans forward, resting his forearms on the edge of the table.

"I thought about that all night." Lifting his eyebrows, he waits until I raise my own in question. "Okay, I settled on the theory that Gramma had always set out to show my soul mate the vision as well so <u>she</u> would realize the mistake and we could move forward <u>together</u>."

This explanation makes more sense than I had expected. If it were <u>my</u> curse, or gift to bestow on Noah, I wouldn't just leave it in his hands to convince the person he was meant to be with; I'd want them to know without a doubt.

"How do we know June..." I almost call her Gramma, but don't. "...showed us what actually would have happened and not just some bullshit. How do we know it's actually what would have happened?"

"That's not the kind of woman she was. She believed in fate, without interference."

"Yet here she is. Interfering," I tease. Jake rolls his eyes.

"I don't think the point is to focus on what life could have been but more so to use it as a jumping off point to get back on track. To make us realize the feelings we have for each other deep down."

I sit back, wanting to dispute that I have feelings for him but unable to lie convincingly. Jake's scar dimples as he smiles. He thinks he has me cornered into his box of reasons. And he might, but our lives have turned so far away from the day I ended our short relationship in the entryway of the school. I'm not sure if I can pinpoint the ways I've changed, because the transformation has taken place over the course of nearly two decades, piece by piece, until I was a completely different person.

"We're not those kids anymore, Jake. It doesn't matter how yesterday made us feel. We've both lived lives and had experiences that have fundamentally changed who we are as people. We don't even know if thirty-three-year-old you and I are compatible in any way." Even as I'm saying this, I'm silently willing him to change my mind. To make me believe I'm wrong.

"We can't be <u>that</u> different. We can grow into the people we know we could have been." He doesn't miss a beat with this. It's something he's clearly thought through. "We just need to mold ourselves into those versions of ourselves. Like clay!"

I can see the over-eager Jake that drove me away as a teenager. Only now, I'm begging to be pulled into his dream. It won't take much to convince me to jump off this cliff if he's by my side.

"We aren't clay, Jake. But if we were, we've already been molded, glazed, and fired through a kiln. Maybe we aren't as beautiful as we could have been, but it's too late to do it differently." This sounds ridiculous out loud. It sounded less cheesy in my mind.

Jake narrows one eye at me, holding my gaze and allowing me to see the gears turning in his head, mulling over what I said.

"Do you want to get out of here?"

One simple question and he's pulled me out of my own head and right along with him. "Sure."

My purse catches on the edge of the chair as I go to pull it. Reaching my hand into the depths, I try to find my keys. I'm taking too long as I sift through crumpled receipts, the handful of chapsticks and crumbs from that granola bar that Noah opened and abandoned.

"I'll drive. C'mon." He stands, dangling his own set.

Six

"This thing still runs?" The Jeep barely ran when he first bought it, and with the amount of work he put into it, never in a million years did I think it would run for a year, let alone another 16 more.

"Ouch!" Holding his hand to his chest, wounded by my insinuation. "Yes, <u>she</u> still runs." Jake unlocks the passenger door and opens it for me. Walking around, he climbs into the driver's seat. "She just keeps on truckin'! Plus, she's less maintenance than most women I've dated." As he says this, he smirks and gives me the slightest wink.

I've always had a thing for a casual wink. Jake <u>knows</u> I have a thing for winks. He once told me that I couldn't date a guy just because he winked at me. Yet here he is sending a wave of flutters through me with my own kryptonite.

The Jeep roars to life with a series of rattles, knocks, and squeals. Lurching forward out of the parking lot, Jake turns east, towards the freeway entrance. Pulling from where it dangles, he hands me the aux cord. With the age of the Jeep, I half expect the cord to attach to a cassette tape. But he's at least updated the sound system.

The Jeep was our first taste of real freedom, our safe haven, and our end. I want to turn and see if the blue nail polish stain is still right where I spilled it. And on that note, does the brake light still blink twice before remaining solid? Even the mechanic in town wasn't sure what he did to the wiring to make that one happen. Does Jake still do all the repairs himself?

"Put some music on." He's practically yelling and I can <u>still</u> barely hear him over the roaring and rattling coming from the front end.

"I thought we could both just enjoy the sound of your low-maintenance vehicle!" I have to shout to make sure he catches my words.

His eyes roll as he takes his fist and pounds on the dash twice in quick succession.

"Just give her a minute. Once she warms up, she quiets down."

Jake was the first of us to turn 16. One month before me and six before Ben. While his dad was opposed to him getting his driver's license, probably because it would mean less control over Jake, his mom knew that his bike no longer being thrown in the driveway and in Dave's way would ease some tension. She probably also thought that a car would be an escape for Jake if things went bad. She drove him to the DMV early enough that he was first in line. I don't want to give her any undue credit, but maybe she did what she could.

Ben and I waited for Jake at Ben's house, our bikes tossed on the front lawn. We expected him to arrive in his mom's Honda Civic, we'd already called the theater three times to get updated movie times by the time the tan Jeep pulled up, clanking and rattling to the curb. I half expected it to flatten and collapse like some sort of cartoon. Leaning over he fumbled the window down.

"Freeeeeee-dom!" He bellowed in his best Mel Gibson *Braveheart* impression.

Ben and I raced, he won but waited for me to crawl between the front seats to sit myself on the small back bench.

Winding through the streets, windows down, we tasted true freedom. So far beyond what our bikes could offer us. The ocean was less than ninety minutes and a single tank of gas away. A distance that would have been unreachable only the day before.

It was a mechanic special that Jake had no business thinking he could handle. The first week on the road he wound up at my house nearly every night, asking my Dad what a certain noise could indicate and how expensive and difficult it would be to fix. My Dad had sent Jake away the first night with instructions to purchase a repair manual, new distributor cap, rotor, and six new spark plugs.

Jake and Ben spent each evening throughout the rest of the week in the gravel driveway on the side of my house learning every nook and cranny of the engine bay while I dutifully manned the boombox. Alternating between my own pop CDs and the Sublime album they bought "for me." We all knew it was just so they could also have a copy at my house. One that wasn't scratched as bad as their own were. For the first time in months, we didn't worry about Jake and what he would face when he returned home. Instead, he seemed to stand taller armed with his own escape hatch.

"What I Got" comes up as a suggestion on Spotify and it stops me with a smile. My finger hovers, but I don't know if he still listens to Sublime. Maybe his music taste got the ultimate sophisticated glow up along with his fashion sense. Maybe he listens to like John Legend. The longer I take picking a playlist, the higher the expectation will be. Best of 2000's playlist is listed under the song and I click it. Pressing the shuffle option, *Hero* by Enrique Iglesias comes over the speakers.

He gives me a sly look out of the corner of his eye. This song was <u>everywhere</u> for a while, and even though he sang it mockingly every time it played, he was really good. As the song builds to the chorus, I'm trying not to look at him, hoping that without pressure, he'll oblige me. Taking a deep breath, he bellows, "I can be your hero, baby!"

Any tension I felt only a short time ago, sitting across from him in the coffee shop has melted into nostalgic joy.

"What do you have going on today?" He glances between the road and me. He's grinning, waiting for my response. I was so caught up, that I nearly forgot that I have any responsibilities at all.

"Uh, well... I have a bunch of emails I need to return, but nothing pressing. Why?" I hadn't given a thought as to where we were going or how long we'll be gone. And judging by his adventurous yet mischievous look, he has absolutely no intention of sharing these details with me.

"Perfect. I want to take you somewhere." He turns back to the road, flips his blinker on, and merges onto I-5 southbound. Coburg fades in the sideview mirror and the time on my Apple Watch lights up with nine-forty-five, reminding me of a certain little boy I dropped off at school only an hour ago.

"Oh. I'm supposed to pick Noah up from my parents around seven." I can't disappear for real, and Jake should probably know that, in case he's planning on driving us to Mexico or somewhere like that.

Thirty minutes into the drive, Jake finally exits the freeway. He takes backroads, staying on Shoreview Drive for a few miles before following a sign pointing north for Pebbles at the Water's Edge.

The pavement ends and as groomed as the dirt road is, this is Oregon, the rain has already caused potholes. Jake speeds up, letting the back tires drift through the corners. He knows the road well and anticipates each twist and turn. His laugh grows each time I gasp. I'm bracing myself, resting one arm on the center console, the other on the door, trying to keep my body as steady as possible as the Jeep relies on its suspension to keep all four wheels grounded.

He's gotten a lot better at off-roading. My body stays stiff, remembering the first time we went off the pavement. It ended with Jake and Ben having to dig us out, wedging branches under the wheels to try and find traction.

Jake rounds a corner and skirts the Jeep to a stop, enveloping us in a dirt cloud. As the dust clears, a neighborhood still very much under construction appears.

"I don't think we're supposed to be here." I give him a nervous smile. I've driven through my share of construction zones by accident and know that they don't appreciate uninvited guests. I may have gotten lost shortly after moving to D.C. and it may have ended with Secret Service agent's guns pointed at my car.

"Eh, I think we'll be okay. I know a guy." Another wink. God, he has to stop doing that. But also please don't stop. Jake inches forward and parks next to a truck with a J&B Designs decal on the door, and a line of vehicles, presumably belonging to the construction crew. "I have a few things I have to do. Wanna help?"

I would sit next to him, saying nothing, just to be near him. Just to feel the hope that seems to accompany him.

Hope. A word often used in such an offhanded way the importance and weight of it is lost. "Hope this email finds you well," dismisses the power of true hope, or the desperation that the absence of hope presents. A person devoid of hope makes choices not believing that they truly matter in the grand scheme of life. On the other hand, someone filled with hope makes even the smallest decisions with a curiosity about how they might play into the future. I'm starting to feel the smallest bit of hope return since losing Scott. It's intoxicating and terrifying.

We walk towards the only house that looks to be in any sort of livable condition. The brown exterior gives it the feel of a cabin in the mountains, only with a more modern flair. Angular windows fill the spaces by the front door. Up the steps of the front porch, plants and a small table to the right of the door add to the charm that the architecture seems to intentionally leave space for. It's gorgeous and in a completely different league than my crumbling house on Crane street.

Jake opens the front door and holds it open. I'm apprehensive about stepping over the threshold; I'll break something, and who knows how expensive whatever I break may be?

The smell of cloves and orange waft through the entryway, reminding me of my own grandma. Holidays spent perched on the stool near the stove, stirring the cranberries as they slowly popped, creating a sticky sweet mess splattered across my hands, the stove, and counters.

Directly above our heads in the foyer hangs a giant spherical chandelier made out of twisted branches, a cluster of bulbs illuminated in the center. It reminds me of a chandelier at a lodge in the Poconos only that one was made out of antlers. But it's also familiar to the style of a fixture my dad made for their backyard a few years back.

Jake closes the door, breaking the spell of the chandelier. An office to my right has bookshelves lining the wall behind a desk. The shelves are organized by the color of the spine of each book. I've given up trying to organize books in any specific way since Noah seems unable to stop mixing it up again.

Straight ahead sits the living room. Floor-to-ceiling windows, overlooking a lake. It's the kind of view you see in a magazine or movie and you just <u>know</u> it doesn't exist in real life. But here it is, existing. I step towards the windows giving in to the gravity of the view.

"This place is incredible," I whisper in complete awe as I turn to take it all in.

"Thanks." His back straightens even more, chest puffing out.

"Shut up! This is <u>your</u> house?" My mouth falls open as I slap his arm in disbelief. It's beautifully crafted, but it's not something I'd expect a thirty-three-year-old bachelor to be living in. It has the vibe of something a man in his forties would build after earning far more money than I could ever imagine having. But also, he brought me to his house? How absolutely presumptuous of him. Jake is not getting lucky, and I hope he knows that.

"I mean, I'm no electrician, but I get by." Jake nudges me with his elbow, calling me back to the profession he spent years working towards in our life that never actually happened. "I don't sleep here, and right now it's mostly just used as the model home, but yeah, it's mine."

I stare, expecting him to explain further. Why is he not sleeping here if it's his, it's by far nicer than any house in Coburg. Maybe he just has a series of homes placed all over the Pacific Northwest. Did I just stumble upon the hometown millionaire bachelor like some sort of Hallmark movie? Jackpot!

"I inherited two hundred acres on the lake and a few buildings in town when Gramma June died. The acreage wasn't really worth that much on its own, so I decided to draw from the rent on the houses and buildings in town for the startup money to get going up here. Someday this will be home." Jake leads us into the office, gesturing to a map framed on the wall.

The development map is broken into three phases with the first colored green. Just below the map on a small table is a 3D model showing the full plan. My fingers trace the rise and fall of the buildings and landscape surrounding them. Placing his hand on my lower back, Jake leans over and touches one of the tiny houses.

My stomach flutters as my breath catches in my throat, the electricity of that first touch is somehow still buzzing through my hand from yesterday. It's taking everything I have to stand still, to not turn around and wrap myself around him. I <u>know</u> how his body feels, though it's never <u>actually</u> been under my touch. The heat radiating from him does nothing to cool me off.

"This..." he points to a house along the shore of the lake in the model "...this is the house we're in. By next summer, I should have these fifteen houses done and rented out for the season." A reservations binder sits next to the model. "When it's all complete, there will be forty-seven houses and another ten glamping spots. Not to mention the trail that wraps around the entire lake."

"Wow!" I don't know how to verbalize the pride I feel. Pride I'm not worthy to feel. I played no part in his success. Never could I have guessed that he was some sort of big-time real estate developer.

Stepping back, Jake moves over to the desk. The absence of his warmth chills my skin, and I follow him, hoping to feel his touch again. It's been so long since I've been excited by anything, let alone another man.

"I have to decide on paint color and flooring for a house right down the lane. I figured you could help with the final decision. Then we can have lunch on the deck and catch up."

Jake walks behind the desk to the coat rack in the corner. He offers me a white hard hat. I take it and follow him out of the office through the front door.

The hat squashes my curls so they all pop out just under the brim. Jake steps off the porch and into mud and gravel. Thank God I opted for a pair of wedges in place of the heels I put on first. My skinny jeans don't have much stretch to them so hopefully the mental image of us balancing on scaffolding above a high-rise is purely imaginative. I dressed for impressing a boy in a coffee shop, not for wandering in the mountains.

Jake grins as he offers his hand to me. I return the grin and take his hand, stepping carefully so as not to twist my ankle.

My cheeks hurt from smiling so much. I've tried to control every aspect of my life over the last year, but just this tiniest act of letting go of that control is liberating. I did <u>not</u> expect the sense of relief and joy I feel at being out of control.

After seeing what he's done to the first house, I know I have nothing substantial to offer by means of design advice. My own renovation is based solely on what I see on social media, along with re-watching every episode of *Fixer Upper*.

We walk side by side with a respectable distance between us. Does he not want to be close to me? Maybe I was the only one who felt butterflies when we stood next to each other in his office. Or maybe he's finally figured out I'm not the same girl he saw in our vision. How is he staying so chill? Down the muddy path we go as Jake outlines his vision for the development.

"It's going to be <u>the</u> Pacific Northwest destination. For those that want to get away, but don't really care for the beach, they can come here." His hands fly out from his sides at an upward angle, encompassing the entire lake, looking like Tevye in *Fiddler on the Roof*. "We're going to have a row of shops over there, and we will have nightly activities and concerts, Saturday markets on the main street. Weddings in the chapel. Something for everyone."

I try to imagine driving up here on a summer night with Noah. Walking through the small main street, eating an ice cream cone while listening to the local Journey cover band that used to play at the bowling alley—if they're even still around anymore. I open my mouth to ask if they are still together and performing but decide better of it as Jake continues.

"Down there..." he points down through the trees towards the water "...will be the marina with kayaks, paddle boards, and paddle boat rentals. And then up past the main street and over north a bit will be the stable, right by the new equestrian trails that..." his voice falls "...I still need to complete."

"Well, when can I move in?" Oh my God, I meant into the community, but now realize as the words hit the air between us that it sounds like I'm asking to move into his lake house <u>with</u> him. Unsure of how to recover, I just let the sticky question lie, praying he'll ignore it.

He tips his hard hat winking, dispelling any awkwardness. The complete ease I feel with him is something I have to get used to again. It's so much like it used to be, even though everything is different.

We arrive at the house in question, walking through the already open door. The walls are sheetrocked in place, and the floor still plywood, giving off the same vibes as my own house. Only this one is <u>actively</u> being worked on, unlike mine. Jake explains the aesthetic.

"So we're going for warm, cozy mountain retreat. These are the samples—"

With a hand on my elbow, he leads me toward the windowsill where the samples sit.

The first option is gray, the second option is ... gray. I see no discernible difference between the two. Maybe one is spelled with an E—that's all I got. Looking from the flooring to Jake and then around the room, I can't help but wonder, am I being Punk'd?

"You're joking, right? These are literally the exact same color." I wait for his laugh. For Jake to admit that he's just messing with me. That of course they're the same. The laugh doesn't come. Jake looks from me to the flooring and back.

"I'm being completely serious. You honestly can't see the difference?" His eyes narrow in disbelief.

I shake my head, eyes wide, begging him to question my sanity. I've been in a number of debates deciding whether the dress was white and gold or blue and black. Just as I was sure that dress was white and gold, I <u>know</u> these two paint samples are exactly the same. It's a hill I'm willing to die on.

"Ok, well this one..." he points to the first "...has purple notes. Whereas this one is just a straight gray."

"Nope." I'm not going to play his game. His eyes bulge like the wide-eyed emoji, and I can't hold back my laughter. He's obviously forgetting how stupidly stubborn I can be.

"You're useless." Shaking his head and laughing, he waves his hand as a dismissal from the room.

My eyes widen. "Wait! I'm getting kicked out?"

"Yup. Go explore the rest of the house while I do this. I don't want your lack of taste rubbing off on me."

"Wow!" I laugh, backing out of the room, hands raised in surrender.

I wander up the stairs and into one of the unfinished bedrooms, still laughing. Jake's lighthearted insult is refreshing after months of everyone treating me like I'll step off the edge if nudged by even a single word.

There had been a time when I shut everyone out. Friends and family alike. This barrier contained my heartache but also prevented anyone from being let in. It was a defense mechanism, ensuring they could not do further damage to me or Noah. Once I found myself sufficiently numb, I shut down any emotion that wasn't essential for survival. Then I started to pick up the pieces of what remained.

Seeing Jake and experiencing whatever yesterday was woke me up. The world I purposely blurred is now crystal clear. I've spent the better part of this last year just trying to make it through a day or a week, and in my frantic struggle for survival, I'd forgotten to look for joy.

Scott often called me Alice, pointing out the same flaw Lewis Carroll gave his heroine in Wonderland. She was unable to take her own grandiose advice which she had no problem bestowing unto others. Scott's assessment of me is pretty accurate. If Scarlett were real, and in my position, I would likely have a great deal of advice for her. Advice that I haven't been living.

Spending the morning with Jake feels like every wall I put in place is being torn down. And that scares the hell out of me.

Jakes laugh with someone, and the sound travels and echoes through the empty house, bringing back memories from times long gone. Late nights and a friendship deeper than the sky.

"Go away, Jake. I'm not in the mood. I just want to sleep." Rolling over, I pulled the quilt up over my head.

"C'mon. I heard about you and Aaron. Let's talk."

He wanted to gloat. He'd told me that I shouldn't date Aaron, and I did it anyway. Jake only wanted me to come outside so he could rub it in my face that he was right all along. I had no intention of giving him that kind of satisfaction.

"If you don't come out, I'm coming in."

It was easier for me to get up and go inside if he made me angry than for me to try and get him to leave in the same instance. Pushing the blanket aside, I sat up, resigned.

Jake backed away from the window, allowing me to leave the house on my own time. Rather than putting on more clothes, I pulled the quilt off my bed and wrapped it around myself.

I found Jake a few minutes later, grinning, swaying on the hammock. "Wipe that stupid smile off your face, Jake Larson." I kicked his foot before sitting down with the billow of quilt following my movement.

"I'm sorry. I just don't see how you didn't see this coming."

"How I didn't see my boyfriend breaking up with me to go out with the new girl? Like I should have known that she's so much better than me so of course Aaron would be crazy about her? Way to make me feel better, jerk."

Heather had moved less than a month before. She was everything I wasn't. Taller than most of the boys. Blond hair curled perfectly, flowing over her shoulders and framing the boobs that she had grown. Meanwhile, I was still flatter than the wall and always had my hair in a ponytail since I didn't know how to do a thing with it. When Heather walked with her hips swaying, the birds chirped just a little bit louder. When I walked, I moved from place to place without any of the magic she possessed.

"That's <u>not</u> what I meant and you know it." Jake took my hand, holding it between both of his. "Aaron is an idiot, so it's no surprise that he'd give you up without realizing how big of a mistake he's making. He sucks. You don't want to be with a jock."

"<u>You're</u> a jock, Jake." I wasn't sure if him joining the football team had slipped his mind, or if he just didn't consider himself to be on the same plane as the other team members.

"I'm not a jock. I just play sports. It's different. I'd be good for you." He squeezed his fingers ever so slightly.

A door closes downstairs, bringing me out of my memory and back to the present.

Moving through the rooms, I pause at each window to take in the view someone will be waking up to in only a matter of months. I notice that there are a number of trees that would be perfect for a hammock. Why hasn't he hung one? Would that be too much of a reminder of our friendship, of the countless nights we laid side by side trying to make sense of the world?

The sun will rise over the lake and spill into these bedrooms, pouring light onto the individuals and families who are here as a respite from their daily lives. I try to imagine the families that will run through these rooms. Will they ever think of the time and effort that was put into each and every decision when it was being built? Will <u>they</u> notice if the correct gray is chosen? I can't help but smile knowing that no one will care about the shade of gray more than Jake does.

Jake never does anything lightly. So our falling back into the comfortable nature of our early friendship can't just be a coincidence. He'd stop it if he wasn't sure it was what he wanted.

It isn't just the sense of familiarity in our conversations and interactions. I feel comfortable with him in a way I've never felt with any man—or woman, for that matter. We saw a possible life together, but who's to say that the pivotal moment in time that could have sent us to a happily-ever-after didn't, instead, send Jake into becoming a serial killer who lures his victims to construction sites and buries them beneath the foundations of new homes being built.

I shake my head. Jake isn't a serial killer, but I open and close the closet checking for possible bodies. Just to be sure.

Footsteps on the stairs startle me, and I quickly move back to the window where I stand looking out at the lake. Goose bumps rise to meet Jake's fingertips on my lower back as he rests his hand there. Straightening my back I welcome the touch, my head falling toward my right shoulder, a gasp escapes through my parted lips. God, I want him.

As quickly as his hand makes contact, it's gone, leaving my back tingling at the absence.

Seven

The gravel mixed with mud squelches underneath our shoes as we leave the construction zone, heading in the direction of Jake's lake house. He's given up on the measured tone he used when he was trying to impress me with his plans for the development and instead has fallen into the rambling nature of old friends.

"So, I decided that putting the homes up on stilts would be the best way to prevent any damage in the event of flooding." He points to a home still being framed. At this point of the process, the stilts look like wobbly giraffe legs.

"Okay, but like, what about if it rains for weeks and weeks and then a mudslide takes out the stilts from this angle?" I swoosh my hands towards the neighborhood. Jake follows the imagined path of destruction with his eyes.

"I guess everybody dies." He nudges me as he looks down and smiles with just a hint of a wink.

"Do they get a refund for their vacation in that instance?" I continue in a mock-serious tone.

"Well ..." He pauses, taking his time to think this through as our footsteps crunch the gravel, pushing the pebbles deeper into the mud. "No, because I'm sure they will have had a <u>lovely</u> time up until that point."

"Until they are killed by your negligence at anticipating a deadly mudslide?" Craving his nearness, I veer slightly towards him. Our arms brush against each other, sending a shiver up my arm despite the sweltering temperature. "Sounds like you've got a liability on your hands, Larson."

He laughs, shrugging. That laugh. It's the laugh that I always felt was reserved for me. It's different than the laugh he uses when flirting with girls, or when he's watching an old Will Ferrell movie. This one is deep and sounds a little like it's trapped in a bubble.

Returning to the lake house, I follow Jake into the kitchen. While the ceiling is not the full two stories the living room is, it isn't much lower. Positioned over a range is a large hammered copper vent hood. White and gray marbled countertops sit atop olive cupboards. A textured backsplash featuring dark wood runs from the range to the hood and over the rest of the countertops. It ends nearly two feet above the counter where open shelving is featured instead of upper cabinets. Filled with coordinating dishes, I feel more than a little self-conscious about the plastic plates and cups Noah and I use.

Situated on the wall to the left of the range is a large apron sink. Windows in place of a wall give an incredible view of the lake and forest on the opposite side. I would never complain about doing dishes again if this was my view. An enormous island sits between myself and the range. The creamy marble countertop reflects the light pendants hanging above it.

I lean against the island, admiring the details apparent in every corner of this room while I watch Jake rummage through the fridge and pantry. His shirt tightens and loosens as he reaches, moving things around in his search. The fridge closes and he turns to me with a frown of apology.

"I haven't stayed here in a while, so I don't have much. I've got frozen pizzas and stuff for peanut butter and jelly sandwiches, if you don't mind possibly expired jam." His regret at what he has to offer would vanish if he realized that as a mom these are two staples in my life. And it all depends on <u>how</u> long ago the jam expired.

"Let's throw in a pizza!" I throw in a little extra enthusiasm to dispel any embarrassment he feels. He smiles, moving to retrieve the box from the freezer.

I move to the oven, pressing buttons in an attempt to be helpful. "What temperature does it need to be at?"

"Four-twenty-five." Jake brings the pizza over to start preparing the baking sheet.

Blocking his access to the drawer he needs, I take a step back so that my back presses against the island. I place the heels of my hands on the granite and lift myself so I'm sitting with my legs dangling over the edge.

I watch Jake cover the sheet with foil, cupping the foil around each edge with his hands before getting the pizza out of the box and placing it in the middle. The oven is only preheated to one-hundred degrees. Now is the time to see if Jake will open the oven and slide the baking sheet in, or if he'll wait for it to preheat. It says a lot about a person. I never wait for the oven to preheat. Jake was always the type to wait, but there is that small chance that time has made him less patient than he once was. He turns to me and shrugs.

I'm not really surprised, and it's not really a revelation. Jake has always been a player in the long game. He befriended me knowing full well that there was little chance I would ever feel the same way about him that felt about me. I, on the other hand, hardly ever think ahead to the next moment. My impulses have landed me in hot water a few times—okay, more like weekly.

With the heels of my hands on the edge of the counter, I press my shoulders forward. Jake takes tentative steps towards me, staying far enough away to not seem threatening but close enough for me to reach him. Maybe I should wait for the metaphorical oven to preheat. It's only been a day, but we have lived a lifetime together, if only for a moment.

Life is short. Fuck waiting. Reaching out my hand, I hook a finger in his belt loop. I don't have to put any force into pulling him towards me. He's more than willing to move into my silent request. This is the moment we should have had years before. Better late than never, I suppose.

He steps forward to stand between my legs against the counter. Starting at his navel and moving my gaze up, I eventually land on Jake's own eyes which are studying me.

He's going to see right through me, and I don't know if I'm ready for that. Can he see how broken I am? I loop my arm up and around his neck, bringing his mouth to meet mine. I expect Jake to be cautious about kissing me, just like he had been when he touched my back in the construction zone. But right now there's no hesitation. I can feel my pulse beating in my lower lip. My lust and desire mixes with his years of unrequited love. Oh my God. It is pure magic. Sparks, fireworks, all of it.

And then the surge of everything slams into me. Months of loneliness, heartbreak, the need to be touched, and the fluttering of new attraction. I'm fighting the tears, and I'm not sure if they are tears of elation, depression, or both. Jake presses himself against my chest, and I can't tell if it's my heart or his drumming. I lean back, the granite cooling my skin through the fabric of my shirt.

I reach up and started unbuttoning Jake's shirt, wanting to feel his skin under my fingers. To know that this is real and not another false memory. He catches my hands, pulling them away from his shirt and straightening himself to break the spell.

He holds my hands in his and looks down. I don't want us to look each other in the eye. I don't want him to know that as badly as I want him, I feel this crushing guilt for wanting him. And he <u>still</u> knows me. He'll see it if I give him the chance. I close my eyes, refusing to let him in.

"Let's slow down." He exhales hard on his last word.

"No!" I reach up, trying to pull him onto me. Jake takes my arm and lifts me to a sitting position. He's right. Of course he's right. I can't just jump headfirst into something physical without thinking it through. Closing my eyes, I breathe in and out, trying to slow my heart down and quell the impulse. "Ok," I agree reluctantly.

Jake moves his head forward, resting his forehead against mine. "That's how our first kiss should have been." He smiles wistfully.

I hadn't been ready to kiss Jake the first time—or really kiss anyone for that matter. Back then, I had a lot of healing to do. The first time Jake tried to kiss me, it ended in tears and me practically running away. I had been caught off guard.

Jake laughs softly. "God, that was so awkward. I was just so excited to be out with you, I tried to move straight to you being my girlfriend without any transition from just being friends."

"It wasn't all you." I don't want to bring up all the reasons we didn't work, but I hope he knows it wasn't anything he did. "I didn't exactly make it easy for you. But <u>this</u> ... this was much better."

Pulled by an invisible force, Jake moves towards me again. He's inches from my face when the oven beeps. Jake reluctantly throws his head back as he turns around to slide the tray into the oven. I slide off the counter and brush past him. My shoulder barely grazes his back and still he leans into it. So it's <u>not</u> just me after all.

Cheeks blazing, I open the refrigerator doors trying to cool off. Sparkling water, condiments, and a single jar of jam are the only contents on the shelves. Picking up the jar of jam, I search for the black printed numbers. It expired more than a year ago. Yikes. I help myself to a sparkling water and close the fridge. Through the dining room, I unlatch the lock and slide the glass door on its track. I leave it open, knowing Jake isn't going to be far behind me and not wanting to put any type of barrier between us.

I set the can on the table as I move to the railing, leaning over. Fresh air fills my lungs and does a decent job of clearing my mind, providing clarity from the electric, stifling air inside.

Sparks. My entire life I've searched for sparks, and I'd nearly allowed the surprise and excitement to take over. Okay, not nearly. I gave it the keys and let it drive. Jake slamming on the brakes allowed me to stop and think about what I was actually doing.

The door slides closed, and I'm finally feeling the humiliation thanks to the clarity the fresh air brings.

"I'm sorry. I don't know what got into me." I lean my back with my hands gripping the railing and my elbows facing out. The breeze from the lake blows against my back, moving my curls over my shoulders in Jake's direction. I'm hoping I look sexy and mysterious, but I probably just look like Medusa.

Jake smiles. He knows exactly what got ahold of me, and I nearly dragged him down as well. This newfound chemistry mixed with our old chemistry as friends is giving way to something unexpected.

Jake leans against the glass door.

"You know, I've dreamed of what being with you for real would feel like." His smile widens as he shakes his head. His voice is so low the breeze almost carries it away. "When I saw you yesterday, I <u>knew</u> that touching you would break my heart. I'd imagined our own happily ever after for so long, the thought of seeing something other than that was terrifying. But I couldn't resist."

The idea of not feeling what I feel for him makes me miss him, even as he stands right in front of me.

"What would you have done if I hadn't seen it all?" I try to imagine Jake sitting in the coffee shop giving me the cold shoulder one second and then trying to convince me to run away with him the next. Would I have thought he was insane? Would I have given it a second thought, or simply brushed it off as another example of how exhausting Jake is?

A shadow crosses his face. He blinks several times, as his mouth tries to form words.

"I honestly don't know," Apparently the thought hasn't occurred to him. Maybe he <u>doesn't</u> always think through everything. "I've never seen anything worth pursuing, but I wouldn't have been able to just drop it and move on. I'd probably have regrouped and approached you later with a plan in mind."

"Ok. So since you have seen something worth pursuing ... what now?"

"I think we see if we can build something even remotely as great as what we saw ..." Jake moves across the deck, placing a hand on either side of the railing, trapping me between the railing and his body. His eyes dart from my eyes to my mouth so quickly I almost miss it.

I can't stop the thought from erupting, ruining the moment.

"And if we can't?" The idea of us not working out hurts just thinking about it.

Jake pushes away from the railing, hands raised in exasperation. "We haven't even started, and you're already looking for an out? Jesus, Liv, why can't you just enjoy the moment while you're in it?" He's annoyed, and I can't really blame him. I'm annoyed with myself, already trying to plan for the failure of our relationship.

I've been trying to talk myself out of a relationship with Jake since I saw him, all the while giving him signals that I'm all in. And I want to be all in. God, I must be exhausting to be around.

"I don't know." We stare at each other, brows furrowed, both trying to figure out why I seem hellbent on self-sabotage.

"Okay, well what about the rest of your list? Do you just give it up now?"

Jake's phone alarm rings from his pocket, startling me and saving Jake from having to answer.

I stand breathless watching as Jake navigates the kitchen, searching three drawers before locating the pizza cutter. With the pan in one hand, Jake uses his free hand to grab an entire roll of paper towels before returning to the glass door. I move quickly across the porch to slide the door open and take the paper towels from under his arm. Placing them on the glass table situated on the far side of the deck, I sit across from Jake and smile sheepishly. I want to return to our carefree conversations, keen to avoid the subject of my pessimism.

Crinkling my nose, I playfully ask, "Any chance you have a can of pineapple in that empty kitchen?" I laugh before he has a chance to react. My love of pineapple on pizza is a controversy that has lasted more than twenty years.

"Liv, don't be gross!" He shakes his head and the controversy continues. He smiles but refuses to join in on the laughter. "I'll have to ask you to leave."

We both know the threat is empty.

"Well, good luck kicking me out. I've only grown more stubborn."

"That's literally the only way you've grown," he quips. Asshole. "I thought maybe you'd hit a second puberty in your twenties, bringing you up to the height of a normal person."

"Ha ..." I hope to God he picks up on the sarcasm in my voice, along with the slow, deliberate eye roll. My height has always been Jake and Ben's favorite subject to try and get a rise out of me. As if their six foot plus height is because of anything they did, and not just the genetic lottery they won. They always made a habit of placing items on shelves they knew for a fact I couldn't reach. The joke's on them since I don't have to crouch to wash my hands or look on the lower shelves of the fridge. So there's that.

I take a giant bite of pizza. Jake's eyes widen as he watches my face, too late to prevent me from burning myself. It's lava. I need it out of my mouth now! The mushed pizza falls onto the tabletop next to my paper towel, looking eerily similar to a blob fish. I catch Jake's eye in my peripheral. His mouth is drawn in disgust. He closes his eyes and shakes his head. Is he embarrassed for me ... or of me? I'm mortified, but there is still some cheese—which is slightly cooler—in my mouth. I cover it with my hand, willing myself to try and swallow faster. I won't blame him if he stands up and leaves right now.

"In case you were wondering ... I'm not any more ladylike than I was as a teenager."

I'm only now realizing that the boy who had once been as messy as me is now polished and put together. He's turned into a catch. I'm the girl who spits out pizza when it burns my mouth.

"Sorry." I'm not really sure what I'm covering in this apology, it's just an all-encompass-ing.

"For what?" His eyes turn from thoughtful to confused.

"I don't know. Not being more impressive? I haven't had to impress anyone in a long time, and I just realized that I'm not exactly putting my best foot forward. I'm not even sure I have a best foot to put forward."

"It's kind of comforting to see that you are exactly the same. It's almost as if no time has passed."

"Almost." My eyes wander down to his chest and back up. Jake is more solid than he had been in the could've been world where he was a husband and dad. He's had extra time to put in at the gym without the need to work two jobs. He puffs up his chest, conscious of my objectification of him.

"You said the other 'what ifs' you saw were dark ..." The last word has to go through a bite of pizza. "What exactly did that look like?"

"Imagine the worst version of yourself. The version that does things only out of anger." Jake's eyes are fixed on something just over my shoulder. "I never wanted to be anything like my dad, you know? He does things specifically to hurt people, and there are some visions where I see him trying to make his way out in me."

"That's not who you are." It's a reassurance that he's nothing like his dad.

Eight

I keep the back door open so Noah will know where to find me, on the off chance he wakes up. I select the "Mom, alone time" playlist I've been curating for years—usually only playing it on quiet drives alone or during my semi-annual bath where I spoil myself with candles and bath salts after begging and bribing Noah to just give me ten minutes.

The patio is the only completed space in the house, which has more to do with the fact it only needed to be power washed rather than torn down and completely rebuilt, but I'm going to take the win.

After Noah goes to bed each night, I come out here and go over renovation plans because I need to convince myself progress will eventually be made. My vision boards burst with ideas far above my budget and skill set, and my contractor is just another old guy set in his ways of popcorn ceilings and red accent walls.

The woodpile against the back of the house has been stacked perfectly by my dad. I told him I could have chopped them myself, but he spent days chopping and stacking. I'm grateful it's not something I have to do right away. There's enough wood to entirely cover the wall and window, and I wonder how far into the fall and winter it will get me. It's a bit beyond my math skills.

Studying the pile of logs, I see the perfect one, only it's not exactly on the edge. I've never won a game of Jenga, but you miss a hundred percent of the shots you don't take, so I go for it anyway. Half the pile comes down in a thunderous crash as I pull the log out from its place. I'll deal with the mess later. Maybe I can convince Noah to stack them back up. Honestly, it might just be easier to burn all that wood in a bonfire rather than trying to put it back.

Kneeling in front of the fireplace, I ball up some junk mail before tilting the wood so they tent over the paper. The paper ignites without any coaxing. I hold the final piece of wood, trying to decide if I'm going to place it with the others or wait till the flames really start going.

"Hey." A deep voice breaks the ambiance.

I turn and without thinking throw the log. The figure dodges it matrix style and stands tall. Starting at my attacker's shoes, I make my way up to his face. Jake.

"You scared the shit out of me. What are you doing here?" My heart beats out of my chest, mostly due to the scare, but also maybe a little because I didn't expect to see Jake again so soon. He'd left me in the Brewtiful Day parking lot at my car only a few hours ago.

"Sorry!" He holds his hands up, surrendering. "I went to the front door, but nobody answered. I was just climbing back into my Jeep when I heard a crash back here. Thought I'd check it out, just to make sure everything was ok." His eyes focus on the source of the noise behind me. I shrug. I'm not going to attempt to make an excuse.

"Well, can I offer you a drink?" Confident the fire is going survive, I stand, brushing my hands off on my sweats.

Jake looks me up and down, smiling coyly. "Does that mean I can stay? Or should I expect another log hurled my way?"

"Ha." I deserve that little bit. "You want wine, beer, Capri Sun, or chocolate milk?" I smile. "I got it all."

"Oh man, I haven't had a Capri Sun in ages. But I'll just stick with beer. I can grab one. Are they in the fridge?" Jake moves towards the house.

"I got it," I insist. His lake house is a masterpiece, while my house looks like it's being torn down and donated piece by piece.

Catching our reflections in the sliding glass door, I cringe. He's no longer dressed in his button-down and slacks, but he still looks like a successful man. I, on the other hand, look homeless. I wasn't expecting company, and am dressed for bed in a tattered pair of Scott's sweats from his high school track team and a white ribbed tank top. And my hair! It was perfect earlier and now it's thrown into the messiest of top knots, not the intentional kind. This is a crawl-into-bed top knot. It's floppy, and floppy isn't sexy. Can I sneak upstairs and change without him noticing? Probably not.

The only beer I have in the fridge is Bud Light Orange. As a single woman without the desire or plan to entertain, I haven't felt the need to buy anything Noah and I won't consume. Now I'm left with the task of bringing out a drink I know he'll mock.

I hand Jake the bottle and watch his face scrunch up. "Liv, I don't know what this is, but it isn't beer."

"Cool. You can bring your own next time." I attempt a wink, but it must look like I have something in my eye.

We sit next to each other, feet propped up on the coffee table, watching the flames grow. The first few logs crackle as sparks burst from air pockets and sap deep in the wood.

"So …" I don't want to ruin the moment, but I'm curious. "What brings you to my house in the middle of the night, Mr. Larson?"

"Ok, well first of all it's not even 8:30. God, Liv, I know we're in our thirties now, but 8:30 is hardly the middle of the night!"

Leaning over, I nudge him with my shoulder. He pushes back gently in response. I think about mentioning that for a parent 8:30 is definitely considered the middle of the night, but I don't know how to do that without also acknowledging that while he isn't a parent, he very well could've been, given the vision we both saw.

"I kept thinking about you and went to text you, but realized I didn't have your number. So I did the totally not creepy thing of driving by. I saw a light on, so I figured you were home from your parents."

"I've been thinking about you too." The words feel juvenile to say out loud—though my thoughts have been anything but childish. Feeling his eyes on me, I turn and meet his gaze with a quiet smile.

His beard scratches my chin as he moves in to kiss me. It's more tender and less lust-driven than the kiss we shared earlier. My heart flutters with the excitement of young love rediscovered.

From his pocket the notification sound of a text rings, causing me to pull back and lean against the pillow. My lips still tingle from his stubble.

"That your _other_ girlfriend texting you?" I joke, but then realize this sounds like I'm assuming the title of girlfriend. Am I his girlfriend? I'm something, but what if he _does_ already have a girlfriend … am I the other woman?

"Could be any number of them." His tone is dry and does nothing to answer the stream of worries that seem to be building in my mind. He sits for a minute without saying anything, all the while I'm starting to lose my mind. "Nah, it's probably just Ben. We usually have some beer and play Ping-Pong on Wednesdays."

And we can sweep the "does he have a girlfriend" worry back under the rug for now.

"Well don't let me keep you from that excitement!" Ping-Pong tournaments in Ben's basement were intense throughout the years. Prior to our friendship ending, I had been undefeated.

"I'll just let him know I'm not gonna make it." He pulls his phone out of his pocket and starts texting.

"Invite him over!"

"You sure?" he looks over at me, his eyebrows pulled together.

"Yeah, I'm sure." I lost Ben in the same moment I lost Jake. Both best friends in one fell swoop. I don't mean to be greedy, but getting <u>both</u> of them back would be incredible.

Jake finishes sending his text and looks up at me, his eyes concerned. Inviting Ben over will also invite questions about <u>why</u> we are together—not like together-together but in the same space—but we can't answer these questions yet. Can we? Does Ben know?

Standing up, I pat Jake's shoulder. "I'm gonna go change real quick."

Jake pulls me down onto his lap. "Absolutely not! The world needs to see this." His finger touches the worn fabric on my thigh. His hand grips me as he pulls me into a kiss, sending my head spinning.

"Well, I'm at least going to put on a bra." I pull away, suddenly self-conscious, and wrap my arms around my chest. I mean they aren't great boobs anymore. They were fine before motherhood. Now they are a bit like deflated balloons.

My blush pink lace bra hangs on the doorknob in my room, exactly where I hung it only an hour before. That will do. Looking in the mirror I quickly fix my hair, pulling the scrunchy out of the tangled, floppy mess and letting the curls spill down. They have kinks in them, and don't look quite as good as they had this morning, but I feel better.

It's hard to imagine Ben in his thirties. Is he as clean-cut as Jake? Or does he still have jet-black hair hanging down over his eyes and ears? Somewhere between skater boy and emo. A combination that was all his own.

The camel cardigan is my final addition before heading back downstairs. Voices from outside carry down the hallway where they meet me on the bottom step.

"What the hell are we doing at Crane House? I thought this place was abandoned?" The voice is heavy with apprehension but still holds familiarity.

"Not anymore," Jake answers Ben in a tone bursting with a secret.

"For the love of God, tell me <u>you</u> didn't buy this as some new project. We are already strapped for cash as it is. Jake, you can't just keep spending. We <u>need</u> money if we want to finish on time. And I'm not touching this place. It needs to be gutted, but not before it's saged."

I continue outside, picking up the Bud Light Orange from the table.

"Oh, I saged the shit out of it." I lean against the doorway, smiling, trying to look way cooler than I know I am. While Jake's transformation was bold, Ben looks exactly as he did in high school—like he belongs in an Abercrombie and Fitch ad. Six foot two and built like a football player. He managed to cut his hair, making him look even more boyish. "Benson Zhao, long time no see."

"Oh. My. God." Ben pauses in between each word. His jaw fails to stay closed. "Olivia fucking Turner!" He strides over, massive arms open.

He crushes my shoulders and ribs as he gathers me into his arms. Lifting me and squeezing so tightly I can hardly breathe. Patting him on his back, I tap out, so he sets me back down.

"Wow..." he looks down at me, shaking his head "...wow." The smile plastered on his face warms every bit of me. Seeing Jake in the coffee shop had not been the warm reunion of two people who had once been best friends; it <u>was</u> the reunion that we deserved, though.

There had never been animosity between Ben and me after the falling out. He smiled when we crossed paths and would occasionally make friendly comments in the classes we shared. We both understood that it didn't change what had happened and that things could never return to normal. Jake had his loyalty. I appreciated his cordiality nonetheless.

I even kept in contact with his mom, Grace, for a long time after I left town. She always sent Christmas cards, but I never sent her my new address when we moved to a different apartment a few years ago. I need to make time to go visit Grace and catch up. It's surprising that a man with as much charisma and intelligence as Ben has stayed in the same town his entire life.

"Ok. Well, take your drink and have a seat before you fall over from shock." I push the drink to his chest and brush past him as he takes it. Ben and I have always had a teasing, almost brother-sister relationship.

The cushion next to Jake is still open where I left it, so I slide a little closer to him, tempted to lay my legs over the top of his. I resist and instead sit crisscross, my bare feet pressed into the cushion. Jake's hand finds its way to my thigh, where it rests. Goosebumps and butterflies are all I feel.

Ben sits in the chair near Jake and locks eyes with him with an intensity that only comes between those who know each other so well; they can have an entire conversation through a series of looks. Scott and I had perfected the eye conversation through countless awkward parties, events, and family dinners at my parents' house.

Ben's eyes narrow in question. I can't see Jake's face, but he shrugs his shoulders and tilts his head towards me. Subtle, Jake.

Ben looks from me to Jake and lifts his brows. Jake returns with a nod. Ben sits back and runs a hand over his face. It's like they aren't even trying to keep their conversation secret. Maybe they aren't as good at this as they once were.

"So, Ben," I start, hoping to end this two-person conversation and worm my way back in. I've had to do this countless times growing up. It came with the territory of being the third wheel to an established duo. "What are you up to these days? Married with a bunch of kids running around yet?"

"You think I'm settling down when I still look as good as I do?" Ben flexes his arm muscles and poses like he's carved in stone.

Jake and I both choke on unexpected laughter. He looks ridiculous, and his cockiness has clearly reached new levels.

"Nah," Ben continues. "I date here and there, but nothing serious. Plus I'm too busy doing all the hard work for Jake. Making his dreams come true and all that good stuff." Ben leans forward and slaps the bottom of Jake's shoe.

"You work with Jake on the lake development?" I'm surprised Jake didn't mention Ben's involvement when we were there this afternoon.

"Liv, I run the whole damn show up there. I'm in charge." Ben's beer sloshes as he takes a swig.

Jake shakes his head. I know he's rolling his eyes, but I can only see a small sliver of his profile with the angle he's turned.

"Ben's the general contractor." Jake turns toward me, offering clarification.

"Exactly, I'm in charge!" Ben roars with his infectious laughter and gulps down a quarter of his bottle. "I make it so Jake doesn't have to worry about breaking one of his pretty little nails while he spends all our money."

"No. No, no, no, no. Don't tell her things like that. I work right alongside you most days."

"Uh-huh, if you say so." Ben's eyes widen, mocking Jake in his reply. "What about you, Liv? I heard you were married. What happened with that? He found out you put pineapple on your pizza and called it quits?" Ben finishes with a barky laugh despite Jake's coughing and head-shaking trying to stop him.

I know he's joking, but there isn't a way to respond without making him feel like shit.

"He uh... Died." I speak carefully, not wanting to darken the mood, but his face falls flat. "I do have a kid though, Noah. He's sleeping." I lean my head toward the house, listening to ensure there is nothing but silence from inside.

"Fuck, Liv. I'm sorry. I didn't know. How is Noah dealing with it all?" Ben leans forward, hunching his back over and resting his elbows on his knees.

I've spent most of the day with Jake, but beyond my first mention of Noah, he hasn't brought him up again. Whether this is due to disinterest or jealousy that I went on to have a child while he hasn't. I'm not sure.

"He's doing better now that we're living here. He really loves it. We've got each other, so that makes it at least a little easier." I know he'll understand. Since the loss of his own father, it's always been just Ben and Grace. "How's your mom?"

"We lost her a few years ago." His voice is devoid of the lightheartedness it had just been filled with.

"What?" It comes out choked. How long ago did I move from the apartment with the orange door ... four years maybe? God, how hard would it have been to send out a change of address note?

"I know you two were close for a while. She said she was gonna reach out to you after she was diagnosed, but I don't know if she got the chance. It all happened really fast."

"If I'd known, I would have been here. I'm sorry, Ben." I have no excuse.

Ben went from having the perfect family—one that both Jake and I were envious of—to being completely alone. We sit in silence for a few minutes, soaking in all the sadness that our lives have endured.

As preteens and teenagers, we'd sit around, dreaming the biggest of lives we planned to lead, yet here we are in the same town we all promised to leave. All single and doing none of the things we dreamt of. The fact that I got out for even a small period of time seems negated by the fact that I'm back.

"Well, Liv is still a complete slob." Jake offers me up as a sacrifice to cut the tension. It's only with Jake and Ben that insults are welcomed. It's the love language of our friendship.

"We all knew there was no hope for that to change!" Ben roars with laughter.

"I mean, I gave it a real solid effort." I shrug. "No luck." They accept the offering, and we return to a lighter mood.

"So what's with the shack? You watch too much HGTV and decide to buy the biggest piece of crap in town, so you can try and turn it into something magical?" Ben nods his chin in the direction of the house. He can see through the sliding door that the kitchen is torn down practically to the studs.

"Pretty much," I admit. "Scott and my dad bought this house last summer. They were going to use it as a rental until they could convince me to give up the big life and move back. But I wasn't about to live in Crane House. He thought I was just a superstitious nut."

"How bad is it?" Ben winces as he asks.

For a second I think Ben is asking about giving up life in the city to move back, but he gestures with his hand and I realize he means the structural integrity of the house.

"Well ..." Should I start with the fact that I need new windows or that my bathroom wall is just Sheetrock at the moment? "It needs a little love."

Ben laughs. "I'm sure it does."

"What about the ghosts?" Jake asks, cocking his head to the side.

"They're always welcome," I tease back. The irony is not lost on me that I live in a house we all thought was haunted, but now I would give anything to see a glimpse of Scott whenever I turn a corner.

"Who's your contractor?" Ben asks. He will do anything to stay away from the topic of ghosts. Still a scaredy cat.

"Tom Sweet." The name comes out as a groan. He promised to have the renovations done a month before I moved in, and yet here I am, three weeks <u>after</u> moving in and still living in piles of sawdust with absolutely no progress being made.

"Oh, man." Ben sighs. "He used to be really good. But he kinda lost it these last few years. He did the Smith house, remember?"

"Oh God, I forgot about that. The one-month renovation took nearly a year. You remember Devin Smith right?" Jake turns to me.

"I remember him. We actually dated in college for like a minute. Is he back in town?" Something crosses Jake's face. Jealousy? Should I not have said that? Should I have kept the fact that Devin and I dated a secret? I don't know the rules.

Moving to New York for college was an adjustment, so when I ran into Devin shortly after rolling into town, it was nice to see a friendly face. We went out a few times before I did the <u>same</u> thing to him that I did to Jake. I pumped the brakes. Back then, people didn't talk about trauma. I was conditioned to believe that what happened to me was somehow my fault. And that not being able to just move past it all was also somehow <u>my</u> fault.

Devin went to Cornell while I was at NYU, so we'd run into each other here and there, but not often. About once a semester he'd call and ask me out to lunch or dinner, and we'd go out and have a fantastic evening that never led anywhere. I always thought we'd just be friends since he was too shy to even test the boundary I'd set up. By the time he got the courage to ask me if I was ready for a relationship, I was already deep in it with Scott.

Even after I moved to D.C., we'd still meet up for lunch. He used to ask how things were going with Scott, and I always felt guilty telling him that things were great. I felt bad for never really giving Devin the chance that maybe I should have.

"You dated Devin?" Jake's eyebrows are so close together that he almost looks nauseous.

"Mmhmm." I give the slightest of nods, enough to answer the question without inviting <u>any</u> follow-up information.

"I think Dev is somewhere fairly close. Maybe SanFran or Seattle?" Ben answers my question. I forgot what an expert he is at ignoring distractions and staying on point. He doesn't have ADHD like Jake and I both do. "I can always step in if you decide you need to let Sweet go."

Tom and my dad are friends. That's the only reason he's still my contractor. I'm not sure how much longer I can go on hearing his excuses before I lose my cool and embarrass myself <u>and</u> my dad. I sure as hell am not prepared to live in a construction zone for a year. It's becoming increasingly frustrating to try and cook any meals in a kitchen without counter space, and an oven that requires me to hold a match or lighter inside for it to ignite.

"If you're serious, I'll one hundred percent hire you. At least I can threaten <u>you</u> openly." Tom Sweet doesn't exactly find my sarcastic jabs entertaining and told me as much.

Jake's body shakes with laughter. Would this have been possible if Jake hadn't seen a life with me? If nothing more comes from our shared experience than rekindling a friendship I'd thought long gone, it's worth whatever else comes with it. I missed this.

"What do you want to do with it?" Jake asks, looking in from the glass door to the room that can hardly be considered a kitchen in its current state.

"You mean, what was Scott and my dad's plan?" I didn't have much say in the original design since I didn't <u>really</u> want the house to begin with.

"That's not what I asked." Jake's voice takes on a serious tone. "Your dad's not going to be living here for the next twenty years. If you could do anything with it, what would _you_ want?"

The house was never my idea, and I've just been going along with the vision Scott had for it all. Not out of any sort of feeling of obligation to his memory, it just seemed easier than starting over. His vision board consisted of every white farmhouse imaginable, with light gray walls and all white cupboards. Light gray hardwood floors and some large windows on the vaulted living room wall looking out onto the evergreens in the backyard. The house would be beautiful and marketable, easily pulling in more rent than the mortgage. That was his argument, that we could have a second stream of income. But now the house won't be rented, and Scott's design is not anything exciting enough to spark excitement at the prospect of living here long term. I've seen what Jake and Ben are capable of. The lake house is proof of that. I take a breath and try to gather every beautiful design I've seen.

"I don't know. I like the idea of a dark gray or black house with some natural wood accents around the front porch. Cozy carpet in the living room, not light but the kind with warm colors speckled in that would go with some really rich hardwood floors. Maybe walnut? That's a dark hardwood right?" No one has asked me what _I_ would do, and now that I've started, I'm on a roll. "Blue cupboards with brass handles, white granite countertops with some blue marbling in it … Oh, and maybe some white subway tile for the backsplash that leads up to the brass vent hood." There's no budget required to dream, but my budget makes even the smallest of changes impractical.

Jake stares at me, mouth open.

"You just came up with all that on the fly, but earlier you couldn't tell the difference between two grays?"

"I watch a lot of remodeling shows, and if they offered sponsorships for Pinterest, I'd probably be sponsored."

"They do offer sponsorships for Pinterest. It's part of being an influencer. Are you an influencer, Olivia?" Ben used my full name, something he only does for the sake of a joke.

"I could be."

"But you're not."

"But I _could_ be." My failed attempt at a wink makes him smile.

The three of us sit reminiscing on adventures we shared. All avoiding the subjects we know will require us to answer for the ways we've wronged each other. We have plenty of time. We can push off the uncomfortable conversations to another day. Instead, we stay within the boundaries that aren't formally established because we know the lines.

A yawn moves through me, with a second starting where the first left off. Both Jake and Ben turn to stare.

"Get it under control, Liv." Ben marvels as a third yawn begins.

I exhale in amusement. I haven't stayed up this late in ages. As the last swirl of smoke leaves the fire, I stand and begin gathering bottles.

"Alright, guys, you gotta go." Pulling the blanket that Jake and I were using on the couch, I reach over to take the other blanket from Ben's lap, folding both over my arm.

"Seriously?"

"Yup, it's a school night. Get going!" I grab both of their keys haphazardly tossed on the coffee table and hand them to their respective owners. I hug Ben, and once his arms are around me, squeezing, I don't want to let go. I'm worried that tonight is a fluke, that things really can't go back to how they were. But something feels different. Ben steps back allowing Jake to come in for a hug of his own, and I grasp for reassurance. "You guys should come back tomorrow night!" I muffle through his shoulder.

"Can't tomorrow," Ben says shortly.

"Oh. Ok." I didn't expect them to turn me down so quickly.

"Saturday?" His phone is out. Checking his calendar maybe?

"Sure."

"Cool, let me put some stuff together and we can start pulling permits for your remodel." Ben's gone, finishing the end of his thought from around the corner of the house. "Fire Sweet before Friday."

"Well now that we got rid of him, you want another glass?" Jake winks at me.

"No, I was serious. It's late. Hold on though." Running inside, I rifle through the drawer I just unpacked. There, under the bundle of knotted charging cords, is a Sharpie. I want so badly to invite him in, to finish what we started on the kitchen counter earlier at the lake house, but Noah could wake up for any number of reasons and I don't want to risk it.

I pull his hand up before I'm even all the way out the door and begin writing my number on his palm. Complete with "Liv" above it.

"You know, you could have just asked for my phone and entered your number?" He's looking at me like I'm a time traveler from the nineties.

"This is more fun." I shrug, a smile growing. "Now you won't forget about me."

"I've thought of you every single day since I first saw you." He moves his hand up to my face so I can rest my cheek against it. "I don't need a reminder to think of you."

Nine

I find my favorite paint-covered ripped jeans and an old shirt from a 5k I ran with Scott and our college friends just after we were married. I'm tempted to wear my new mustard top that twists on itself in the front. It makes my boobs look <u>really</u> good, but I remind myself that manual labor requires proper clothing. I don't want to embarrass myself in front of guys that do this for a living.

Noah stands on the counter, the kitchen chair slid from its place at the table to be used as a step stool.

"What are ya looking for, buddy?" What could he possibly be trying to reach up there?

"The long cooker we use to make French toast." He stands on tiptoes, looking on the top shelf of the mixing bowl cupboard.

"Well, the <u>griddle</u> is down here." The chair slides roughly over the uneven linoleum. I grab the griddle and return the chair so he can climb back down. Noah already has the bread on the cutting board resting on top of a long piece of wood balanced precariously on two plastic saw horses I borrowed—or stole, depending on who you ask—from my dad's workshop. Someday I'll have a real kitchen island.

With Tom Sweet out of the picture, the house might have a shot at being functional sooner rather than later. My dad tried to convince me to keep him on board, but when I mentioned that Jake and Ben would be taking over, his entire demeanor shifted.

"So you all made up then? About time!" He said it in the way parents do when their kid does the thing they've been telling them to do for years. "You should see what those boys did up by the lake." He beamed.

"I saw."

"You did? So you saw my chandelier?"

It turns out that while Jake and Ben ended their friendship with me, they had remained close with my dad over the years. So when they started designs for the lake development they went to him.

I mean I get why he didn't tell me, but I wasn't the one that ended the friendship and it still just doesn't feel fair that my dad got to be included when I was all but exiled.

Opening the fridge, I retrieve the cream and eggs. Noah has a knife as I reach around to set the ingredients near the griddle.

"Why are you slicing the bread?" I give his back a tickle as I walk to the pantry in search of cinnamon. Noah continues slicing while his words come out in a jumbled sprint.

"Well, remember those French toast sticks we got at that restaurant on our drive from D.C.? I thought if we cut them, it would be just like those ones." Noah has asked me countless times to return to the burger joint we stopped at for breakfast. I'm <u>never</u> returning to Nebraska. I don't care how good the French toast is. And the French toast <u>wasn't</u> very good, though Noah loved it. I sat with slimy, nearly raw eggs, answering the waitress as she continued to ask why Noah and I were traveling without a man. Like it was the 1950's and we were some sort of oddity to be marveled at. Making French toast sticks at home is a far better option.

"What a great idea buddy. You'll want to cut some more, though. My friends are coming over today to help us work."

"Is it Jenn and Dre?"

"No." Calling Jenn is still on my to-do list. It just keeps getting moved down the list because I'm still being a shitty friend. I have to call her this week, but I need to figure out how I'm going to explain Jake before I do.

"I thought you said we'd see them more when we moved here."

"We will. But today you get to meet two of my very best friends from when I was only a few years older than you. Jake and Ben."

"Huh." Setting the battered bread onto the griddle, Noah asks, "If they were your best friends, how come they aren't anymore?"

"Sometimes friendships just can't make it past bumps."

"But you're friends again?"

How do I tell him that nothing changed? Essentially everything is the same. We're just ignoring the things that led to the demise of our friendship.

"I don't know, buddy. Maybe we are just old enough to move past the hard stuff."

"Did you talk about why you weren't friends?" he asks in a very momish tone. It's the same one I use when asking if he talked with his friends about something that upset him.

"No." A real great example I'm being here.

"Oh."

"Oh, what?"

The edges of the bread strips seem to be pulling away from the griddle just enough so that they might be done on that side. Flipping them, I mentally pat myself on the back because they are perfectly cooked.

"Won't you just end up getting mad again and not be friends?"

"I hope not."

The possibility of it all coming back to haunt us is real. After nearly two decades we can hopefully navigate the past with more grace and understanding than we were capable of at sixteen.

Noah places each stick, once cooked, thoughtfully onto the mountain he's created. Ignoring my advice on building a proper base, he simply towers one on top of the other. The newest addition to the heap threatens to topple as a knock at the door distracts Noah. He drops the slice in his hand haphazardly on top.

"I GOT IT!" Noah screams as he runs out of the kitchen towards the front door. I have to practically dive to right the teetering tower.

"Hey! You must be Noah. I'm Benson, but you can call me Ben. All my friends do." Ben's voice carries down the hallway. His interaction with Noah reminds me of my first day of school, just after moving to town. Ben introduced himself while Jake stood back, nervous. It took Jake weeks to open up and months to begin to trust me. Ben has the type of presence that makes a person instantly feel like they've been friends forever.

"Yeah, we made about a hundred French toast sticks. C'mon!" Noah exclaims, only slightly exaggerating.

"Hey!" I say when Ben and Jake are in sight. Ben's wearing a pair of cargo khakis that are covered in paint, and what I assume is plaster, along with a shirt with the "J&B Designs" logo printed on the chest. Jake's wearing a matching shirt, in significantly better condition, and a pair of form-fitting jeans. He looks good, and now I'm wishing I wore the new mustard shirt that I decided against. Well, I hope he feels silly being dressed up—at least as ridiculous as I feel in my tattered clothes.

"Hey, hey." Ben walks around the sawhorse island and squeezes me in a half hug, just the one arm over my shoulder.

"Grab a plate and help yourself." I slide the stack of paper plates towards Ben as Jake comes around. "Hey you," I whisper as his mouth brushes my cheek. Maybe it's just in my mind, but it feels like way more than a quick friendly peck of a greeting.

"Hey you." Taking a plate he leaves his hand on my lower back—ok, so maybe it's <u>not</u> just in my mind. He wiggles his fingers back and forth where my back meets my side, attempting to find the ticklish spot he only knows about because of our fake memories. Squirming, I turn and push him towards French toast stick mountain with a serious "not here" look. I don't even know <u>what</u> is going on with us, so I can't exactly explain it to Noah when I can't even explain it to myself.

"So, Noah, I heard you made a new chandelier for one of the lake houses," Ben says as he grabs what must be his seventh helping.

"You know about the lake houses?" Noah asks around a mouthful of syrup and bread. He bursts with excitement. I didn't know Noah was helping my dad with the chandelier.

"Dude ... I am in charge of building the lake houses!" Ben gestures wide with his arms, showing off his T-shirt.

I can clearly see that Ben is Noah's new hero, finally replacing the guy on YouTube who plays video games while yelling into the void. Good riddance.

"Ok. So what's the plan?" I ask as Ben dips another strip into the pile of powdered sugar he has on the side of his plate, followed by syrup. An ungodly amount of syrup.

He needs to slow down on the syrup if he has any intention of making it to forty. Defying every law of physics, he transfers it to his mouth without a single drop falling onto his plate or table. Noah follows Ben's lead, doing the exact same with his own stick, though with less practice he drips the syrup down his chin. Awesome.

"It's demo day, baby." Jake beams at Noah as he delivers the good news. Noah returns Jake's smile with one of his own. And they just sit there sharing toothy grins.

"That sounds awesome! Can I help?" Noah asks, hardly able to stay in his seat.

"Of <u>course</u> you can help, little man." Jake winks at Noah.

"But like, what exactly are we demo-ing?" My face scrunches up. How much more in shambles can my house get?

"I looked over your budget you had set up with Tom." Jake pulls a folder out of a bag he slung over the back of the chair. What budget? I don't think the tiny amount of money I have sitting in an account for the remodel can really be considered an actual budget. "Since we're doing all the work ourselves at the steep discount of free, and we can use extra materials when we have them available, I think we can come in under budget, by like a lot." Jake passes the plan across the table to me.

"Uh, under budget is _not_ what we decided on," Ben interjects. "There is _going_ to be some big unknown problem, guaranteed. With a house this old and..." he pauses, rethinking the word on his tongue given that Noah is sitting next to him "...crappy." He smiles, proud of himself.

"I am _not_ having you work for free. I will pay you."

"You can't afford us." Ben says confidently. "Tell her what you found, Jake."

Jake slides his iPad to me, where a logo of a hammer and saw is above the words "HGTV Retreat Redo."

"I don't know what I'm looking at." I look between Ben and Jake, searching for an answer. Jake points to the screen below where a series of paragraphs outlines the parameters of the retreat redo contest.

"HGTV is doing a design challenge, updating remote homes. Those chosen will be featured in a special they are filming for Christmas and a cash prize of a hundred grand for the designers. So we can use your house as a sort of marketing opportunity for J&B Designs, and _when_ we win, it will help pay for everything we don't just write off as an expense."

"What makes you so certain my house would get featured?"

"It's terrible, and everyone loves an extreme remodel." Jake leans over, swiping the screen to a new app where I see my house as it is now, in a 3D model. It's much better quality than the blocky Minecraft version Scott and Noah built while living in D.C. With the press of a button, it transforms into the house I described on a whim in the magic of the firelight only a few nights before. "Plus we're really good at what we do."

Ben was right. They are worth every penny that I obviously cannot pay them.

"You did this?" He heard me, like really heard me, and made my words into something I could actually hold in my hands and see.

"I didn't do it. That's _your_ vision. I just digitized it." He looks at me and everything else seems to fade.

Ben addresses the plan to Noah rather than to me. I'm barely listening. I'm far away from breakfast. I see something in Jake's eyes, and it's taking everything in me not to cry. I didn't ask him to do _this,_ to pay attention to the smallest details I gave and build this model. It's incredible and gorgeous.

"We're gonna demo everything that way we have an empty canvas to paint our master-piece on. We'll start by replacing the windows in the living room, then everything outside that needs to be done so we can work inside when it gets colder and wetter. Sound good?"

Noah squeals.

"And where exactly do we sleep while our house is torn apart?" I ask, still locked in Jake's stare. At the question he suddenly lowers his gaze, rediscovering his plate of French toast. Ben laughs, refusing to take the fall for the answer Jake doesn't want to give me.

Ten

"You've been back in my life less than four days and you've already managed to ruin it. I should have known you were bad news, Larson." I'm only kind of teasing as I march the duffle bags I packed for myself and Noah down the stairs.

"You lived with them for eighteen years. I think you can handle a couple months. I believe in you." Jake takes one of the bags from my hand and walks alongside me to the curb, where we load them into my trunk.

Ben and Noah don their safety glasses and hard hats found in the back of Ben's truck. With crowbars and sledgehammers in hand, they set to work. Ben arranged for a dumpster to be delivered later in the morning so everything we tear down doesn't just get thrown in a pile on the side of the house, something Tom Sweet had been doing whenever he actually showed up to work on the renovation.

Noah and Ben start with the fun part of ripping and destroying. I don't exactly want everything I own in the wake of destruction. So Jake and I pack everything I had literally <u>just</u> finished unpacking a few days ago, loading them into the storage container also now taking up residence in my driveway.

Empty boxes come in above my head while Jake brings filled ones out. We exchange smiles and winks, a silent acknowledgment of our attraction. More than once Jake catches me unaware with a squeeze or a kiss. Each time I find myself checking to make sure Noah isn't watching.

Reaching around me, Jake takes the frames down from the top shelf near the TV, placing them in a box. He holds my wedding picture in his hand, studying the me he never knew. The woman who broke his heart and left. A wave of guilt crashes over me as I watch him place Scott in the box. The symbolism isn't lost on me, and from the twitch in the corner of his mouth, I don't think it's lost on him.

"I'm gonna go work on the laundry room." I move out of the living room, waiting until I'm around the corner to press my back to the wall and breathe long and deep. Scott isn't just a picture to be packed away. This entire remodel was his idea. By packing away the picture, I'm making room for Scott's dream to come true, but I'm also making room for Jake.

The house would never be finished with Tom Sweet. I know this. Jake and Ben are the only real shot I have. I can't afford another contractor. I don't <u>want</u> another contractor. Spending time with Ben and especially Jake is something I enjoy. It's only the nagging guilt that's giving me any pause.

Taking the box down the hallway, I catch Ben and Noah's conversation, stopping just shy of the bathroom the two are in the process of demolishing.

"So, how are you liking living in Coburg?" Ben asks.

I asked Noah the same question only days before, only to receive a shrug in response. Yet when Ben poses the question, I can feel an answer formulating.

"I like some stuff a lot. I like boy's day with my grandpa, and I have a lot of friends in my class, and I like that ..." Noah trails off as if he's debating adding something less pleasant. I'm desperately hoping Ben receives my telepathic plea to probe a little more into how Noah feels.

"Well, what's the worst part?" Ben's tone is still light enough to prevent Noah from getting discouraged but also sincere so that Noah knows he matters.

"My dad doesn't get to try all these new things with me. He always talked about wanting Grandpa to teach him how to build stuff, but now I'm learning and he doesn't get to. Mom used to watch her house shows while Dad would talk about fixing up this house. Now I'm getting to help, but Dad won't even get to see it." The sound of the hammer hitting the counter replaces his voice.

"It sucks huh?" Ben's tone changes from carefree to something much lower. "My dad died when I was a teenager. I've never stopped trying to do all the things I remember him saying he wanted to do."

"Do you still cry sometimes?" Noah asks in earnest.

For the love of God, Ben, please tell him it's completely normal to cry. Not only normal but necessary. I close my eyes and grip the box a little tighter, waiting.

"Not as much anymore. But sometimes, it's too exhausting trying to just be happy all the time, right?" There's no response, but I imagine Noah nodding his head. "I had to tell everyone that I just needed some alone time. That's when I would do something my dad and I would do together and just let myself be as sad as I could be. It gets easier, but it's always going to suck."

Stepping away, I leave them to their new camaraderie. A club that no boy wants to join.

We work through the day only stopping when pizza is delivered. We each have a slice in our hand as we assess what's been done and what is still left to do. As much as we've done today, it honestly feels like we've made nearly no progress. After pizza, I take Noah to my parents' house so he can relax and play video games. He's been a good sport, but I can feel his enthusiasm waning.

By the time the sun sets, the house resembles the haunted shack from our childhood more than the work-in-progress Scott left me. If there was a basement, a clown might have thought about setting up shop in it.

"That kid is pretty great, Liv," Ben declares, entering the master bedroom.

"He really is." I smile, proud that he figured out what I already know. "Thank you. For letting him help today, and for talking to him about your dad."

"Scott sounds like he was a good guy."

"You would have loved him, Ben. He was incredible." All those times Scott asked to meet some of my childhood friends when we were in town visiting, I steered him toward Dre, who he hit it off with, but I knew he would have loved Jake and Ben.

"Who's incredible? Me?" Jake jumps into the conversation. He crosses the floor and pulls me into a dip. Once upright, he moves his mouth to mine and kisses me slowly. My cheeks burn knowing Ben is watching.

Jake breathes as we separate. "I've been dying to do that all day."

My face tingles where his beard rubbed. Eyes closed, I smile and nod in agreement, deciding against the smart-ass remark that he _has_ been doing exactly this throughout the day. In corners and in passing, nothing as bold as this, but he hasn't exactly been restraining himself.

"C'mon. Back to work." Ben launches his hat, hitting Jake in the back of the head with the bill.

Demolition can't be completed or even really started past what Noah helped with until the house is empty. Honestly, we should have packed everything first, but I mean who doesn't want to swing a sledgehammer. Leaving D.C., I opted to hire movers rather than pack the apartment myself. The cost of doing so had hurt, yet as I tape the box filled with the contents of my dresser now, I'm tempted to send a belated tip to the movers. They were worth far more than I paid.

Packing is as close to Sisyphus as a person can get, pushing the boulder up the hill only to have it roll back down. Each box I think will surely make a dent, only to turn around and find more stuff in the same place I just cleared.

Jake and Ben dismantle my bed as I empty drawers in the bathroom.

"So you and Devin huh?" Jake calls as he holds the headboard while Ben quickly removes the bolts holding it in place.

"What about it?" I answer, allowing my tone to be slightly teasing.

"Was it serious?"

"Guess that depends on what you consider serious." We hadn't been serious by any standards, yet letting Jake know that would take away the fun. "We didn't know anyone else in New York, so it just seemed natural."

"I wouldn't have thought he was your type," Jake says in an accusatory tone.

"You wouldn't think that funny, smart, and kind was my type?" I _know_ he means physically, but I'm not about to let him say it without _saying_ it. Jake always fixated on the appearance of boys I had even the smallest crush on. Constantly comparing himself to them, and wondering why I could be attracted to them, and not him. Old habits die hard I see.

"No, I didn't mean—"

The questions he holds back are as loud as those spoken.

"Is it weird?" Ben asks, saving Jake from himself. "Knowing you guys could've been together all these years, but really not knowing each other at all?" So Ben _does_ know about Jake's little power, or curse, or whatever it is.

Silence follows as Jake and I try to wait the other person out, hoping to hear their response first. Jake wins because I hate silence more than he does.

"Yeah. I mean mostly when Noah is around, because to him Jake _is_ a stranger. That's a pretty big reminder that this isn't real."

"Your feelings aren't real?" Jake's words come out in a huff.

"Well, I mean my feelings _are_ real, but they aren't based on like actual reality and experience." As soon as the words are out, I know I didn't word them right.

"Seriously?" Dropping the drill, he stands and faces me. Ben rolls his eyes downward so he's unnaturally focused on the bolt he's removing. Neither of us is new to Jake's ridiculous, over-the-top reactions. Teenage girls have nothing on Jake Larson.

"It's not a bad thing, Jake. I think you're taking it the wrong way. I just meant that it's weird to be in love with someone I haven't seen in eighteen years, after only a few days."

The words hit him with a force, softening his face.

"You're in love with me?"

"Of course I am, you idiot. How could I _not_ be after what we saw?" I knew _immediately_ after the vision that I was in love with Jake. That wasn't ever a question. My problem lay in what that meant when mixed with my grief over losing Scott.

"Hear that?" Jake kicks Ben lightly in the shoulder, nearly knocking him over. "Liv Turner's in love with me." His grin isn't exactly a return of the sentiment, but it calms the young part of me that still worries my feelings will be left unreciprocated.

"I heard nothing." Ben swings his hand attempting to make contact with Jake.

The house is empty of any personal belongings by Sunday afternoon. The demolition phase is set to commence Monday with Ben's crew. Walking through the house after Jake and Ben leave for the night, I can't help but wonder if Scott would be happy about the direction I'm taking with the house or if there would be disappointment at the abandonment of the plan that had been set out.

Scott was happiest when I was happy. If this direction in design makes _me_ happy, it would have made _him_ happy.

Sliding down, I sit against the wall in the living room that faces the gaping hole where the new windows will soon be installed. Scott sat with me in this same spot almost exactly five years before, laying out his vision of the future.

"Imagine Christmas morning..." he said, holding his hands up as if by the motion alone he could conjure the image. "The tree would be over there..." Scott pointed to the corner "...and the couch over there, so we can sit and watch the kids open presents."

"Kids?" I questioned.

"Kids," he insisted. "We have time. We can try again."

Tears fall as I remember the pregnancy tests scattered on the counter. The early flutters that stilled far too soon. The perfect but tiny girl, eyelids nearly translucent as I held her lifeless body in my arms. I wanted her more than life itself. Noah was unable to understand what had happened to his sister, why she wasn't growing in mommy's tummy anymore. It broke me to hear Scott explain to three-year-old Noah that sometimes babies don't make it.

Amid my grief, he'd again spoken of moving across the country to the house on Crane Street. If I had agreed when he'd first suggested it, would he still be alive or would fate have found another way to take him? Sobs take over the silent tears as I sit alone, in our house, allowing the grief to release into the universe.

"Forgot my phone!" Jake's voice breaks the silence of my memories. His footsteps echo loudly against the empty walls. Turning the corner, he nearly steps on my leg splayed out in front of me. Finding the wall next to me, his back slides down until he is seated by my side, his arm settled against my own. "You good?"

I shake my head, unsure of how to encompass all that I'm feeling in a simple explanation. The sobs return.

His arm wraps around my shoulder as he pulls me into his chest; as he did so many times long, long ago.

Jake holds me as I cry for what seems like hours. Never asking for an explanation or making me feel as though any justification is needed for my tears. He's there, in the way that make the years fall away, so we are just two kids holding onto each other, hoping to ease the unfairness life deals.

His thumb traces my hand. As it circles, I catch the faded heart above the "I" where I'd written my name.

Eleven

Moving in with my parents is something that I promised myself I'd never do. The fact that it's temporary makes me feel slightly better about the arrangement, but only marginally.

My mom nitpicks.

"Wouldn't your hair look better if you cut it? Your face looks too long the way it frames it right now," she asks as I come out of the bathroom after spending an hour curling it.

"Is that really an outfit for a mom in her thirties?" She looks my outfit up and down, lingering on my Converse.

"Do you think Noah doesn't like books because you didn't read to him enough as a baby?"

It's like the woman gave Heather and her cronies lessons on how to just tear me to bits. I'm never enough. And even now I find myself accomplishing so much and still feeling that it's not enough. Comparing myself to what others have done. I am not this insecure when I have a couple thousand miles between my mom and me.

When I leave the house for any reason, she asks where I'm going, why, and how long I'll be. She cares now, but when I was a kid she was one step away from neglectful. Can't she just go back to not caring?

My dad doesn't really seem to notice I'm here.

But Noah is here, and he still looks at me like I invented banana splits.

"You ready for school tomorrow?" I run my fingers through Noah's hair as he stands straight, toothpaste spit still dripping down the corner of his mouth.

"Can't I stay home and help build the house?"

"Nope."

"Aww, please. I'll be really helpful, I promise."

"I have an idea." Walking behind Noah, I steer him into his room—Dad's old office with the couch against one wall and the computer desk on the other. His suitcase sits open on the floral wingback chair near the window. Noah climbs into bed, pulling the covers up to his neck. I sit, creaking the springs in the old pull-out couch. "You know how Dad's favorite part of all the house shows on TV was when the people got to see their house for the first time, when it was all done ... what if we do that? Make it a total surprise for you when it's done."

"I'm not gonna cry like they do on TV."

"You might. You never know. 'Oh this bathroom is so beautiful, look at that pretty toilet,'" I tease, poking his sides. Laughter escapes from Noah.

"I'm definitely not going to cry about a bathroom."

"I don't know, I think you might." My eyebrows lift as my grin grows. Standing, I make my way to the door. "Alright, now get some sleep and dream about bathrooms and toilets. Love you."

"Love you, Mom."

I'm dead to the world, but still somehow unable to fall asleep.

"Can't sleep?" My mom's voice comes from the dark hallway, making me jump. My legs are slung over the back of the couch in the way I've been reprimanded by her for more than a thousand times.

"I'm watching a scary movie. You can't just sneak up on me like that!" I whisper harshly, reaching for the remote and pausing the movie.

My mom crosses the room and sits on the cushion so her head rests nearly on my legs. Her passive-aggressive way of telling me to get them the hell off the back of her couch. Rolling unceremoniously, I return my feet to the floor, feeling adequately chastised without her having to say anything. The message is loud and clear.

I bob my head slowly, waiting for my mom to speak. We've never been particularly close, which I've always attributed to her ability to turn every discussion into a teaching moment. Trying to solve my problems rather than simply listening. I pat my hands on my thighs after an uncomfortable amount of time passes.

"I saw Jake Larson over at the house when I drove by earlier."

"Oh, um yeah, he was there."

"You two patch things up then?" My mom knew something had happened between us as teenagers. She spent months pushing me to fix things, though I hadn't given her any details about what transpired. Did she see the kiss we shared on the front lawn or just the friendly argument about which method would be best for the siding of the house?

"I mean, I guess you could say that." I'm suddenly aware that Jake and I haven't exactly worked through any of the reasons we parted ways, acting as though the vision was a blank slate of sorts. I've never been one to look a gift horse in the mouth.

"I always thought you two would end up together until you went and moved across the country to get away from the poor boy."

"You thought I'd end up with Jake? How? I wasn't even interested in him." I could argue that I didn't move to the East Coast to distance myself from Jake, but it was exactly what I did.

"Everyone did. You were interested. You may not have known you were interested, but given time you would have come to the realization sooner than later, I think. You didn't quite know how to cross that bridge between friends and lovers."

I cringe. "Please don't say lovers, Mom."

My mom noticed more than she'd let on. My feelings for Jake <u>had</u> grown, just a little too late for it to make a difference.

"The problem now is going to be if you both move to being..." she pauses, clearly searching for a suitable word to replace lovers "...together before you figure out how to be friends again. Just try not to screw it up again this time, Livvy. He's a good boy. He deserves to be happy."

<u>He</u> deserves to be happy? Not her widowed daughter. Clenching my jaw, I hold back from unloading that it hadn't been <u>my</u> fault we ended our friendship. Sure, I didn't want to hear and accept his apology, but he hadn't exactly offered an apology. Not a real one, at least.

My mom pats my leg before pressing her weight onto me to steady herself as she stands. I hear the popping as she straightens her legs. With each step towards the hallway, I realize—maybe for the first time—that my mom is visibly aging.

She'll be sixty before the end of the year. Her hair has shifted from the bright yellow I remembered as a child to a silvery blond well on its way to white. The lines on the side of her mouth have deepened over the years, giving her the slightest look of a marionette. My maternal grandma passed away in her early sixties, leaving me to wonder how many years I can reasonably expect to have my mom around.

Her words are left as an echo as the door latches closed at the end of the hallway. The idea that any number of people believed that Jake and I were destined for each other only furthers Jake's theory of fate. Had we really danced around and somehow misstepped away from the life fate intended? The notion that my entire adulthood had been a wrong turn doesn't sit right with me. Scott and Noah were the result of that turn, and there is nothing I would trade to give up my time with Scott, or the boy sleeping down the hall. But if I hadn't missed fate, would Scott still be alive, living a happy life with someone else somewhere in the world? Would Noah have found his way to me or Scott in that reality?

My mom is way off base, claiming we're skipping friendship and moving straight to something more. It seems to me that we picked up right where we left off, still able to anticipate the other's words and moves. Still able to make each other laugh and smile with ease. We'd been on the cusp of being more than friends when it had all come crashing down.

But is there the possibility that going in the direction we're going is doomed to fail in the same way our friendship had been doomed?

The sudden need for fresh air moves me to turn off the tv. Pulling my cardigan off the back of the kitchen chair, I slide my feet into the shearling slippers near the back door and slip out into the cool night.

Walking past the Harmons' house, I know the path my feet are taking. This was the same route I took endless times as a girl, ending at Ben's house. Just around the corner from the old abandoned Crane House. My house.

With only a couple of blocks between my parent's house and Crane House, I decide that a walk there and back will give me the fresh air I'm craving, allowing me to fall asleep without staring into the void of my ceiling. Or worse, sitting with my thoughts.

Scott had taken me on this same walk during a holiday visit, the entire time painting a picture of what our life could look like if we made the move from D.C. to Oregon. I didn't need Scott's description. I lived the life he wanted and had escaped. Barely.

It wasn't easy to tell him "no." He wasn't the type to ask for what he wanted.

After three semesters, I gave up on Scott working up to courage to talk to me and took matters into my own hands. Walking into the summer semester of international relations, Scott was the only face I recognized. The rest of my usual classmates returned home for the summer rather than taking classes, so I really had no choice but to force Scott to be my friend.

We spent the entire semester together. When we weren't in class, we could be found wandering the streets of New York, trying our hardest not to melt into the pavement.

Scott took me to the underground jazz clubs, where I affirmed that I am not a fan of jazz. But Scott remained vigilant, promising that we just hadn't found my particular flavor of jazz. As if it were some sort of curry. We sat in a nightclub late one night in June as the singer stepped up onto the stage. She was breathtaking. Her dark skin shone in the spotlight. The sequins of her slinky yellow dress danced and reflected onto her skin, furthering the sparkling effect.

I braced myself, ready to fall in love with jazz, certain that <u>this</u> woman was going to serve the jazz I'd been waiting for. A slow rendition of Ella Fitzgerald's "My Heart Belongs to Daddy" began. The woman in the yellow dress sang the lyrics so seductively that when she sang the line about Daddy, I couldn't hold my laughter in. We were quickly escorted out of the club, both laughing uncontrollably.

"That is the most uncomfortable I've ever been listening to someone sing. Ever." I said, putting an end to Scott's quest to make a jazz fan out of me.

Oblivious to his feelings, I thought of Scott only as a friend, the same type of friendship I'd gravitated towards my entire life. I never quite fit in with normal girl groups. While I always got along with girls and women my own age, I never had the same camaraderie that seemed to come effortlessly with boys and men.

Knowing I fell short of my mother's expectations, I assumed that judgment would carry over with my female peers. Scott brought comfort in his friendship, allowing me to fall quickly into its security.

The first day of class, fall semester, Scott introduced me to a friend as his girlfriend. I had spent years regretting the way things had ended with Jake. The idea of my friendship with Scott ending similarly had been enough to prevent me from correcting him. It took another three months for Scott to kiss me, giving me plenty of time to adjust from the idea of being only friends with Scott to being more.

Scott grew up everywhere and nowhere while his parents provided legal and medical aid to refugees. They moved wherever an influx of refugees were found. He'd dreamt of the small-town life while living the big city and international dream I had wished for. His parents died shortly before he and I met. I wasn't ever sure how that may have clouded his description of them. Could someone really be as close with his parents as Scott claimed he'd been, like calling them five times a day to tell them a funny thought he had kind of close? Or in their absence did he place them on a pedestal, ignoring the flaws in their relationship?

The reason for their bond, I suspect, was that they moved around the world together and were the only constant in each other's lives. Scott losing his parents was something he never got over, not fully. Scott became insistent that we move closer to my parents shortly after Noah was born. He never understood why I would voluntarily live away from everything I'd ever known. All he ever wanted was stability and comfort, something he thought we could find in Coburg.

The street curves, giving way to Ben's old house. My pace quickens, hoping to get a peek at any changes the new owners have made. Will the wobbly tire swing in the backyard still be visible from the street or has it been removed?

A shudder moves through me as I remember Jake launching from the tire swing at its peak height, soaring through the air before landing hard on his shoulder, dislocating it. The sharp point of his shoulder. His limp arm. The howl echoing through the trees.

The house is the only one illuminated on the block. Lifting my wrist, my watch reads a few minutes past midnight. As I near the house, I can identify the two vehicles in the driveway. A truck with the J&B logo on the door covers almost the entirety of Jake's Jeep.

No changes have been made because there isn't a new owner. Ben still lives in the house he grew up in, and Jake, as with most of our childhood, is here. I imagine them lounging on the green velvet sofa, a VHS playing on the old box tv in the basement. The idea makes me chuckle as I remember the grandeur of the lake house and juxtapose that with the idea of Jake and Ben still sitting on the same old furniture from the nineties.

Before I think about what I'm doing, my hand is raised, ready to knock. I stop the movement just before making contact. With no legitimate reason for being here, I lower my hand to my side. Stepping down from the step, I turn to make my way across the grass, returning to the sidewalk, and my path towards the house on Crane Street.

Light spills onto the grass, transforming the blackish green to a brighter, rich emerald. An elongated shadow spreads across the lawn.

"Liv?" Jake whispers loudly from the doorway.

Embarrassed at being caught creeping around at night, I stand with my back to Jake. The light vanishes as the door closes behind him. His footsteps pad lightly on the steps before they hit the grass, where the shuffling bends the blades under the force of his weight.

"What are you doing here?" His question echoes my own. What _am_ I doing?

"I needed some fresh air," I stammer, trying to explain to both Jake and myself why exactly he found me standing outside. Turning slowly, I face him. Basketball shorts and a tattered YMCA shirt are a stark change from the jeans and button-up shirt he wore earlier. My own ripped sweats and white ribbed tank match his pretty well. "I was walking to Crane House, and I saw your Jeep and thought about saying hi, but it's late."

"You should have knocked. I'm still up." He smiles sweetly, dimpling his scar just slightly.

The words don't register with me, until they do. Jake and Ben weren't hanging out; they both live here. In Grace's house. He has a million dollar lake house, yet he's here in Ben's 1200-square-foot childhood home.

"How did you know I was out here?"

Jake throws his thumb back towards a doorbell camera I missed.

"Can I join you?" He takes large strides, closing the distance between us in only a few steps. Leaning down, he takes my face in his hands, cupping my cheeks in his calloused palms. I tense, bracing myself. At some point, my body will have to realize that we aren't going to transport into a parallel universe, but tonight is not that time.

"Won't Ben wonder where you went?" I ask.

Jake's lips meet mine, and we forget what I just asked. In every kiss I find that I'm searching for the Jake from another life. The Jake who had something to prove to me and the world. Instead, I only find this new Jake so absolutely sure of himself. The unfamiliarity could be disappointing, but it brings flutters of delirium. It's a new love found in the oldest of my loves.

"C'mon." Pulling away, I take Jake's hand and lead him towards Crane House.

The house is stripped, covered in plastic with scaffolding around most exterior surfaces. Moving plastic aside, we cross the threshold into the house. It no longer feels like the same house I moved into a month ago nor the house Ben and Jake helped me pack up only two weeks ago. This is not the house Scott envisioned. This is <u>my</u> house.

I gasp as Jake shines the flashlight from his phone on the path before us. The carpet and linoleum which was part of the 1970's renovation are gone, exposing the original hardwood, which Ben refinished with a walnut stain after I left here earlier today. The warmth of the stain transforms the entire home.

The staircase is being relocated from the front entryway into the large open living room. The railing is still absent, a task I stupidly agreed to take on with Jake's help. Large beams have been installed on the vaulted ceiling, which now extends to the spot where the ceiling lowers for the kitchen. There had been a wall separating the rooms, but with the wall gone, the space is open and inviting.

"It's coming along." Jake's voice is that of someone impartial to the renovation, trying to sound professional and unfazed. I want to shake him. There has to be some excitement in there somewhere.

"This isn't even the same house. I mean, God, Jake, this is incredible. The beams, the floor!" My voice rises to just below a shout so it bounces off the ceiling before returning as a hollow echo.

Moving to the center of the room, I lie on my back. Eyes closed, I reach my arms above my head and back to my sides like a seven-year-old carving a snow angel into the wood. Goose bumps rise on my shoulders and upper arms as I breathe deeply, still able to smell the stain on the floor.

Jake's knees crack as he moves to lie next to me. Taking my hand in his own, he moves each finger between mine until they are intertwined, resting on the floor between us.

I trace the beams with my eyes, following them from the openings where the windows will soon be installed to the landing at the top of the new staircase. On the exposed trusses, I find a dark spot which might be a knot in the wood, though it's too dark to really tell.

Soft, slow breaths come from Jake. Is he asleep? I don't know how long we've been lying here, but it's certainly not long enough to justify the quiet snores. Rolling over, I straddle him, leaning down to wake him. My scruffy Snow White or Sleeping Beauty. Why are there no fairy tales where a woman saves a man with a single kiss? It's more believable if you think about it. A gentle moan escapes his lips as he opens his eyes.

"This wife-beater is really doing it for me." Jake moves his hand under my shirt as his sleepy voice turns into an almost growl.

"Don't call it that!" I argue, still allowing his hands to wander freely.

"It's a ribbed white tank top. What else would I call it?"

"I mean not a wife-beater. That's offensive."

"My dad wore one all the time." The connection to the shirt and wife beating needs no further explanation.

"Not helping with the mood here, Jake." I move my own hands to the waistband of his basketball shorts as he cups my breasts under the thin fabric. It's new _and_ familiar. Exciting and terrifying. I need to get out of my own mind and just be here.

"Can I ask you something?" His breath catches on the last word as I trace one half of his well-defined abs.

"No." The answer comes out in the same way I answer Noah after he asks for ice cream after I've already told him no. I don't need anything else to cloud my mind.

Each time we get close to any kind of intimacy past kissing, Jake finds a way to pour cold water on us. I'm starting to think he might be a secret virgin. Or maybe he's just not that into me.

"I'm serious."

Rolling off of Jake and returning to the floor next to him, I sigh. I'm desperate to lose myself in this moment but I guess I will settle on an opportunity to connect on a deeper level. Even if it comes with a side of sexual frustration. My mom's voice telling me to learn to be friends first is on a loop in the back of my mind.

"Okay. What's your question?"

"Why didn't you tell me?"

"Tell you about what?" A pit drops in my stomach.

"Heather told me what happened with you and Aaron that night at the beach."

The trajectory of my life has been determined by things fucking Heather has said. I take a deep breath, promising myself to think before speaking.

"And _what_ exactly happened at the beach, Jake? Please tell me what happened because you were _there_. And I don't know how Heather could have misconstrued the truth into another crazy story about crazy Liv."

"I know I was _there_, but you never actually told me what happened."

"I didn't think I had to." He'd _held_ me, he'd _fought_ Aaron without once asking me for an explanation.

"Heather said that—"

"I'm gonna go." I stand and move to the hallway as Jake sits up, stunned. "I'm sorry, Jake. I'll see you tomorrow. I don't want to hear what _Heather_ says about _my_ life."

"Liv!" Jake calls after me.

The memory of that night is one I have worked for years to keep down. And now it's coming up, and I can't stop it from surfacing.

"Livvy," Aaron called from the far side of the fire. The wings of his hair poked out from under his Von Dutch trucker hat. Scooting over, he motioned to the log beside him.

Heather and Aaron had only broken up a few weeks before, after dating for nearly two years following my own breakup with Aaron. He'd dumped her and I knew it was still a sore spot for Heather. I moved around the crowd before straddling the log and facing Aaron.

"Hey, A." I arched my back, hoping my chest would look a little more impressive.

"It's been a while." Aaron moved to straddle the log, scooting so close that my knees rested against his upper thigh. "How you been?"

"I've been good. How've you been?"

He pursed his lips in the way he always did when he wanted someone to think he <u>really</u> cared about what they said. I knew it was all an act, but one that I was willing to play into. The butterflies I felt every time he was around years before suddenly returned. He was a dick, but that didn't stop me from feeling some feelings for him, even if I knew he was nothing but bad news.

"I'm better <u>now</u>." His hand rested on my thigh.

With more than a dozen of our peers surrounding us, I felt eyes from every direction. I wanted to mess with Heather, but I wasn't comfortable putting on a show. I wasn't even sure I wanted anything to happen with Aaron, just the fact that Heather would <u>think</u> something might have happened was enough. Show her that she could make fun of me all she wanted, but the guy she was still crazy about wanted me, not her.

I leaned in. "Wanna go for a walk? There's a cave that's probably still dry for a bit." The tide was moving in, but I figured we had enough time to check it out before it was submerged.

I didn't look towards the football game as we walked past, but I could feel Heather's glare. For the first time, it felt warranted ... and a bit welcomed. Heather had done so much to make my life unbearable over the years, completely unprovoked. It felt better to me that next time I would at least deserve a bit of the hostility.

The water lapped at the rocks of the cave entrance. We had a little less time than I expected.

"I like to explore the caves and see if I can find starfish. Usually, I don't find anything, but they're just kind of magical. You know?" I moved my hand along the cave wall, which despite having been above water for most of the day was still oozing water from the cracks above.

Aaron's hand moved over my own, straightening my back as the shiver moved through me. I turned to see Aaron staring at me intensely.

"I don't know why we ever broke up," he mused as if he hadn't been distracted by shiny Heather and dumped me without thinking twice about it.

"Yeah, I couldn't tell ya," I lied.

His hand moved to my face. The breath caught in my throat as my eyes closed. We were both only here because of Heather, and yet the flutters were all too real. There was <u>nothing</u> to like about Aaron. He was cocky, ingenuine, and just all-around the kind of guy that I knew only cared about his appearance and reputation. There was nothing below the surface of Aaron, and in that was the security that I wouldn't need to be vulnerable with him. I wouldn't need to spill my secrets. I could just enjoy it for what it was. But what <u>was</u> it?

His lips touched mine. I always imagined my first kiss would be special, and while there was nothing special about Aaron, the cave somehow muddied that in my mind so I could pretend he was more than he was. I pulled back as his tongue pressed to my closed lips. I knew this was part of kissing, but it felt intrusive and unexpected, and I didn't know if I wanted it. At least not so fast.

Aaron pulled back, insulted. "Sorry, I just thought—"

"No, it just caught me by surprise." I couldn't let him leave and let everyone know that I didn't know how to kiss. I pulled him back to me, catching my upper lip on his teeth. A tear welled as I winced.

Aaron took this as a sign to move faster instead of slowing down. Stepping between my legs, he pushed me against the cave wall, pressing a rock directly into my spine. His hand moved from my neck down to my breast, where he cupped it roughly.

"Aaron ..." I moved his hand from my chest to my waist.

Immediately he gripped my shirt, pulling it upward. Was this normal? Was this what he and Heather did? Was this what everyone was doing? I didn't like it, and I didn't care what he told people. I just wanted to leave and get back to the bonfire.

"Aaron," I repeated, attempting to pull back, pushing the rock deeper into my back. My hands gripped his shoulders, hoping to relieve the pressure and send the message that I was done. "Aaron, stop." My demand went unmet.

A wave lapped against my ankle. I'd misread the tide. The cave was under siege. Wriggling against the wall, I made another attempt to move enough so I could get either a knee or a fist between his legs.

He moved his body closer so <u>any</u> move of self-defense was impossible. His mouth covered mine. His hands inched up little by little, pulling my shirt with them. Each movement I made to fight him only seemed to further his quest to remove my shirt.

Stop. Stop. Stop. The demand repeated in my head as I frantically moved through the possibilities of how to get away from Aaron.

"Let's get rid of this, huh?" Aaron swiped his finger under the bunched-up fabric now pinned by my arms.

"Aaron, this isn't funny. Let's go back to the party." Reaching up, I pulled the fabric, fighting him with all my strength while it took next to none of his to keep my shirt up.

Grabbing my wrists in his hands, he pulled my arms through the sleeves.

"Aaron don't!" My scream fueled his laughter, proud of his success despite the fight I put up. He tossed my shirt behind him. A new slightly bigger wave hit my calf before receding, pulling the sand away from my foot and letting it sink under a new layer. The water sat ankle-deep.

His mouth pressed so hard against my own that my protests sounded like nothing more than moans. Moving my own mouth, I found his lip and bit down until I felt a crunch.

Aaron pulled his head back, and with the side of his hand, wiped away the blood that was pooling below his lips, just above his chin.

"Aw, c'mon, Liv. We're just having fun."

"This isn't fun, Aaron. God, you're such a douche" The heels of my hands slammed into his chest, pushing him backwards. Stepping away from the cave wall, I searched the ground for my shirt. Each wave pulled it further toward the entrance, and I moved slowly, sloshing through the water to retrieve it.

My feet were swept from beneath me, knocking the wind out of me as I fell into the few inches of water that now covered the sand floor of the cave. Straddling me, he kept me down, arms pinned to my sides under his knees as I tried to catch my breath.

As the first gasp began to replenish my desperate lungs, a wave moved over me, filling me instead with the salty sea.

The wave receded and I tried to cough, but the weight of Aaron on top of me made it impossible to breathe. Spurts of water left my mouth as I tried to scream. "Aaron, I can't breathe."

"If you couldn't breathe, you wouldn't be talking right now," he mocked.

Lifting, I reached my neck, hoping to stay above the waterline as the next wave moved in. Aaron put his hands on my shoulders and smiled as he pushed me below the surface, just as I took a breath and hoped it was enough.

I was going to die, I thought, calmer than I should be. I couldn't hold my breath and inhaling water would give me none of the relief my body expected in the action.

Then the weight was gone. I coughed, gagged, and puked as water expelled itself from my lungs.

"I was just trying to have fun. You need to chill." Aaron kicked water into my face as he stood. "Heather was right. You _are_ a bitch."

My arms shook uncontrollably as I moved to sit, the next wave crashing against my bare back. One strap of my bra had broken in the struggle, allowing the cotton fabric to fall from the top and hang, still covering me but barely.

The ocean claimed my shirt as its own. I knew I would never find it, even if I had the strength to stand and look for it. My lungs burned as I began to cough again, attempting to empty the remaining water.

Aaron almost killed me, all the while laughing. The entire encounter cycled through my head. Was there something I said or did that pushed him to do it? Did I ask for it in some way?

"Liv?" Jake's voice cut through the noise in my head. "You're missing all the— Liv!"

His feet splashed, sending water down my back. The gentle touch of his hand on my shoulder was the permission I needed to fall apart. The sobs intensified, the shivering that was already racking my body making it more difficult to breathe.

Jake pulled me onto his lap, holding me against his bare chest, as I cried without explanation.

"Will you take me home?" I asked when the water level reached my navel.

"Yeah."

Standing, he set me on my feet and began looking around.

"It's gone." I knew what he was searching for without him needing to say it.

"I can go back and grab _my_ shirt if you want to wait—"

"No, it's fine. Let's just go."

Making our way silently toward where we had left the Jeep that promised us freedom, I felt anything but liberation. I felt small. Weak. Powerless.

"I think Ben's probably gonna want to ride back with Brendon. He finally made a move on Andie, and it seems to be going well."

I wanted to express my happiness for Ben but knew it would come out wrong given what I'd just been through, so I simply nodded.

The laughter from the group grew louder as we neared the parking lot. I hoped they would be too enthralled in the party to take notice of me. Steps away from the Jeep, the crowd turned in our direction.

"Jake!" Aaron congratulated as he moved towards the Jeep. "She have anything left over for you?"

Jake flew from my side with a speed that seemed unnatural. His fist met Aaron's face to a chorus of shrieks and cheers from our peers. Aaron righted himself and threw a returning punch. My stomach churned as I watched the two circle each other, throwing jabs where the other was unprotected.

"I'm going to destroy you for what you did with Aaron." Heather's threat came from just behind me in a quiet, menacing whisper.

I'd gone with Aaron to hurt Heather and instead ended up punching <u>myself</u> in the face. Now there would be retaliation, and I had no one to blame but myself.

"You stay the fuck away from her!" Jake yelled to Aaron who lay on his back after a particularly hard blow.

I moved to my door and opened it. Stepping up and climbing in, I heard the hardest punch Aaron could throw. "You're just fucking jealous, man, because she'll never want you in the way she wanted me."

Jake climbed in, refusing to give Aaron the satisfaction of seeing his words land. But I could see the impact.

TWELVE

"I know it sounds stupid, but I thought this would be easier after what we saw. There is just a lot of past." I sigh. I shouldn't have left. I should have stayed and told Jake exactly what had happened that night with Aaron.

Jake and I returned to Crane House to tile the main bathroom upstairs—a task from Ben. We've been working in relative silence, neither of us sure of how to make peace with how we left things last night.

"So we should move past the past." Jake says in a tone that makes me question if he is entirely serious or not. I laugh, despite trying not to.

"I mean, yeah, ideally. I've been in therapy for like ever though, and I'm still not past it all, with more adding to the pile seemingly every day. Are you in therapy?" I already know the answer.

"Do I, the man who with a single touch can see an entire life that never happened, go to therapy? No. They'd lock me up."

"They don't just lock people away anymore, Jake. This is America. You'd need a really expensive insurance plan to cover that kind of inpatient care." I've been paying out of pocket for my own <u>and</u> Noah's therapy. Our insurance company agreed to cover the cost only once we reached our out-of-pocket maximum for the year, which I know will never happen unless catastrophe strikes ... again.

"They'd find a way."

"Given the shitty childhood you had, therapy would probably be really beneficial to you."

"Noted." Jake's tone is flat and dismissive, letting me know that he's not interested in my recommendations for therapy.

I recently returned to the therapist I'd seen in my teens, catching her up on most of the last chapters of my life, knowing that my parents will no longer be given a report card based on what I tell her.

In therapy, I've discovered that so many of my issues stem from the fact that I've never felt heard and listened to. I thought I was past it all, but being back here is the ultimate test that I feel like I'm failing. My mom knew the way things should be and my input wasn't needed. My dad didn't ever get a say with her, so when it came to me, he had no problem letting me know what he thought. I was so used to being dismissed, pushed aside, or just ignored that when it came to my relationships, I just sort of expected it. It was different with Scott. It was different when I didn't live in Coburg. Something about this town takes away the power of my voice. Unable to find the words necessary to assert myself, I let people talk over me. I'm trying to be better.

"What if," Jake offers, "we take a break from the past? We have plenty of time to catch up on all that we missed. Why don't we focus on the now? With a little bit of the life that could've been."

The phrase "could've been" grates a little hard, but I agree that the sentiment is rooted out of genuine intentions.

The next hour passes with little said between us. We both open our mouths, on the edge of speaking, before closing them and rethinking what we're about to say.

"Okay, I have a question," I say, triumphant in being the first to find something to say in line with the new guidelines. "You and Ben still go out on the boat each Fourth of July, right?"

Jake nods slowly, eyes drawn together. "Yes?"

"If you're planning on having big holiday celebrations at the lake, won't that ruin the tradition?"

"Nope. There is a floating dock where fireworks will be set off. Someone has to be in the boat near the dock, in case anything happens. So while everyone is up having a fantastic time in the town square, Ben and I can still be out on the boat, watching the fireworks from the same place we've always watched them. Only now they won't be in the distance. They'll be right there." His arm reaches up, grabbing and pulling an imaginary firework towards himself.

"Who's gonna run the party?"

With Ben and Jake both in a boat, there are a number of issues that can arise during such a large event.

"Dre and Brendon," Jake answers without a second thought.

Scott was really close with Dre through the years but never mentioned his friendship with Jake. It shouldn't be surprising; they played football together, so it's not like they didn't run in the same circles. Dre just didn't run in <u>my</u> circle at the time.

We fall back into silence, waiting for the next "safe" topic to come up. It's harder than I thought to not talk about the latest half of our lives.

"Is Devin still into wearing silk Yu-Gi-Oh! shirts?" Jake pokes.

His fixation on Devin is entertaining. I haven't thought about him in years, not until Ben brought him up. Jake seems to think it's something quite a bit more than it had been. I could tell Jake that Devin was well on his way to becoming a doctor, and was dressing as a reflection of that, last I saw him. That women were attracted to him in social situations because of his welcoming demeanor. That if things hadn't gotten serious with Scott, there was a real possibility I might have ended up with him. Since it's against his own rules, I have no choice but to deny him the answers he's so desperately seeking.

"Nuh-uh. That's the past. Why is Ben single?" I pivot the subject, working to keep the conversation moving.

"He dates, but never really anything serious anymore. I think he has commitment issues stemming from losing his parents, amongst other things."

"He seems happy, though."

"There has never been a happier, more fulfilled man than Ben. His ability to find the good in everyone and every situation amazes me. He's Uncle Ben to all the kids in our circle, and he's so much like his dad in that way, it's impossible for anyone not to love him."

The admiration he holds for Ben is unrivaled. If he's not going to even entertain the idea of therapy, I'm glad that he and Ben have each other.

"He's always been good people."

"Good people?" Jake questions, sliding a tile into position. "He's a person, not people."

"It's a term, all-encompassing for when someone is the kind of person that you want in your group. They're good people."

"Yeah, if there is more than one of them. He's a single person. So he'd be a good person, not good people."

"Being a good person is different than being good people. Ben is both a good person <u>and</u> good people."

"I'm not ever going to use the phrase 'good people.'" He pauses for a long time, working the tile into its level position. "So what exactly is a political consultant?" Reaching behind me, he pulls the stack of tiles to the space where the previous stack sat between us.

Jake continues to work, spreading the mortar to an even thickness as I lay each tile in its place. He never leaves clumps or dips, making me believe that either he's chosen the easier task or that he makes the harder job look easy. Given my inability to frost a cake, I opt to leave the question unanswered instead of trying my hand at it to make a point.

"Depends on the year, candidates, political climate, and all that." My mouth shifts from one side to the other as I think of a way to easily explain my job while still sounding impressive and cool. "Okay so politicians are—"

"Smarmy?"

"I was going to say calculating, but I suppose that works too. I do the calculating. I run the poll numbers to see if the idea they want to run with is popular, if it has a shot in hell at succeeding, or if it will result in their political suicide instead."

"You're basically a statistician for politicians?" Jake sits back on his heels, eyes drawn together in distrust. I'm not sure where the look stems from; he always enjoyed math.

"Not exactly. I take into account public discourse, people's temperature on certain issues that sometimes can be ignored by many if not all polls. It's a lot of digging in some cases, especially on local issues. I had to make a recommendation for a congresswoman who wanted to vote against a bloated defense budget. She knew that all the money would only go to contractors with little to none making it to the troops themselves. The problem was she represents a district that has several military bases on it, basically putting her at jeopardy of losing her seat if the people didn't understand <u>why</u> she would vote down the budget. In those cases, I come up with a plan of action, a campaign to inform voters of the details of a specific issue. To take some of the risk away—" I notice Jake's eyes glazing over.

"That sounds... fascinating," he says dryly. "Actually, no, that sounds absolutely horrible." He laughs at his outburst of honesty.

"Well, I enjoy it," I say once his laughter subsides.

"There's something for everybody, I guess."

Our conversations flow freely throughout the afternoon, both of us making a point to avoid the forbidden topics. I know we'll need to sit down, sooner rather than later, and get everything out in the open. We've pretended it's all in the past, but the way we each react when the past is brought to the surface makes it clear that we are far from being able to move on from our grievances.

We've hurt each other and been hurt by people in ways the other has no way of understanding. I hope that we'll be able to put it all out there and somehow be able to find a way through. There is something so genuinely innocent in our affection when we ignore reality and dig into the fantasy that we've always been meant for each other.

"Fantasies aren't real," Scott's voice reminds me.

Thirteen

After taking Noah to school, I stop at Crane House to clean up the construction mess. Jake bounds in, excitedly demanding I drop everything to go with him. In his Jeep, he asks me to cover my eyes while he zips through neighborhoods. I comply, despite not knowing where we could possibly be going. He used to take me on these types of adventures long ago. I'm channeling younger me—the me that had complete faith in Jake to deliver something exciting.

Jake stops, parks the Jeep, and jumps out, I wait for him to open my door and help me out. I'm worried I'll face plant if I am left to do so blind. Jake picks me up out of my seat and carries me a few feet before setting me down. We stand in grass, the blades brushing against my ankles between where my Converse end and my jeans begin. I shift from one foot to the other in response, looking for relief from the tickling. Both my hands cover my eyes, but Jake places one of his own over mine to ensure I can't peek. I've promised him I won't, but we both know I lie about that kind of thing.

"Okay, you can look." Jake pulls his hand off of my own.

Lifting my hands from my eyes, I blink twice, allowing my eyes time to adjust to the sun. Summer is still hot and sticky, though the mornings and afternoons give a tease of the reprieve from the heat that's just around the corner. Across the lawn from where we stand is a small green house. <u>Our</u> house. This was the house <u>we</u> lived in. Together. The house we bought when our small one-bedroom apartment proved too small for us and little Scarlett.

We've spent a week abiding by our "nothing from the past" rule, and as a result, it's been bliss. Butterflies in each touch and desperate need in each kiss.

The house in our could've been life had been mostly bare in the front, due to my inability to keep anything green alive. This house, however, has hydrangea bushes nearly up to the windows. The purple-blue of the blooms contrasts with the olive-colored siding, which gives the house a warm and welcoming vibe.

"It's our house." I don't know if I want to cry or squeal in excitement. I turn to Jake, my grin so wide it feels like my cheeks are going to push my eyes out of the way.

"I found it! I mean it wasn't hard. My mind knew where to go and sort of got me here on autopilot. I don't know why it took me so long to just get in the car and find it. I met the current owners. They're a young couple who just bought it a few years ago."

I imagine a couple, not unlike Jake and I, with a kid or two in tow. Running through the backyard with sprinklers, eating on the porch when the weather is nice enough to escape the sweltering heat at the end of summer. I have a lifetime of memories in this house that I've never stepped foot in. Tears well as I feel the pull to move closer.

"Do you think it would be weird if we asked to see inside?" I ask, wanting to find the doorframe where Scarlett's height was marked, knowing I won't find it and knowing that it will break something inside me when I don't. Yet the need to be inside the home that holds so many fond memories is intense.

"The owners moved out yesterday. I closed on it this morning."

"You what?"

"I offered them more than it was worth, making it possible for them to move into a bigger place." Jake leaves me standing as he moves towards the door, keys jingling in hand. "I figure I can use it as a rental property. I just...needed it."

"You bought a house on an impulse?" I still worry my debit card will get declined after all my groceries have been scanned, and he's over here buying houses like he's playing Monopoly. Something Ben said that first night on my back porch about them needing money for their development nags at me, but I push it down. I _really_ want to go inside.

"Welcome home, Liv," Jake announces as the key turns in the lock, freeing the handle to twist, avoiding the question of his purchase, and baiting my curious nature.

"Ooooh!" My squeal surprises me.

The house is bare without the secondhand furniture I envisioned filling it. The echoing silence is a gut punch that catches me off guard. Running my fingers along the wall, I follow it to the living room, finding a hardwood floor where we instead had carpet. The spot where I crashed through the coffee table when we tripped, caught in passion, draws my attention for a moment as I move toward the bedroom. My hand runs over a patched section of wall in the hallway, where a hole has been repaired. It stops me dead in my tracks.

"How?" I breathe the question as much to the universe as to myself.

Scarlett crashed her bike into the hallway wall. But Scarlett never existed in this world. There is no reason there should be a hole here.

"That's not even the craziest one. Come see this." Jake leads the way through the house to the main bedroom. Walking across the plush carpet to the far wall near the window, Jake points to a series of nail holes.

"Did you do this?" I know he didn't, but if he did, it's not funny.

"Nope, I found it this way."

Nail holes form the constellation Cassiopeia exactly where I remember hammering nails, attempting to hang a picture. The nails were cheap and kept bending under the pressure of the hammer. Jake took the hammer from my hand, insisting it was something I was doing wrong. When he stepped up to the wall, he pointed out the constellation I'd inadvertently pounded into it.

"How?" I brush my fingers across the holes. A chill moves through me.

"I have no idea." Jake moves his fingers over mine.

Electricity moves from my fingers through my arm before settling in my chest. This time it _is_ a spark between us, nothing more. My breath quickens in response. His fingers linger, making the slightest circles on the back of my hand, and oh my god my knees are weak.

Turning my back to the wall, I meet Jake's look of anticipation with one of my own. We stand staring at each other still as can be. Shallow breaths move through me as I watch Jake's chest rise and fall at a similar pace. This is it. As long as both of us keep our mouths shut and don't ruin this moment.

Jake moves first, pinning me against the wall, his hands on either side of my head. My calves flex as I rise to my tiptoes, reaching towards his face which lowers to meet my own. Jake's stubble is softer and less scratchy.

The apprehension he's displayed over the previous weeks is absent. His breathing is fast and ragged, his fingers rough as they pull me closer. Being back in _our_ house has somehow done what we've tried to do for weeks. Allowing ourselves a little bit of what our life could have been to occupy our reality. At this moment, we are no longer strangers trying to navigate uncharted territories. We are the boy and girl that fell in love and built a life together, in _this_ house.

Jake reaches behind me, lifting until he stands upright. I wrap my legs tightly around his waist, wishing desperately for any piece of furniture. Jake lowers me to the place where our bed should be. I'm 33, I'm way too old, and my back is going to hurt ... not that it's going to stop me.

We make love on the carpet. Between groans of pain and discomfort from lying on the hard floor, followed by giggles, we find ecstasy in each other. My fingers curl, digging into Jake's back, trying to pull him even further into myself, needing to erase the space between us.

He watches me with a smirk on his face as my hands press against the wall behind me, giving me the leverage needed to arch my back. Eyes closed, a noise escapes that I'm damn sure I've never made. Something primal in me is released, along with the tension that has built in me over the last year. I'm barely aware of Jake as he joins me on the mountain peak.

Jake collapses on me before rolling to my side. I lie next to him, eyes closed, completely spent. Holy shit.

Jake's fingers trace the curves of my body, pausing on the stretch marks that cover my abdomen. I don't push his hand away, even though I want to.

"I tried all the fancy creams." I'm quick to make excuses for the part of my body I'm ashamed of.

His body has spent as much time in the gym as mine has spent on the couch. My body is perfectly fine holding on to at least ten pounds I could do without, along with stretchmarks and loose skin where it never fully went back to the way it was. Fertility hormones, pregnancy, motherhood, and time have all left their mark on me.

His fingers lift and are immediately replaced with soft stubble as he kisses my stomach.

"Don't ever be embarrassed of what life has done to your body. You made a whole person in there."

I don't correct him. I don't mention the countless miscarriages and the stillbirth.

We move from room to room. Jake's dressed only in his purple boxer briefs, me in my bra and panties, which I _would_ have paid more attention to and at least had them match if I expected the day to go this way. They aren't even top-drawer undies because I was working on the house, with absolutely no plans for this little rendezvous.

We explore the scars the house shares with the one we lived in. With each mark or hole, we share the memory of how the damage occurred. Memories that seem to spark electricity between us.

When we come to the doorframe of the coat closet, we find a growth chart in the exact place Scarlett's had been. We sit on either side of the frame. Jake leans against the open door, holding his hand out on the ground. I take it, allowing his fingers to wrap around my hand.

"Do you think Ketchup is buried in the backyard?" Jake asks in quiet horror.

We'd adopted a stray cat, we named Ketchup. Scarlett had fallen in love but a few days later the cat died mysteriously. After a proper funeral, Ketchup was buried under the tree in line with the northwest corner of the house.

"Oh my God, I don't want to find out!" I bend over in disgusted laughter. Giving even the slightest bit of interest in the idea will fuel Jake's curiosity. I don't want to watch as he digs up whatever might be out there.

"What was a dead cat for us, might be a treasure box in reality," he offers.

"Or it might be a dead cat." I stand, moving towards the bedroom where my abandoned jeans and T-shirt lie.

Jake reaches out, pulling my ankle out from under me. I fall onto the ground with an "oof" as my breath is knocked out of me. Jake moves on top of me, looking down as my desperate gasps for air turn to laughter.

"Should we sell our houses and move in here?" he asks, lowering himself so our noses brush.

"As long as Ben tags along too," I tease. "He and Noah can have bunk beds in Scarlett's room."

Jake shakes his head, grinning. Rolling to the side of me, we lie shoulder to shoulder, eyes fixed on the fan above our heads.

"Can we always be this happy?"

"Probably not," Jake answers truthfully, without his usual optimism. "But we have forever to try." There it is.

Forever. The word's been used in my life when it comes to things that have, in fact, not lasted forever. Jake and Ben and I carved "BFF" into a tree near the corner of my backyard. A grim reminder over the years that our friendship had not lasted even close to forever. On my wedding day, Scott promised me a lifetime of happiness. Ten years hardly counts as forever in my opinion. Forever lacks the permanency it promises. Fuck forever.

Being in the little green house with Jake is a true escape from reality. It's a trip to an alternate universe. One where I teach high school civics and Jake's an electrician.

The illusion has to end as the time grows closer to needing to pick up Noah. I become desperate to make each moment last just <u>that</u> much longer. I outline how I would update and renovate the little greenhous, changing it from the home we knew to something modern.

We both know that Jake is the expert, but he listens as I talk of moving walls, adding an addition, and updating the fireplace. He nods as though we'll do anything I'm suggesting.

"But like honestly. What are you planning on doing with this place?" I ask in reverence

"I like how little it is. It was enough for us, and I think that's all I really want. To rent it out to a young family. Maybe one day I'll have a kid that needs a starter house. Or us, I mean I know you have Noah, but maybe Scarlett is still somewhere out there in the universe."

I need to tell him that I'm not sure if I can even have any more children, not without thousands of dollars spent on interventions. That the odds of me conceiving naturally are nearly nonexistent.

But his dream of the future is too appealing to not allow myself to buy into the fantasy of forever and of kids. We need a win, and reality can wait until we return to the real world.

FOURTEEN

I arrive at the lake house as the black of night turns to the deep blue that promises daybreak. Jake's Jeep is parked in one of the two spaces designated for the house. Pulling into the other spot, I get out and pop the trunk.

Jake and Ben stopped by just after four-thirty this morning, pulling a still sleeping Noah out of bed and into the backseat. All to the grumbles of my dad who's bitter that he's not the person taking Noah fishing for the first time. They'd invited him to join, but he made an excuse about needing to work on his honey-do list and sent them on their way.

I kissed Noah on the head with the promise of seeing him in a few hours. The plan was for Noah to go fishing while I stayed behind to finish the reports I've been putting off. I've been putting them off because I've spent most of my time at Crane House, completing projects Ben lays out for me. I've fallen behind on my actual job. The one that pays the bills.

These reports shouldn't take all that long, and once they are done I'll be able to actually enjoy the weekend. The Labor Day hang has grown from the small get-togethers we used to put together as kids, into a real grown-up weekend. Hikes, camping, fishing, and bonfires all up at the lake. Jake and Ben are treating this as a trial run for next summer. Hoping to work out any kinks before opening to the public. I'll meet Noah, Jake, and Ben after fishing for a hike with the group.

Jake pulled the Jeep away from the curb and since then my imagination has made it impossible to focus on my computer screen. Images of Noah falling over the side of the boat into the freezing waters, Ben pull starting the engine only to have it explode, and a gigantic fish jumping up and slapping Noah with its tail, knocking him unconscious forced me to close the laptop and give up the pretense of work. I loaded myself into the car, knowing I'd arrive long before everyone else. It's the anxiety that comes with losing someone in an accident, I know the thoughts are mostly irrational, but that doesn't keep them at bay.

So instead of calling Jake, and telling him that Noah can't go fishing I'm going to try and work where I can at least see Noah. But if anyone asks I'm just here in case anyone shows up early and doesn't know the code to the front door.

Placing the grocery bags onto the kitchen counter, I pull out the packs of hot dogs and turn to begin filling the fridge. Thankfully Jake hasn't gone shopping since we were here for lunch. So there is no rearranging needed to fit the hot dogs, soda, and rest of the groceries. I do however throw out the long expired jam. Let's not put food poisoning on the schedule for this weekend.

The large cream couch against the windows has a perfect view of the lake. The small silhouette of the boat sits idle in the middle of the tree-framed opening. Pulling out my laptop and setting it on my knees, I begin typing, looking out to the lake every few minutes. I do tell myself I can't look more often than every five minutes. So the clock is getting about as much attention as my report is. Even so, the report takes less than an hour to complete. I shouldn't have put it off. I've been stressing about this for days and it only took me a few minutes. It's that last-minute deadline is closing in stress— without it, I get nothing done.

I move to click the send button and am met with the ping of a popup.

Retry with internet connection.

Yeah, that might help. Of course, I don't have enough bars of service to use my hotspot. Standing up, I stretch my back, allowing each vertebra to crack, before wandering towards the office by the front door. If this is where business surrounding the rentals side of the development takes place, there has to be a placard informing visitors of the WIFI password. While the report can wait until Jake returns, I'll probably forget again and Julie is expecting it before noon.

I find the frame on the wall where we stood only weeks before, remembering Jake's fingers on my back as he explained the plans for the development. The electricity between us was something I hadn't experienced in years. Honestly, I'm not sure if I've ever felt it as strong as with Jake. With Scott, it was like the waves that move toward the shore—the ones perfect for surfing—while with Jake it's like those giant waves that swallow ships.

Same, just more intense, bigger. Wanting him to reach out and touch me, but scared of what admitting that could mean. The vulnerable feeling of desperately needing validation but terrified to receive rejection instead.

I move from the frame to the bookshelves that line the wall, forgetting the search for internet and letting my fingers run across the spines. I try to see if the titles can give away any piece of who Jake's been on his road to becoming who he is. A mixture of classics, business, and architecture books arranged by color rather than subject or author makes for a beautiful if not a little confusing display. I pull out a book titled *Turkish Art and Architecture* and sit in the office chair to flip through the pictures. Spinning around, I set the book on the desk and lift the cover.

The book is huge and doesn't fit in the space provided, at least not without moving a few things. Reaching up to move the object blocking the top left corner of the book, I find a photo. Inside the bronze frame is a picture of Jake and Ben standing where I am right now, only before the house was built. They're each leaning on one side of a sign that reads: New development by J&B Designs. Coming Soon! I can feel the joy radiating from their faces. And though I know I never would have fit into their business venture, there is still some jealousy that I wasn't there to share in their joy, their failures that led to their success.

I move to set the picture down further back on the desk out of the way of the book when a second bronze frame catches my eye. Jake stands on a beach in a pair of blue Hawaiian print board shorts. In his arms he holds a blonde wearing a tiny white bikini, her arms around his neck as they both smile broadly for the camera. I don't need to look any closer to put a name to the face. He's holding Heather.

I had to give it to Heather, she was a woman of her word. She pillaged my life upon conquering it. I had never understood why she'd singled me out. She found joy in my destruction long before the incident with Aaron at the beach, but after that night she kicked her diabolical plan into high gear. Heather made any space she was in unbearable for me. Eventually, she managed to take what I valued most in the world. Jake.

She didn't even wait a week after mine and Jake's fight before digging her claws into him. I'd been on my way to talk to Jake, to try and patch things up. There had clearly been a misunderstanding. I couldn't have been the one to call CPS, I had spent the entire day trying to figure out how to tell Jake that I was desperately in love with him. This made the fact that he believed I could do something like that to him all the worse.

He avoided me for days, so I showed up to school early enough that I could catch him when he arrived. Only as the Jeep shuddered to a stop, it wasn't just Jake and Ben stepping out. But Jake, Ben, and Heather. Ben's sympathetic looks from across the parking lot as Jake and Heather walked right past me was salt in the wound.

Jake's smile as he holds Heather in the photo tears something I thought long healed. He can't be older than early twenties, dating the picture to at least a decade before. It's weird to keep a picture of someone from ten years ago on your desk unless it <u>isn't</u> completely over, right? Is Heather seriously <u>still</u> fucking up my life?

A knock on the open door causes me to drop the frame. I don't see but I do hear the glass crack as it meets the walnut desk.

Jake stands in the entry, smiling. "Hey, you."

Our eyes move to the frame on the desk together. Taking a step through the doorway, Jake slides the large barn door closed. We haven't spoken about Heather since the night in Crane House.

"You knew we dated." Crossing the room, he takes the now broken frame from the desk. His fingers trace over the cracks in the glass. "We were engaged. Did you know that?" His eyes meet mine. I <u>didn't</u> know that. Makes sense though. Football player and cheerleader, senior year prom king and queen. Why wouldn't they have ended up engaged?

"What happened?" I'm trying to keep my tone measured, the last thing I want is to start crying. A sense of dread rises in my throat. The feeling of a crack in the dam of our past, all the history we refused to acknowledge is threatening to break through.

"A lot. Heather got an offer for a fellowship as an art historian in Turkey. We tried to make it work long distance, but it was just too hard. Then she moved to Canada a few years ago." A wistfulness in his voice is all I need as confirmation that I was right, she's still in play.

Oh. My. God. Are they <u>still</u> together? Has he been talking to her since we first ran into each other?

"She made my life miserable." The words escape through my quivering jaw.

"I know." He says this like it's a reason rather than a regret of his relationship.

"No. You don't know the half of it." I'm hoping to see an ounce of regret cross his face. He winces but his eyes remain trained on the picture. There isn't regret, at least not in regards to me. "Are you still in love with her?"

"Do I still love her? In some way, yeah." He's quiet for a moment before adding, "But you still love Scott, so ..."

What the fuck?

"Oh, did Scott torment you as a teen? Did Scott destroy your life for the sheer fun of it?" My voice rises despite my best efforts. His comparison is unfair and misplaced. Scott never personally attacked Jake. <u>Scott</u> can't come back at any moment and disrupt the life we are trying to build. Scott was a decent person which is more than I can say for Heather.

"Destroyed your life? That's a bit dramatic don't you think, Liv? You never even gave her a chance." Is he trying to piss me off? Or am I just trying to pick a fight? Either way, let's go.

"Dramatic?" I scoff, leaning back in the chair. I'm holding my hand to my chin trying to keep it from quivering. "Scott's dead, Jake."

Regret passes over his face. "Liv, I'm sorry." Jake moves to close the book I'd taken from the shelf and forgotten on the desk. "Yes, I do still care about Heather. She and I were in love for a long time. You will always love Scott, I know that. I know that no matter what I do, I am always going to come second to someone who is going to be on a pedestal in you and Noah's minds. I already know that I can't compete. The guy was perfect." He must think that this is some kind of balm for his words that not only sting but hurt. All he's doing is telling me that I can't compete with Heather. Pausing for a moment, he allows his own anger to show. "It's just hard to think that Heather would never have even been around if—"

"If what?" I know it will always come back to the same thing for him. A lie he believed without question. A lie that took our years of friendship in its grasp and crushed it to dust like it was nothing.

"Just forget I said anything."

"No, no, you meant something. If only <u>what,</u> Jake?" I can hear how crazy I sound but I can't stop myself. Enough avoiding it. We can't move past something we won't face.

"If you didn't rat me out to CPS!" His words come out as a bark. Loud enough, I'm sure, for Ben and Noah to hear in the other room. We're back to this. Back to him thinking I turned him in. That I'm the reason he was taken from his home and sent to live with his grandparents. "If you would have kept your promise, and kept your mouth shut, I wouldn't have even thought to go out with Heather. We could have lived that perfect life in our little green house." The level of vitriol in his voice pins me to the back of the chair. "Instead, I have lived through eighteen years of heartbreak and toxic relationships, searching for anyone that could fill the void that <u>you</u> tore in me. Only to have you come back and show me how much better my life could've been!"

"God, you <u>still</u> believe that's what happened? Not once in all this time have you stopped to ask yourself if that is something I would actually do. You didn't know me at all, did you?" I should stop now, but once I get going, I just can't. "You didn't <u>have</u> to go to Heather. You <u>chose</u> her to <u>hurt</u> me. You hurt me and you hurt me and yet you never take responsibility for <u>any</u> of it. I am not the only reason your life turned out the way it did. I didn't show you anything. <u>You</u> showed <u>me</u> a life that I can't have, the daughter I'll always want and never be able to hold, yet again somehow I'm the only one at fault?"

"That life <u>could</u> have been real. Instead, we've wasted all these years, and for what?!"

"Wasted?" My voice is only the shadow of a whisper. "Noah is not a waste."

"I didn't mean Noah ..."

"No." I hold my hand up. My eyes burn from the tears I refuse to let fall. My throat tries to close around the words, causing my voice to crack. "I trusted you. I trusted you more than anyone I have ever trusted in my life. And the <u>one</u> time I needed you to trust <u>me</u>, you chose to trust Heather when she told you it was me, without even asking me if there was even a shred of truth to what she said. How is it fair that eighteen years later <u>I'm</u> still being blamed for choices <u>you</u> made in your own life? I picked myself up. I made a life for <u>myself</u>. I'm tired of feeling like I'm somehow responsible for <u>your</u> life, on top of mine." I'm crying now. The release of my resentment is liberating, but I wish I could take it all back. Jake looks how I felt only moments before, like I've slapped him.

Tears stream silently down my cheeks. I've been given promises of lives I could live. Promises that can never be kept. No matter how hard I wish, I won't ever get another day with Scott. Jake and I will never live the life of growing together through our choices and mistakes. I will never have a single day with the daughter I was promised. My anger gives way to a profound sorrow. I live a life crafted of broken promises.

"Jake ..." My face softens along with my voice. "I have made mistakes. I've made <u>so</u> many mistakes. But they led me to Scott, who gave me Noah. I wouldn't take back those decisions for the world. The mistakes <u>I</u> made also led me back to Oregon and you, at a point in my life when maybe I'm more ready to be with you than I was at sixteen. What we saw was not real in any way. It was incredible and magical, and I'd be lying if I said I didn't feel things for you that I never thought imaginable. It was like reading a book and falling completely in love with the character, only to find out I'm allowed to take that character home with me and start my own love story. Sure, it's not the same as the story in the book, but it's better because it's <u>real</u>. This..." I motion between us "...this is real."

"Yeah." His shoulders slump in defeat.

We hurt each other with words we can't take back. We aren't actually fighting over a picture of Heather or a memory of Scott. We are still fighting the same old argument, using a picture and a memory as daggers aimed at each other.

"Liv." My name hangs between us, attracting our unspoken thoughts like a dream-catcher.

The rapping on the door breaks the trance.

"Hey, uh..." Ben pokes his head in, tentatively looking between us "...I sent Noah out to the campsites with the other kids. But uh, everyone else is out here. Just a heads-up." He smiles apologetically in my direction as he backs out of the doorframe. Shit. How much of this did everyone hear? And <u>who</u> exactly is everyone?

"Liv," Jake repeats, grabbing my hand as I reach the doorway.

"Jake, I never ratted you out. I never said a goddamn word to <u>anyone</u> about your dad. Ask yourself why Heather would say I did." Wiping my eyes and breathing deeply to help with the flush I can feel in my cheeks, I slide through the opening, leaving Jake with my confession.

Fifteen

"Not even eight A.M. and Liv's already up and breaking hearts," Dre bellows as I step into the living room.

I smile sarcastically, narrowing my eyes and scrunching my nose. I've known Dre as long as I've known everyone in this town. Even if we weren't friends until he and Jen got together it feels longer.

While not quite as tall as Jake, Dre is still an impressive five-foot-eleven. He cut the afro fade he sported as a teenager into a short hard part fade, a move that instantly gave him the credibility of a serious man that Jake once declared a beard would give <u>him</u>.

Jenn's only a few inches shorter than Dre, though the height of her red curls gives the illusion they're nearly eye to eye. Her skin's nearly translucent, painted with freckles, on the opposite side of the melanin spectrum from her husband. I've been all around the country and they are still the most striking couple I've ever met.

Kate stands, pushing away from the armchair in the corner. I haven't seen Kate since graduation, but her warm smile as she approaches me reminds me of why everyone only has the best things to say about her. Married to her middle school sweetheart Brendon, and raising three kids. Kate looks how a mother should, soft and slightly disheveled, but happy.

"Hey! It's been too long," I speak over Kate's shoulder as we embrace.

"I'm so glad you're back." Her voice is as comforting and warm as her smile. "My older kids already met Noah. Lincoln and Leah are out running around with him right now."

"I thought you had three kids?" I'm questioning my memory.

"Lane is out on the deck with Brendon and Andie."

Is Jake still in the office? Did he leave and go somewhere? Why is he not out here facing everyone with me? Coward.

Steph's in the kitchen, watching with a look on her face like she's smelling something unpleasant. I've been greeted more warmly than I deserve for someone who left and never looked back. The fact that Steph refuses to pretend she's happy to see me is a relief. But as Heather's once right-hand girl, I have to wonder if she heard my fight with Jake.

I set to work packing lunches into backpacks and filling water bottles still wondering where the hell Jake is. Everyone keeps looking at me thinking I don't see them.

Jake joins the group in the kitchen long after the bulk of the work is done.

"We're going for the afternoon, not the weekend." Jake avoids my eyes as he holds an armful of filled water bottles, like he's struggling in an infomercial.

"I've never been on a hike. I don't know how much water is necessary." I shrug.

"It's better to have too much than not enough," Kate adds. I smile at her, knowing that as a fellow mom she knows the catastrophe that is kids without their food and water needs met _immediately_.

"Can we circle back to that point about Liv never having hiked before?" Dre asks the room.

"Nope." I brush past Dre, slinging my backpack over my shoulder.

The trailhead is only a short walk from Jake's house. We set out in one large group, quickly spacing into pairs and trios as we make our way into the forest so densely populated with trees that if we don't follow the markers, the trail will be impossible to see.

Noah runs off to the side of the trail with Lincoln and Grayson. Balancing on fallen logs and boulders, the ground suddenly a dangerous lava route. Leah trails behind, yelling for the boys to wait for her. Her legs aren't quite long enough to give her the stride of the older boys, and I find myself wanting to scream at them not to leave her. Us short girls gotta stick together.

I'm walking with Jake, but something's off. I can feel the tension. It could be that he has more he wants to say with regard to our fight earlier. The wound is still fresh. If we just keep hiking, I'm sure the awkwardness will subside, and it will make the conversation easier when we get back. While the way we said things maybe wasn't the best way to say things, I'm at least grateful things are out in the open.

"Kids nowadays don't have acne," Brendon muses completely unprompted behind Jake and me.

"They do too," Kate contends.

"Not to the degree we had. They have all these creams and drugs that basically make pizza face as dated as cable TV."

"Plus, preteens nowadays know how to apply makeup in ways we never dreamt possible," I add. "They just make their nose all but disappear. Poof." I move my hands quickly in front of my face pantomiming a magician. Jake gives me an amused side-eye.

"You mean they don't just slather on the body glitter and lip liner?" Kate laughs.

"I'm just waiting for Leah to get old enough to teach <u>me</u> how to contour," Jenn hollers from behind us. "Give me the illusion of completely sunken cheeks."

"You girls were all pretty enough. You didn't need all that stuff," Dre chimes in.

"Aww," all the girls say in a chorus, partly mocking, partly touched.

"Says the guy who wouldn't give me the time of day in high school," Jenn responds in a teasing tone.

"I came around." Dre throws his arm over Jenn, kissing the top of her head. "Took me less time than Liv coming around to Jake."

"Ben could have used some makeup to cover up his ugly mug," Jake yells loudly enough so that maybe Ben can hear up ahead. It's an attempt at distraction from Dre's observation. Typical Jake, deflecting his pain with humor. So he <u>is</u> still hurt from our argument.

Ben walks with Steph and Andie, tagging along with the group of kids. I suspect it has something to do with his athleticism needing the speed of kids rather than the moseying nature of the thirty-somethings back in the pack. Ben doesn't hear Jake, but the laughter that erupts from our group is loud enough to catch his attention.

No one can dispute Ben's good looks. Not a blemish to be seen, eyelashes that almost make him look like he's wearing eyeliner, hair always perfectly messy, and a chin with more structure than a house.

"I don't know what you said, Jake, but screw you!" Ben yells back, causing further hysteria.

The group spreads further and further apart as the hike goes on. Dre and Brendon, with Lane on his back, have sped up their pace to keep up with the kids, joining Ben and Steph. Andie falls back and is now with Jenn and Kate, stopping at a viewpoint under the guise of taking pictures. They confide in Jake and I that it's more to give them some space from the rest of the group. So that Kate can have a longer break from her kids.

I debate whether we should go ahead or stop at the viewpoint with the girls. But I'm hoping that if we keep walking, just the two of us, we'll be able to bury the hatchet and get back to holding hands, making everyone nauseous with how in love we are.

We hike on in relative silence, only speaking to warn the other of roots or branches. I don't know what I should say. Do I start apologizing for earlier or do I keep waiting to see how he's feeling about it all? The awkwardness is killing me.

A series of steps carved into the dirt, with logs and branches forming them into permanency, moves into view. Jake takes the steps as easily as walking up a staircase. Each step, however, hits above my knee. With legs considerably shorter than his, I take each step slowly, bracing my arms on my thigh to propel the trailing leg up to meet the other. Jake neither goes ahead nor comments on my struggle. And now I know something must be wrong. Jake never lets an opportunity to mock my height go by without acknowledgment.

Jake stands at the top of the last step and holds out his hand. I take it, allowing him to pull me to the top. My quads burn. The top of the steps opens to a lookout point. Jake leads me through the clearing and under a branch, the path no longer in view. I'm growing nervous, but I'm curious. Passing a cluster of bushes, we find a bench sitting on the cliff's edge. Taking my hand, he sits on the far side of the bench and pulls me down to sit next to him.

"This is my favorite place on the lake." His eyes scan the horizon slowly, taking it all in. Following his gaze, I look out and am struck with a sense of awe. The lake reminds me of a mirror my grandma kept on her vanity, the raised gold frame, and the way it sat stagnant while reflections danced on its surface.

Along the edge of the lake, I'm able to locate Jake's house almost directly across from where we're sitting. It's so hidden in the trees that if I didn't know what I was looking for, it would blend into the forest.

"Will your development ruin this?" The question comes off as more accusatory than I intend.

"No." He sits back with a start, his voice curt. Then he pauses for a minute, thinking. "Well, we are trying to prevent that from being the case. I started this because my grandpa had this lake that only he and his friends could enjoy."

I want to ask why his grandpa left the lake to him rather than his parents. But I know that his parents' rocky marriage wasn't exactly a secret, and no father would want to give his daughter something knowing it would be taken by her abusive husband. Did Jake's parents try and fight for it?

"I had to tear down about a hundred private property signs when I first took over. I want others to be able to enjoy everything that's up here, without destroying it. That's why we are so focused on sustainable development. I don't want to build something only to have it destroy the place I love the most."

There seems to be a double meaning in his words, but I'm not quite sure where he's going with this.

His voice is far away. "You really didn't talk to Miss Grownski about my dad?"

"I never said a word."

We sit with the knowledge that our friendship ended over tempers and misunderstandings, and that there's nothing we can do to change that.

"I need some time."

"Time for what?" He might as well have said 'we need to talk' the way it's twisting me up into knots of anxiety.

"I've never met anyone who makes me laugh the way you do. You were my best friend because of the pure joy I felt whenever you were around, and not only because I was pining after you for years." He squeezes my hand ... in what? Reassurance? "My gramma wanted me to finish this list, and what if _this_ isn't my fate? If you and I are really it, shouldn't it be easy Liv? It's going to break me if I lose you completely. I don't think I can risk not even being friends again, you know?"

"Things are different now." I wish I believed myself. Deep down, we're the same people. Our issues still remain. We opened the wound without doing anything to stop the bleeding.

"Are they? We say we're friends, but we hurt each other."

"That's not fair." I hate how wobbly my voice is. He's breaking up with me because I _didn't_ turn him in to CPS? And somehow this is supposed to be a good thing?

"But is it wrong?" he asks softly.

"No." He's right. We've hurt each other in ways neither of us have fully moved past.

We sit with this for a long time. Tears silently roll down my cheeks as I realize I'm losing him and I can't do anything about it. We can say we're going to step back and be friends, but we've already crossed that line of no return. People say you can't go back because you can't. The moment we saw our life together, that was it. There was no way for me to make my life make sense with Jake and I just being friends.

"So what do we do now?" Neither of us have said we don't have feelings for the other. It's the opposite really. How does a relationship end when both parties don't want it to?

"We do what I did for years." Jake stands, holding his hand out for me to take. Placing my hand in his, he pulls me to my feet. Leaning down he kisses me softly on the lips with a heartbreaking tenderness. "We push our feelings down and move forward as friends, knowing that it's the only way to avoid complete and total devastation. I finish my list, and maybe ..." he trails off, leaving the maybe as a possibility of everything and a promise of nothing.

"I don't know if I can do that." Pretend my heart doesn't break every time I see him? Pretend I don't say things just to hear his laugh?

"I have faith in you." His lips press against my forehead. How did we get here? Can we start over?

I've experienced many breakups in my life, some awkward, some anger-fueled, some that seemed to come out of left field. Never have I experienced a break up that makes me feel more loved, and as a result more heartbroken than this one. It has more and yet none of the finality that normally accompanies the end of a relationship.

Sixteen

J ake and I are the last to arrive back at camp. I can only hope that the look of pure devastation I am sure is plastered on my face will be confused for simply exhaustion after a long day of hiking.

The large bonfire pit spans nearly ten feet, allowing for a large group to sit around its edges in a selection of Adirondack chairs. A smaller fire burns in an adjacent pit of significantly smaller proportions.

The glamping sites are something I'd expect from a photoshoot rather than a real place. Bistro lights hang inside each tent, where an assortment of bed sizes make for accommodations to suit anyone hoping to get away from the worries of the world, but comfortably—though not as comfortably as a real bed in a real house.

Noah, Lincoln, and Leah sit on chairs around the small fire, sodas in hand. Steph's son Grayson, who is in Noah's class, stands at the edge of a long table, crafting a s'more with the blackened marshmallow perched on the end of his roasting rod.

Two women descend the pathway towards the fire, holding hands and giggling. As they enter the glow of the fire, I recognize Ashley. Jake's 7th grade Sadie Hawkins date.

"Ash! Mish!" the chorus greets.

"That's Ashley's wife, Michelle," Jake whispers helpfully. I nod in appreciation, feeling like Meryl Streep in <u>The Devil Wears Prada</u> getting names fed to me.

"How was <u>that</u> vision of life lost?" I tease, wondering how in-depth he'd gone tracking down exes. Did middle school dance dates count?

"Nothing bad, but certainly not happily ever after. I'm not her type" Jake laughs a strained laugh. Brushing his hand along my lower back, he moves toward the group.

Sending me a mixed signal from the conversation we just had. He can't do things like that. Jake takes a chair next to Dre, accepting the beer offered by Jenn as she returns to her chair on the other side of her husband.

I can still feel the phantom touch of his hand as I make my way to the smaller fire, where the kids are all set up with their hotdogs and marshmallows roasting. Leaning down, I wrap my arms around Noah. My cheek presses against his own.

This. This is my constant. Noah is the one who anchors me to the earth.

"Hey, buddy, how was your hike?" I squeeze, hoping his day was better than my own. Noah leans his head back against my chest. It's almost as if he can feel my heart breaking. After the last year, he's more in tune with my emotional state than any kid should have to be.

"It was so fun." Exhaustion heavily paints his tone.

"You drink enough water today?"

"No, and my head hurts a little."

I walk to the cooler and dig until I find a bottle of water, cracking it open I gulp a quarter of the bottle before handing it to Noah. "Drink the rest of this, and let's see if that helps. If not, I can get you some medicine. But it's about time to head to bed and some sleep should help too, ok?"

Noah nods tiredly.

"Can I sleep in the tent with the other kids?" He looks up to meet my eyes. A tent is set up with two sets of bunk beds on either side of the tent and a large rug in the center. I know Kate and Steph are going to let their kids sleep there, and I don't want Noah to be the only one left out.

"Yeah, I think that will be ok." I kiss the top of his head.

"Hey, little man." Jake moves into the seat next to Noah. "Can you throw another marshmallow on there for me?"

Noah perks up. "You want a s'more?"

"Yeah, I was going to roast some Starburst. You want one?"

"Those used to be my dad's favorite!" Noah turns over his shoulder. Seeing me still standing there, he lifts his eyes, dismissing me.

Geeze what am I? Chopped Liver?

I watch from my seat at the large fire. Noah laughs as Jake's stick leaves the fire empty, the Starburst lost to the flames. Distracted, the marshmallows on Noah's stick catch fire. Earlier today I would have seen this with different eyes, the eyes of a mom hoping the man

I'm with will be worthy of my son. Now I'm watching as my childhood friend extends his friendship without any motives.

The biggest surprise of the trip isn't the breakup. It's that the kids settle into their bunks easily. Exhaustion from the hike, and the late hour, results in silence from their tent within minutes.

The group, apart from Kate who disappeared into her tent with baby Lane, sits around the large firepit on the far end of the camping area, where noise is less likely to carry to those sleeping in tents.

"So is this like a tradition?" Michelle asks from the hammock she shares with Ashley.

"Yeah, this is what ... our eighteenth year doing the Labor Day bonfire?" Brendon answers. "We used to do them down at the coast until Jake offered the lake. Then we moved them up here. But none seem to be as exciting as that first one."

A nervous chuckle moves through the group as they <u>all</u> remember the fight between Jake and Aaron. Only I remember what led to the fight.

"Oh, why was that one so exciting?" Michelle's question prompts all eyes to turn to Jake and me.

Neither of us offer a response. I can only hope that this is where the conversation shifts to a new topic.

"Well," Steph speaks the singular word in a tone that sends a chill down my spine. "Liv decided to throw herself at our <u>good</u> friend Heather's boyfriend. And when he turned her down, she threw a tantrum and Jake ended up beating the shit out of the poor guy."

"Excuse me?" I demand in sync with the group erupting into a chorus of "Woah"

"Steph," Jake warns.

"What?" she challenges, looking completely innocent.

I open my mouth. Setting the record straight will make my life easier in several ways. Jake could finally understand that Heather was never to be trusted. My reputation could be wiped of the blemish the rumors marred it with, and Steph would be publicly shamed in a way she's probably deserved for years.

"Aaron has never been a 'poor guy.' He's an asshole and always has been." Ben leaps to Jake's defense—or my defense, I'm not sure.

"No, he's not!" Steph argues. Is her face flushed or is it just the firelight? I don't think I've ever seen Steph get flustered.

"So you guys broke up because of what an awesome guy he was?" Jenn tosses it back to Steph. I don't know the story, but I love the way this is turning out.

Steph leans forward, finger-pointing. "That's low, Jenn."

"Well!" Jenn throws her hands up in a "What are you gonna do about it?" way.

Drama lingers in the group of people who grew up together but never fully put adolescence behind them.

The talking and shouting is chaotic enough that no one seems to notice when I slide out of my chair and back away from the group.

The pebbles on the shoreline clack together as the weight of my footsteps shifts their positions. The moon is just shy of full, and as its twin shines up from the glassy water, I'm reminded of the night me and Jake shared on the shore of <u>this</u> lake on a full moon. The night that resulted in Scarlett. The night that <u>wasn't</u>.

I find an old log washed ashore and settle onto it. Sliding my feet back and forth, I dig a small trench in the rocks with my bare feet.

I hear the footsteps of my follower, I don't need to look to know who it is.

"Hey, you." Jake sits on the spot next to me. He buries his own feet next to my trenches.

"I'm fine. You didn't need to come look for me."

"I know you're fine. You're always fine, till you're not."

He's acting like nothing's changed.

The silence between us is packed. I open my mouth to speak, but what <u>should</u> I say? I have no idea. Jake wants to be friends, but we <u>aren't</u> friends. Not anymore. With so much history behind us, we'll never be <u>just</u> friends again. Were we ever really <u>just</u> friends? Even as kids there was always something deeper. I just hadn't recognized it at the time.

And yet his list, the possibilities of fate somewhere out there, is enough for him to step away. He told me he hadn't seen anything worth pursuing, he said it was so bad he had to stop looking. Is it that bad with me that he could really want to go back to searching?

"You don't owe anyone an explanation. You know that <u>right</u>?" His hand is warm as it lays over mine.

The tears are working their way to my eyes. If one comes out, I won't be able to stop. It isn't <u>just</u> Steph, or the memory of Aaron, or the breakup. It's that if Scott was alive, I wouldn't <u>have</u> to deal with <u>any</u> of it. Every ache and every struggle seems to lead back to Scott, and that seems to amplify the unfairness of it all. I close my eyes and nod briefly in reply.

"What Steph said over there," I begin. "Is that ... is that what Heather told <u>you</u> happened?"

"Yeah." I can't hold it against him. I assumed because he never asked me what happened that it meant he didn't want to know.

"What is it about Heather that makes everything she says <u>so</u> believable?"

"I don't know," he answers honestly, a hint of regret in his voice. "You've always seen through her in a way that none of us ever could."

The water moves across the shore, ebbing and flowing with our thoughts.

"I think it's that she offered answers to questions she <u>knew</u> we would need answers to. Making it convenient to accept. It doesn't help that you never stand up for yourself. You just let people say what they will about you."

He's right. I run from the accusations and confrontations and anything hard. I could have spoken up when Jake accused me. I could have destroyed Aaron by coming forward. I didn't have to date Scott just because he called me his girlfriend. I just find it easier to go along with it all than to say something. Sometimes it works out, but not always.

"I figure people that actually know me would know not to believe what people say about me."

"That's expecting a <u>lot</u> from people."

We sit in companionable silence for a long while. So long that I start to think maybe we can actually be friends. Maybe this isn't the worst thing in the world.

I don't know if everyone noticed when we disappeared, but they don't say anything when we return. We rejoin the conversation without missing a beat.

At some point in silent agreement, the fire is no longer fed with new logs. The fire wheezes its dying breaths. In a few minutes, the glow of the embers will be all that remains. Ben, Dre, Jake, and I sit in silence, watching the coals pulse with life.

I can feel my eyes getting heavy before fluttering closed as I fight to stay awake. The conversation shifts to sporting events. This Adirondack chair reclines just a bit more than the others, which does nothing to keep me awake. My eyes burn, refusing to open. I'm still awake, barely, listening to the conversation.

"Oh man, when Scott and I were in Phoenix for the Super Bowl—"

"Wait," Jake interrupts Dre. "Liv's Scott?

"Yeah," Dre answers nonchalantly.

"That's the Scott you've been talking about all these years? You never said he was married to Liv." Jake sounds almost offended that this information was withheld.

"Well, yeah," Dre responds. "I didn't want you to hate him right off the bat." His serious tone hits the mark on Jake's grudge-holding.

I don't mean to, but I laugh, giving away that I am, in fact, still awake. I pry one eye open narrowly and smile at Jake. He meets my smile with curiosity.

"Wait, so that like hour-long video chat we had when you were in Phoenix for the Super Bowl?"

"Liv's Scott."

"Huh... I liked him," Jake says the words methodically, almost as if they surprise him. Dre is nodding. It was impossible _not_ to like Scott.

"He was a good guy," Dre agrees, his voice cracking. _Was_. The word that brings the happy reminiscing down with a crash. Hearing people remember Scott doesn't seem to get easier, especially when they show the vulnerability of their grief. I've been avoiding Dre and Jenn, worried that I would be a mess in my grief without ever thinking about how much Dre must be hurting too.

Ben jumps at the opportunity to change the subject to keep the tone light, reminiscing about the hockey game they had all attended the spring before. I lie back, looking up through the trees to the sky filled with so many stars it's hard to distinguish one from another. A tear escapes from the corner of my eye.

Scott applied for several jobs and was offered a campaign manager position in Portland only days before he died. That he applied without talking to me resulted in an argument. Scott reluctantly agreed to turn the job down, lamenting that I needed to grow up and move past whatever teenage drama I was still holding on to.

God, he would have _loved_ this group, and that sucks. It's only in his death that I've been able to even start moving on and restoring friendships I thought were gone. Another tear rolls freely down my face and around my neck, where it rests. The only reason I was even invited tonight was because I was _with_ Jake.

What would the last month have looked like if after running into Jake, and seeing all that we had that day, I returned home to Scott? Not the ghost of him, but alive and well. Would I have been able to continue living with Scott, completely ignoring the feelings the vision instilled in me? Was it possible to love two men wholly and simultaneously? Except it is possible because I do. And I've lost them both.

Grief lurks like a physical pain dampened by opioids. It's still very much present, waiting in the shadows to emerge in full force. Grief from the loss of Scott crashes intensely in waves against the wall I keep as a barrier. Added to this is the grief from the loss of Jake, which is new and still unbelievable. I don't have to look at Scott as I deal with the reality that he is gone, yet with Jake I have to push aside the weight pressing down on me for the sake of our friendship.

I may never experience with another person what I have with Jake. I allowed my pettiness and jealousy to drive Jake away in the same way I let my fear dictate so many of the choices Scott and I made. I have no one to blame but myself.

The coals are now gray as smoke barely rises. Jake stands and grabs a bucket of water, dumping half its contents onto each of the fire pits. Pockets of heat erupt with a loud hiss as the water hits them. Plumes of smoke billow.

Dre holds up his hand in a mock salute as he makes his way toward his tent. "Night, guys."

"Night, Dre. Night, you two," Ben calls as he follows Dre, making his way to the tent two down from where Dre enters.

Jake stares at the hissing smoke, deep in thought.

"Jake?" I ask after it's clear we are truly alone.

"What's up?" His eyes strain over the pit to meet mine.

Rather than tell him that I <u>know</u> we are making a mistake, I swallow the lump growing in my throat.

Instead of saying, "I'm sorry for everything. I love you." I say, "Nothing. Sleep well." I hope he hears what I mean.

"You too, Liv."

His smile reminds me of that first day in the coffee shop, unable to fully reach his eyes yet still dimpling the scar. Closing his mouth, he nods at me and turns to find his tent, leaving me with a chill and regret at words left unsaid.

Seventeen

Jake all but disappears after the campout, timing his arrivals and departures at the old Crane House so we are two ships passing in the night. I thought there was real hope after the bonfire, but now I'm not sure.

I decide to be a less shitty friend and take Jenn and Dre up on their standing offer for dinner. Noah and my dad locked themselves in the workshop earlier today, working on something I'm not allowed to see yet. My mom invited me to help with a quilt, but I would rather organize my sock drawer.

"Jake came by Crane House," I announce, building myself another cracker sandwich from the charcuterie board.

"He told you he'd help you with the balusters," Dre says.

"I mean, he did. But that was before."

"Before you agreed to be friends?" He says this in a tone that makes me feel defensive. My eyes dart around the living room looking for Jenn. She'll take my side.

"Ok, yes. But I haven't seen him in weeks. Not since the campout." I forgot how frustrating it is to complain to a man, who just wants to fix things, not listen and commiserate.

Jake and I left the Labor Day campout with a kiss on the cheek and the promise that Jake would call me in a day or two to check in. It's been more than two weeks of radio silence until today when he stopped by to help me cut the balusters for the new staircase. I wasn't expecting him, so I had my headphones on. My music was loud because it had to be so I could hear it over the saw. I turned around to grab another piece of wood, and he was just standing there staring at me. My soul nearly left my body.

"He's not avoiding you, Liv. He's probably just really busy."

"That's bullshit and you know it, Dre! Without Liv's house, their whole project is doomed." Jenn swoops in with the save, returning from the kitchen with the box of pinot under her arm. We've been back and forth from the fridge refilling our glasses and this conversation is going to need more wine.

Dre shakes his head as he gulps his glass, which houses a rum and coke. "We didn't see you for like a month after you moved here. Were you avoiding us, Liv? No, you were just busy. Just like Jake is."

"I was one hundred percent avoiding you."

Afraid of the pity I knew would occur, returning home as a widow and without the job I loved, I purposely avoided getting together with them. It wasn't until the campout that I was reminded of why my friends were my friends in the first place. During the most awkward moments of my life, they're there. Able and willing to distract me.

Jenn's friendship is never one that comes with expectations or requirements. It's exactly the kind of friendship I should have nourished over this last year instead of pushing her away. I worried that seeing them in person would change the easiness in some way. Forcing me to spend my days reliving memories of Scott, making it impossible to move past my own grief instead of wallowing with others in our shared grief.

And on top of it all, I rolled into town and nabbed a boyfriend almost immediately. It's embarrassing that Dre and Jenn, and the rest of our friends, even saw me <u>with</u> Jake. Like I came back to town searching for love. Like I'm some kind of cheesy Christmas movie. I assume there's been a good amount of judgment. I'm sure they are all talking about how I'm desperate to jump into a relationship, while the same people were likely genuinely happy for Jake being given a second chance with a lost love. The double standard is infuriating. Or maybe there isn't a double standard, and I'm just imagining it?

"You were avoiding us?" Jenn asks. "Why?"

"I mean, at first because I didn't want you guys to see how pathetic and sad I still was. And <u>then</u> because I didn't think I should be so happy so <u>soon</u>. You know."

"Why is it that you women always feel as though you're undeserving? What is it you think you've done that makes you unworthy?" Dre muses, taking a Ritz and piling salami, gouda, salami, and muenster before adding a top cracker. His eyes widen at the tower in front of him.

If he wasn't so focused on his Lunchable, he would see the exchange of looks between Jenn and me. The look that conveys exactly what we've done to become unworthy of happiness. We're women, raised in a society in which we are expected to live in a certain way that upholds the standards set by those in power. These standards often mean women are penalized in some fashion for our infertility or our promiscuity. For our ambition to build a career, but also for our choice to stay home with children. For bouncing back too quickly after childbirth or the slowness at which our body returns to what is considered normal or acceptable if it ever actually does return to its previous state. We can't win.

After years of infertility, Jenn and Dre are just waiting on the final paperwork before they can bring their daughter home from Haiti. No one asks Dre what's wrong with him, or why he can't father a child; they assume it's Jenn.

I enjoyed ten years with Scott and bore his child. Something that people think should be enough to keep me happy for a lifetime. That by engaging in a relationship, I'm somehow dishonoring Scott. My happiness too soon after Scott's death can somehow be taken as an admission that I never actually loved him. Yet if my grief continues too long, it's also sad and I'd be told it's time to move on. As if the time to move on isn't dependent on a thousand different factors. Dre doesn't have to live with any of these realities.

"Look, all I know is that I haven't seen Jake this happy in years." Dre allows his question to remain another secret of women he'll never fully understand. "How'd you two make up anyway?"

I can't exactly tell them that Jake touched my hand and we saw a life different than our real ones. That we had a baby, got married, and lived happily ever after. They'll certify me. But it's best to stick to the truth as much as possible.

"We ran into each other and got to talking about how different our lives could have turned out if we'd done things differently." I shrug like it's as much a mystery to me as it is them.

"That's it?" Dre's eyebrow cocks. He's not buying it. Shit. "The guy whose senior quote might as well have been 'Fuck Liv Turner.' <u>That</u> guy just got nostalgic and moved on?"

While hyperbolic, Dre isn't wrong. Jake was anything but quiet about our rift. While I can't remember what it was, I <u>think</u> his senior quote was something about backstabbing or betrayal, disguised in the form of a literary quote to make it past the yearbook advisor who would have most definitely denied "Fuck Liv Turner."

My own, on the other hand, was nauseatingly cheesy; about a caterpillar emerging as a butterfly. About as unique as getting a dandelion that blows into a flock of birds tattooed on my side, but I was so proud of it.

"Yeah, I don't know. I don't think he's fully moved on. Otherwise, they'd probably still be together instead of talking about how he showed up to help her with the balusters after avoiding her for weeks." Jenn is eager to get back to the topic at hand. "So what <u>did</u> he say?"

"Almost nothing!" I throw myself backward in exasperation. "It was like pulling teeth. So I asked him how long it would be awkward for, and he shrugged. He shrugged!"

I was in actual physical pain, aching for Jake to say or do anything that would give me any indication that he was as crazy about me as I am about him. Our breakup only intensified the feelings Jake told me to suppress. And according to Dre, Jake is the happiest he's been in years. I'm miserable, and he's out living his happiest, best life. Fuck!

The whole time we were working on the balusters, Jake kept his eyes down and focused on cutting, sanding, and staining the wood with minimal words passing between the two of us. When I pointed out how weird and stiff it all felt, he shrugged and told me it would just take time. That I should be patient. He took the exact words I'd used when I'd broken up with him, <u>knowing</u> I couldn't argue.

Something Jenn said nags at me. "What did you mean his project is shot without my house?" I ask, remembering her comment from earlier.

Dre leans forward conspiratorially. "Don't tell either of them I told you this, because they specifically didn't want you to know, adding extra pressure to your renovation. But Jake bought a small house in town using the money they needed to start the next phase of building. Ben is livid but wouldn't tell me why Jake bought the house. My guess is he's moving out of Ben's place." Dre spills the tea like he never intended to keep it to himself in the first place.

I widen my eyes, pretending this is the first I've heard of this. I can't tell them Jake bought the house for me. I can't tell them about the afternoon we spent examining the scars of the home and reconnecting in a way we only had in a fantasy. That's ours. Sharing that would lessen the magic.

"But if he was moving out of Ben's house, why wouldn't he just move into his lake house mansion?" Jenn counters. "And if he's not dating Liv, we aren't going to get any insider info about what's going on. Cause God knows you can't keep a secret." Smirking she nudges Dre.

"I mean, he <u>did</u> invite me over to hang out tomorrow. But he didn't seem super sincere about it, so ..." Not that he'll tell me he's moving out of Ben's, because that's not what the green house is for.

"You're going, right?" Jenn sits up straight at this first bit of good news.

"I don't think so. What if it's <u>just</u> as weird and awkward?"

"Then you text me and I call pretending to be your mom telling you that Noah needs you. You have to go! Plus, Ben will be there, right?"

The idea is tempting. We're running so far behind schedule <u>because</u> Jake is avoiding me. If we want any shot at making our deadline on the house, we need to patch things up. I <u>need</u> to get out of my parent's house, and Jake <u>needs</u> this renovation to go well so he can finish the lake development. I feel guilty that because he did something for <u>me,</u> there is a real chance that it delays everything he's worked for.

Plus there is always the chance that by the end of the night he won't be able to keep his hands off of me. That he'll decide his list isn't worth it, and we can go back to the way things were. I'm not even paying attention to Jenn and Dre. Did he just say something about Heather?

"Heather?" I ask hesitantly. I really shouldn't have zoned out.

"Yeah, Jake and Heather were pretty serious. Toxic, but serious." Dre jumps in.

"Toxic how?"

"I don't think <u>they</u> thought it was toxic. But she likes to have things her way, and Jake is so used to making everyone around him happy at his own expense, so he just kinda went along with whatever she decided," Jenn adds in explanation.

This is something I can't relate to. Jake's never had a problem advocating for himself with me.

"I <u>really</u> hate her."

"Cause she dated Jake?" Dre asks incredulously. He obviously missed the years of drama.

"Are you being serious, Andre?" Jenn turns to Dre, matching his drawn expression. "She was always starting rumors about Liv." Finally! Someone remembers how bad it was.

"The whole thing with Aaron at the beach?" He pinpoints the one rumor I don't want to address. By keeping this to myself, maybe I've been protecting Aaron and Heather too long.

"Aaron assaulted me and then tried to drown me when I fought back." I've never said this out loud to anyone other than my therapist. This secret has crushed me, and I never realized it until the weight of it was removed. I've found liberation in speaking the truth.

"Are you serious?" Jenn's eyes fix on mine.

"When we left the bonfire, we found a cave and went exploring. He kissed me, but I'd never been kissed so it caught me off guard. We kissed a second time and then he just went crazy. He pinned me against the wall and ripped my shirt off of me. I bit his lip until I heard it crunch and tried to leave. That's when he knocked me over and held me under the waves, laughing the whole time. Heather got pissed that I was with Aaron at all and told me she'd destroy my life. She did a pretty good job too."

"But Heather couldn't have known. Aaron probably told her the version she told everyone." Is Dre seriously trying to stand up for her? I didn't just tell them my most horrible moment for Dre to turn around and be the Devil's advocate.

"Liv, I had no idea," Jenn starts, giving Dre a serious look. "Her story never quite sat right with me, but you and Aaron were both so quiet on the subject, I didn't know _what_ to believe. Does Jake know?"

I shake my head.

"I think you should tell him. He couldn't have known how awful she was before he started dating her. No matter what happened between you two, I don't think he would have if he knew it would hurt you."

"I'm pretty sure that's exactly why he started dating her. Because he _knew_ it would hurt me. I just don't know at what point it quit being revenge and became something real."

I regret talking about Heather. I'm worried that if we say her name a third time it will summon her like Beetlejuice. She'll manifest just to mess with my life for a second time—or is it third ... no, this would be four. God, at this point I can't even remember _how_ many times she's just fucked everything up for me.

Dre hangs around, shit-talking Heather with me and Jenn, up until the theme music to _The Bachelor_ starts. Standing, he excuses himself to do literally anything besides watching _The Bachelor_, and I've never been more jealous of him. I've made it my entire life never watching a single episode of the show Jenn treats as a religion. But I owe Jenn for the months I've been a shitty best friend so I snuggle next to her. The same way we did as teens, popcorn bowl perched atop our blanket, trying to mentally prepare for the trash we are about to consume.

"You're throwing a housewarming party once the renovation is complete right?" Jenn's question comes at the beginning of the commercial break, starting the stopwatch on the conversation.

"Wasn't planning on it. I'm not much for entertaining."

"Dre and Brendon will handle food. Kate and I can help with everything else. It's really just music, mingling, and good food. But we're all dying to see how you all have taken the haunted house of Coburg and transformed it."

"I mean, I guess we could do a little something."

"Perfect." Jenn returns her gaze to the TV, raising the volume as the show resumes. Conversation over.

The idea of a party adds a new pressure to the renovation. I just wanted the house to feel like home. When Ben and Jake decided to enter it to be featured on HGTV, my opinion was no longer the only one that mattered. I <u>know</u> that Jake and Ben's business is riding on the publicity they're hoping the contest will garner. If my house somehow isn't good enough, it won't only mean they've wasted time and money, but now they'll have no way of finishing the next stage of the development thanks to Jake and his lack of impulse control and the little green house now in his name. The pressure weighs heavy on me.

It was all so much simpler when I was living in a construction zone with Tom Sweet dragging his feet on renovations that didn't excite me past the point of the house functioning again. It was only myself and Noah being inconvenienced, and we're flexible. Everyone else may be less so.

Eighteen

Since the moment Jake extended the invitation, I let my mind create elaborate evenings similar to those that Grace had created for us as teens. Whether it was red corn syrup dripped down the side of glasses for Halloween, paper lanterns to celebrate the lunar new year, or even just a spread of fresh-cut fruit, there was always something to look forward to in the Zhao house. Stupidly, I expected the magic to be in the house despite the source of the magic being gone.

Instead, I find the home unrecognizable once inside. Modern furniture replaces the old worn couches that once filled the space. A large abstract painting hangs where Ben's school pictures had smiled on us. The smell that always lingered from Grace's constant cooking is nonexistent, instead a sandalwood candle burns, filling the bachelor pad with a clean, masculine scent.

"So what happened?" Curled up on the couch, I nurse my whiskey. Seeing Jake lounging in his grey sweatpants, a whiskey of his own hidden beneath his fingers, sends twitches of longing, and I have the hardest time focusing on Ben's answer. Damnit, what is it about guys in sweats? I have to remind myself that Jake is no longer mine. That he's never _really_ been mine. Not for more than like a minute.

Jake had been so desperate in the beginning to convince me to be with him, only to pour cold water on the relationship as it was heating. Without any real communication, I'm not even sure if Jake is actually working on his list or if it was an excuse to end things.

We're never fully on the same page, both circling around what my mom deemed inevitable—only I'm circling towards it while Jake spirals away.

"Then Caleb got a job in Silicon Valley, but my mom was sick," Ben continues. "He's married to some tech guy now. They just had a daughter this last spring."

"And you haven't dated since?" I ask, wondering if there is a part of Ben that's still hung up on Caleb.

"Nah."

"No," Jake interjects. "You went out with Steph for a bit after her divorce."

The idea of Ben with someone as fundamentally mean as Steph is more than I can wrap my head around.

"Ew." Whoops. That was supposed to be an inside thought.

"Liv, people can grow and change beyond who they were as teenagers," Jake chides.

"You do know I saw and interacted with her Labor Day weekend, right?" The sneers and snide remarks from Steph might have been looked over by everyone else, but I caught them.

I know better than to believe that Steph feels any different about me now than she had nearly two decades ago. I'm the woman who returned and took her best friend's man, even if Jake and Heather have been over for years. Unless in Steph's mind, they aren't quite over.

Heather's name is on Jake's list. Whether it's crossed off yet or not is the question. Has Jake already seen and dismissed a life with Heather, or is _that_ the possibility that made him rethink moving forward with me?

"If you could see what your life was like if you'd followed Caleb, would you want to know?" I ask Ben, attempting to round the conversation towards the answers I hope will come.

"Hell no." He all but shouts before the question is even out. "I think it's all bullshit. I mean look at you two, your real relationship after seeing it all probably wasn't _anything_ like what you saw. It creates unrealistic expectations, and I think then you judge every interaction with that lens."

"God, why don't you tell us how you really feel?" Jake's heard this all before and seems frustrated hearing Ben's take on it once again.

Was Jake keeping tabs on how I measured up to the me that he'd wanted? Had I failed a test I was unaware I'd been taking? Self-doubt creeps in, replacing every tingle I felt near Jake with a pit. I don't think I was judging Jake against a nonexistent version of him. If anything, I've been judging him against my marriage with Scott. Which while equally unfair, isn't the same.

"Did I think it was cool that you could do it at first, I mean yeah. But who's the one that's had to deal with the aftermath of it all. Me. Then you see the _one_ thing you were hoping to find, and it's _still_ not enough." Ben stands, flexing his hands in frustration as he walks out.

Holy shit.

The silence is stunning. All the tension returns from where it receded.

"I _have_ to finish it." The list. It's all about his goddamn list.

"Why?"

"You know why."

"But I _don't_. Ben has a point. You told me that you've never seen anything worth pursuing. What if all that is waiting for you is just more of what you've already seen?"

"Then that's what it is. But I _promised_ her." Grandma June, the woman who took him in and loved him unconditionally in the way his mother didn't.

I can't be the reason Jake doesn't fulfill his promise. The resentment would destroy any shot we have.

"Okay. Then let's do this." If this is what Jake needs to be in any kind of a place where he can move forward with his life, with me or not. I'll pick up where Ben became exhausted and quit. I'll stand in the aftermath with him.

"Do what?"

"Find them. Track down the rest of the names on your list. How many do you have left?"

"Nine. But you don't have to—"

"Jesus Jake. Did you date every girl in the valley? Doesn't matter, Let's get to it."

Jake sets his hand on my thigh, appreciative of my offer. It's painful how badly I wish his move is something more than the innocent friendly gesture it is. The muscles in my cheeks twitch with longing and heartache.

There's a real possibility that Jake will reconnect with someone who doesn't come along the baggage we do. Someone who can fit seamlessly into his life without any of the messy history. It's a possibility that's worth the risk. Jake deserves to be truly happy, even if it isn't with me. But God do I hope it's with me.

"It's getting late. I better get going," I say, needing to break the hold he has on me.

"I'll walk you home."

"I'm just gonna go say goodnight to Ben." Standing, I take his empty glass along with my own to the kitchen, setting them in the basin.

"I had fun." Leaning against the doorframe, I smile at Ben lying on his bed, phone held just above his face.

Lowering his phone, Ben returns my smile, and there is nothing but adoration in it. "I'm glad you came by."

"It's nice to be back. Almost feels like nothing changed."

"Except everything did," Ben counters. His eyes convey the seriousness of his words while his wide smile remains.

"Except everything did," I agree, wistful.

Outside a few cars are driving down the road, briefly shining their headlights onto the sidewalk.

Jake and I move slowly, gliding toward the direction of my parents' house rather than simply walking.

"I'm glad you came over." Jake breaks the silence.

"Me too." Twisting my mouth, I weigh what I'm about to ask. "What's your wildest hope? I mean, with all this." The darkness and breeze give a sense of security in speaking the words I'd think twice about in the light.

"I don't really know," Jake begins. "The first time it happened I wasn't even sure what <u>had</u> happened. I think by the time I realized the magnitude of it all, I'd already experienced so many heartbreaking outcomes that the magic and awesomeness of the situation was sort of already gone, ya know?" Stepping into the road, Jake kicks a large rock toward the sidewalk, out of the way of traffic. "I think I gave up hoping a while ago. At this point, it's just enduring to the end. What about you, though? If you found out you could see <u>any</u> outcome, where would you go? Who would you track down?"

I've spent sleepless nights mulling this over since the possibility first presented itself.

"Well, I didn't exactly date a ton in high school, same with college. So I don't think that's really a fountain of missed opportunities waiting to be rediscovered."

"What about Devin?"

"Devin was a friendly face when I needed one. But I wasn't ready for a relationship. I needed time. And by the time he asked, I was already with Scott. I'd be curious how life would have gone if I hadn't pushed him aside. If I'd given him a real shot."

"What about Scott? If you could, would you want to see what your life would be if he hadn't died?"

The question is packed. I'm not sure if Jake <u>really</u> wants me to unpack it, but what the hell?

"Honestly, I think I'd be too curious to <u>not</u> see. But I think I'd regret looking if I had the chance. Seeing a life that I have zero chance of ever being able to live is heartbreaking. With you, there was at least the possibility of building something from what we saw, but with Scott, it would all be unattainable on every level, and I don't know how I'd get through that."

Jake's silent with what I assume is some sort of self-reflection.

"Do you ever think about Scarlett?" I ask, hoping to keep the conversation moving.

"Of course I do," Jake answers without pause. "It feels like part of me is missing, part of me that I never really deserved to have."

"Yeah."

"You feel it too?" He looks over at me, surprised by the admission.

"Of course." I pause, trying to determine how much to share. "I have congenital adrenal hyperplasia, which made it incredibly difficult to become pregnant with Noah. I had a half dozen miscarriages before him. I managed to get pregnant when Noah was a toddler but we lost her when I was twenty-two weeks along. We tried and tried but never conceived again. Seeing Scarlett just sort of brought back all those feelings that my body isn't good enough to grow another child. Which I know is ridiculous, but my mind goes there anyway. It's something I'm supposed to be able to do, and I can't."

"I'm sorry."

"No, it's fine. You made the right choice not wanting to be with me, though. I don't even know if I could give you what you want." I try to make a joke out of it, but my tone falls flat, leaving something sad in its place.

"How do you know that's what I want?"

We reach the lawn of my parents' house, causing me to worry that this conversation will be over just as we hit a breakthrough.

"I guess I just assumed." Stepping up onto the porch and sitting on the swing, I leave plenty of room for Jake to sit next to me. Instead, he takes the rocking chair perpendicular to the swing, moving the red throw pillow from the back and holding it on his lap. "So what <u>do</u> you want? What is all this for? What would be the thing that makes you stop looking?" I hoped it would have been me. With the knowledge it isn't me, my curiosity grows. What is it that he hopes his life will become?

"I think I'll just know when I know. I want to feel like I'm the happiest I possibly could be. Until I met up with you, that never included a kid. But God, she was beautiful wasn't she?"

Jake talking about Scarlett warms the part of me that is reserved for my children. Both Noah as well as the children I dreamt of raising but was never able to.

"Liv. I never said I don't want to be with you."

He never said it. He just ended things. What other message could that possibly send?

Nineteen

Renovations move along so much faster with Jake and I no longer avoiding each other. In turn for Noah not being able to see the progress, I've agreed to stay out of the workshop while he works alongside my dad, creating something special for the house. He lights up each time he talks about it.

After dropping Noah off at school each morning I head to Crane House, setting to work on whatever task Ben has ready for me. Once I'm shown the basics of how to do something, I'm able to do it on my own—well, for the most part. The work is repetitive enough to keep going with minimal issues.

Cutting and installing baseboards is pretty relaxing. Headphones on, my playlist turned up, I'm good for hours. I bring the miter saw I borrowed from my dad's shop from room to room, measuring and cutting the boards to fit around the perimeter. I've never built anything that didn't come in an IKEA or LEGO box before, but this isn't as hard as I imagined it would be. Once the house is complete, the majority of it will have my handprints on it, and _that_ is really fuckin cool.

The smell of sawdust in Crane House brings me back to afternoons in the workshop with a glass bottle of root beer and my dad explaining shop safety for the hundredth time.

Once Noah was allowed to use the lathe, he began bringing me candlesticks. Like sooo many candlesticks. I lined them on the mantle, slowly removing the pictures my mom keeps there. Over the last month, it's become a bit of a showcase of the evolution of Noah's skill, with more grooves and body cut into each candlestick. I stopped by a local shop soon after the first candlestick made its appearance and purchased a cream-colored taper candle I thought would complement the wood nicely. Placing it in the holder on the mantle before Noah returned home, I waited to see how long it would take him to notice. I figured a day, maybe two? It was the first thing he saw at as he entered the room, a warm smile spreading across his face as he embraced me in gratitude.

There are now well over a dozen candlesticks on the mantle, with only the one tapered candle.

"Can we please get more candles?" Noah's disappointment in returning home from school and yet again seeing the empty candlesticks reminds me that I forgot to order a box. Again.

"I forgot, ok. Yes, let me get on Amazon and order some right now." I pull up my app. I paid like three dollars for the one I bought locally, but the ones online aren't much cheaper. "Geeze, dude, they want like twenty bucks for a dozen."

My mom, who hasn't said anything since we walked in the door, calmly stands and walks to the closet in the hallway pulling out a box. Noah and I are still on the small tiled square next to the front door, watching as she carries the box to the kitchen table. Reaching in, she pulls out a bundle of strings and a large cream brick, showcasing them like Vanna White through the large doorway.

"Noah, go out to the shop and tell Grandpa I need the old can. He'll know what I'm talking about."

Noah runs through the kitchen, letting the screen door slap against the open frame.

"Mom, I'm supposed to meet up with Jake and Ben to go over some samples." Candle-making is anything but a quick activity. It's been years, but I've been roped in more than once as a kid, only to realize I lost an entire afternoon or evening. Looking back it wasn't a loss, it was bonding and memories, but it's hard to explain that to a ten-year-old who just wants to go ride her bike.

"Call them and tell them to come over here. I've got lasagna in the oven, and it's more than enough for them too. I'm sure it's been a while since they've had a home-cooked meal."

"They're in their thirties. I'm sure they are capable of cooking."

"I meant a meal cooked by a mother, and I know they haven't had one of those. Call them."

I close myself in my room, unsure of whether I should call Jake or Ben. Settling on Ben, I dial his number.

"Hey, Liv."

"Hey, so I know we need to go over those samples. But my mom wants you guys to come over for dinner. She's making lasagna." God, I feel like a child even saying this. "Is it possible to bring them over here and we can—"

"JAKE!" He pulls the phone back, but the yell still comes across the line, making my ears ring.

Ben doesn't even let me finish. They are at the door within minutes.

"Jacob! Benson! It's so good to see you two." My mom greets them in the maternal way she always has. I'm sure they are crouching down to hug her as she kisses their cheeks. "Olivia! The boys are here!"

Finding everyone in the kitchen, I notice one of the kitchen chairs is now in front of the stove where Noah stands, watching his grandma, eagerly waiting for her instruction. It's been years since he's needed a chair to stand at the stove, but the stock pot she uses is so tall that even my mom needs a stool. She returns to Noah's side from the table, her long wooden spoon held horizontally with a series of weighted wicks tied to one end.

Coaching Noah through his first steps, she speaks in a calm grandmotherly voice, one I haven't noticed in her before. Has she always had it or is it developing now that she's spending so much time with him? "Now we dip. Straight down. Perfect. Okay, that's long enough. Pull them straight up now. Okay, bring it over to the cold water and dip it in there. Oh, nice work. Okay, now we do it all over again."

"What's with the candles?" Jake stage whispers to the table.

Motioning with my head, I bring Jake and Ben into the living room where I'm now Vanna White, showcasing Noah's hard work.

"My dad has been teaching him to turn wood on the lathe, so now we have an ever-increasing supply of holders and no candles to go in them."

"Noah!" Ben shouts over his shoulder. "I want to buy some of these from you."

Noah pops through the kitchen nodding as if he expected this to happen the moment someone saw his handiwork.

"Okay, I think I'm going to sell them for twenty dollars each. But if you buy three, I'll include candles with them." Noah answers like he's already thought this through. We exchange a smile between the three of us, trying not to break into laughter. My little businessman.

"How do I turn down that killer deal?" Ben asks, still grinning.

We can hear my mom trying to talk Noah down on the price of his candlesticks, giving him advice on a more reasonable price that people might be willing to pay if he wants to try and sell them.

"No, it took a lot of time and work to make them. Twenty's fair," Noah responds firmly.

Ben moves towards the kitchen, clearly ready to bargain. "Okay, how about this? I give you forty-five for three of them and ..." he adds in response to the look Noah is giving him. "I let you pick any two comic books from my collection."

"I don't read comic books. No deal."

"Some of them are worth hundreds. By the time you are old enough, they might just pay for your first car."

More quiet whispering ensues as my mom tries to convince Noah.

"I guess that would be alright," he agrees, though a bit reluctantly.

I collapse on the couch, listening to the mixed conversations of comic books and candle-making coming from the kitchen. I just need a few minutes of quiet and I'll be ready to help with dinner. Mom can't see me, so there is at least a small chance I'll get this reprieve. I close my eyes.

"The baseboards look great," Jake says as he sits, causing the couch to shift under his weight. The springs are so shot we slide towards the center, our legs only inches apart.

"Thanks. I haven't done the stairs yet, but I'm hoping I can get them done tomorrow. I just need to watch a few more videos so I at least kind of have an idea what to do."

"I'm free in the morning, I can come by and give you a hand ... If you want."

"That would be nice. Just know I have full music control," I answer without opening my eyes. I don't know if I even <u>can</u> open my eyes.

I don't realize I've drifted off until my dad's booming voice startles me awake. I must have leaned over onto Jake when I fell asleep. His fingers brushed my upper arm, leaving a wake of goosebumps on the flesh beneath my sweater.

"Sorry." I apologize, sitting up. "I didn't think I was that tired."

"You're good."

We stand, smoothing our clothes. My cheeks are on fire. Either from embarrassment or excitement, I don't know. Maybe both?

I make it to the kitchen in just enough time to catch Noah piling bread and lasagna on his plate, skipping the bowl of salad completely.

"Forgot your greens, dude." Palming his head, I turn his body back to the counter. I know he'll maybe take a bite or two of the salad at most. Hopefully if Ben eats salad then Noah might follow his lead. And two bites of salad is better than none.

"Here," Jake offers from where he stands in front of the salad bowl. Moving the tongs, I see that he sets no more than five lettuce leaves on Noah's plate before covering each one with an obscene amount of ranch. "<u>That's</u> a salad." Jake winks and Noah smiles conspiratorially.

Scott would have done the same thing.

"How's the house coming along?" my dad asks from his seat at the head of the table. His voice warm. He may have offered to help at first but was more than happy enough to be let off the hook.

My dad can always be found in one of two places at home, either in his workshop or on his lazy boy in front of the TV, two places I've rarely found my mom. I thought this was normal growing up until I got married myself, and realized how little my parents did together. My mom was constantly busy cleaning something or at her sewing machine in their bedroom, half of which she'd transformed into a quilting workshop.

I don't think my parents are in love.

I realized it around fifteen, and Jake was the only person I told, confiding in him that I'd never seen them kiss or even touch. I knew they weren't crazy about each other. But they've always at least been on the same page. Both equally unenthused by their marriage. It works for them in a way I know it would never work for me.

Then again, maybe there is love. It just doesn't fit my personal description.

"It's going good. I think we'll be done before Thanksgiving," Ben answers between bites of salad.

"That soon huh?" My dad's brows furrow, doubting Ben's timeline. Like Ben isn't a full-blown professional in the industry.

"Yeah, you got all the hard stuff done with the plumbing and foundation last year, so our work is mostly superficial," Jake adds, knowing my dad thrives on compliments. Things always seemed to get fixed faster on his Jeep when he'd butter up my dad.

"Mom." Noah squishes the words through a full mouth of lasagna. "Can we walk to Ben's house to get those comic books tonight?"

Noah's not much of a reader, so I will jump at the opportunity to further his interest in reading, even if my parents try to argue that comic books aren't "real books."

"Yeah, we can do that," I answer only after glancing between Jake and Ben for permission.

We've only just begun sifting through the shelves of comics when Ben's phone buzzes. A brief apology, and next to no explanation, and he's gone. Leaving Jake, Noah, and I to ourselves. It feels right, and I have to fight it off. Jake is not ours. Jake is not mine.

"Alright so you know Superman, right?" Jake pulls one from the shelf.

"Yeah," Noah replies skeptically.

"Did you know <u>his</u> dad died?"

"Yeah, when he was a baby, right after they sent him to Earth."

"No not that Dad. His other dad, the one that raised him on Earth." Opening the pages, Jake runs his finger over the page. "Ben read this one a lot after his dad died."

"Did <u>you</u>? When your dad died." Noah asks.

"My dad is still alive," Jake replies cautiously, confused by the question.

"Oh, my mom said you didn't have a dad ..." Confusion and embarrassment color his voice.

I made the comment without wanting to overshare Jake's history, but now I see how it was misconstrued.

We exchange a look in which I apologize and Jake forgives me then asks permission to tell him. I close my eyes and nod.

"My dad," Jake begins, "wasn't like your dad. He wasn't a good guy. He used to hit me when he'd get angry."

"What?" Noah's alarmed at the thought of this. The idea of a grown-up in <u>his</u> life hurting him is unconscionable.

"Yeah, I used to sleep in the hammock in your grandparents' backyard sometimes when I needed a safe place. When I was sixteen, I went to live with <u>my</u> grandparents. So no, I don't have a dad, even if he is still alive. But what I did have was your grandpa to teach me how to work with my hands, Ben's dad to teach me to be a good person, and my grandpa to show me what it felt like to be safe."

"They did all that, even though you weren't their kid?"

"Good guys, like your grandpa, don't need a reason to step in."

Noah is surrounded by good men, the kind of men who can shape him in the way Scott would have without ever feeling the need to replace Scott.

"It's not really fair," Noah speaks after flipping through the Superman comic Jake passed him.

"What's not?" Jake and I say in unison together.

"That <u>your</u> dad gets to be alive and mine has to be dead."

"Noah." Oh my God. I mean he's not wrong. As far as fairness goes, Dave walking around while Scott can't is definitely <u>not</u> fair, but he said it out loud. I don't even know how to explain to him <u>why</u> he shouldn't say that.

"No, it's fine." Jake holds his hand up to me. "It's <u>not</u> fair. I told your mom the same thing when Ben's dad died. It should have been mine. And if I could trade my dad's life for your dad's, I would do it in a second. You deserve to have your dad here. Your mom deserves to have your dad here."

Tears prick the corner of my eyes. It's impossible not to love Jake with his selfless and easy nature and the way he says what we need to hear.

TWENTY

"You awake?" The voice on the phone is alert and excited.

"Jake?" My voice is still caught in sleep, coming out only as a silent croak. Clearing my throat, I try again. "It's the middle of the night. Is everything ok?"

"Can you come outside?"

"Yeah, I'll be right out." Rolling out from under my warm quilt, I pull a pair of socks out from my drawer before returning them and opting to go barefoot instead. I'm too tired for that.

We left Jake's only a few hours ago. The comic books Noah borrowed from Jake and Ben sparking a light in him. We've been over to their house multiple nights this week, exchanging comics like it's a library. I don't even know why I go; Jake and Noah ignore me the entire time, debating who the best and worst characters are. Ben joins their arguments on occasion, but he's been busy lately crunching numbers and doing paperwork on the table while Jake and Noah giggle happily. I know Dre said not to say anything about their business being in trouble, but it's getting hard not to; Ben is looking more and more weathered by the day.

When we left, Jake commented on getting to work. So I assume he's here to talk about the little green house. I know he probably has to sell it, and I wish I could buy it. But I can't.

My bedroom door's top hinge is prone to deliver a drawn-out, high-pitch squeak. I've asked my dad to oil it countless times, but he always refused, calling it his budget alarm system. Insert an eye-roll every time he makes this joke. However, when the door swings open quickly, the squeak is absent. I don't understand <u>why</u> this happens—something with science, I'm sure—but it's a fact I've conveniently kept from my parents.

I slide silently into the hallway, finding my cardigan over the back of the floral wingback chair near the front door. Pulling it on, I unlatch the front door and creep out into the night.

Jake isn't on the front porch where I expect to find him. The crisp edge of the early October night nips at my chin, reminding me of autumn in the east. Unlike the green of Oregon, I lived most of the year in D.C. waiting for the fall foliage to turn from green to every imaginable shade of red, orange, and yellow, before ultimately resigning to brown and falling, covering the ground in a soggy, slimy blanket of decomposing leaves.

Only the movement of the hammock swinging gently in the trees at the far corner of the yard gives away his position, though I already know where he'll be. The grass is in the process of an overnight frost. I hop lightly through it to prevent my feet from staying in any spot too long, causing them to freeze. I should have put on the socks. The shadow of Jake pulls me closer. He sits on the edge of the hammock, using his feet against the ground to propel him forward and back.

The fabric shifts as I move to join Jake on his left, forcing us both backward so we lie against the opposite edge, our legs dangling off the side.

Stars fill the spaces where the trees open to the sky. It's the kind of night we hoped for when expecting meteor showers as teens, only to be met with a storm or just enough clouds to prevent any decent stargazing from occurring.

"I know you're not going to know half of what I'm about to say, but I just needed someone to get it out to, and you're the only person who knows, and you <u>did</u> say you would be an ear if I needed one."

Oh, so this <u>isn't</u> about the green house. It's about the list. Clearing my head from sleep and remembering I told Jake I would be here to hear about any parallel universe lives he encountered, I nod.

"Alright." Jake breathes in deeply. "So I drove to Portland—"

"When?" I was with him most of the evening and there certainly wasn't time between when we left and now.

"This morning. I just didn't exactly get a chance to talk to you earlier. So I drove to Portland to find Kelly. She moved to town the summer you left. Her dad came to work at the RV factory. Anyway, she and I had a thing."

"Weren't you dating Heather?"

"We took a break after graduation."

"Why?"

"Do you want to hear what happened with Kelly or not?" The deflection is obvious, but it's clear he's willing to talk about Kelly, not Heather.

I wave my hands above us, indicating that he may continue. The hammock moves backward as Jake pushes with his foot against the pine needle-covered earth below. His arm against mine, we swing in silence as Jake finds the place to resume his story.

"When I met her, it felt like I knew her from somewhere. You know that feeling?" He nudges me, triggering my head to begin bobbing. "She was crazy, and a complete bitch, but she was incredible in bed."

"Didn't need to know that," I add quickly.

"It's pertinent, I promise. Anyway, so I told her she was crazy once, and then we started going at it, which was super-hot until she pulled a fuckin knife on me!" He chuckles at the memory, confusing me even more about where the hell this story is heading.

When I agreed to be available for him to help work through his visions, I never expected him to give me details on his sex life.

"So I threw her out. Naked and everything. I'd put up with my dad's shit and wasn't about to accept it from some chick."

"This was real life, not the ghost of Christmas that never actually happened?"

"Right." His finger taps the air above us once and then a few more times in an echo of the first.

"I don't understand why you would want to see what a life with her could have been in the first place." I leave my thoughts about me being the better choice for him unsaid. "You know, curiosity killed the cat."

"Funny you should say that. So I find her working in a hotel lobby in Portland and go up to the counter, pretending to just be a guest. I didn't think she'd recognize me, cause I have a beard now."

I narrow my eyes in question. "Do you think your beard is a pair of those nose and mustache disguise glasses?"

"Well, I might have thought that ... until tonight. So anyway, I make to grab her hand—"

"Creepy."

"Pay attention." His hand gently swats my thigh in reproach. "She recognizes me right off the bat. But it's too late for her to pull back, the memory reel starts going." The teacup ride of our memories comes to mind, and I can't imagine doing it over and over again, especially alone. "I'm swirled to when she pulled the knife on me, and instead of kicking her out, I had a calm rational conversation with her. And we make up. The next few memories are blah, just boring normal stuff. Until we get in an argument about what fat level of milk to buy ..."

"Whole."

"Exactly. She wanted skim milk like a psychopath. I told her it was the wrong choice, and then she came at me with something in her hand and everything went black."

"Wait what?"

"I think she killed me," Jake whispers ominously.

"Are you serious?"

"Yeah. I thought that meant I died in real life?"

"That's only in dreams, I think." I yawn, despite my best efforts. "What do you think ol' Granny means for you to learn by this experience." I feel his shoulders shrug against me, as though he hasn't worked it out for himself quite yet.

The expectation of insight from me is present, though what wisdom I'm meant to impart, I don't know. The only thing I keep thinking is that he should have just stopped looking after seeing <u>our</u> life together. But that's not exactly helpful. And I <u>really</u> do want to be helpful.

"Maybe you were meant to realize that just because you were partly to blame for some of your relationships ending, that doesn't mean they shouldn't have ended?"

"And how exactly was I to blame at all for the way things ended with Kelly?"

"You called a woman crazy."

"She was crazy!"

"Doesn't mean you voiced that in the best possible way."

"She still shouldn't have taken a knife to me. What the hell, Liv!" He lifts himself onto his elbows, looking down at me in disbelief.

"Of course, she shouldn't have. Fuck, Jake, calm down. I just meant that overall it doesn't sound like a healthy relationship."

"If I told <u>you</u> to calm down, I'd probably get murdered ... again." He's back to his flirtatious tone. The one that melts me a little inside.

How has Jake been able to keep the last fifteen years of his life straight with countless alternate realities circling through his mind at all times? When he touched <u>my</u> hand, everything I experienced in life was suddenly mixed up with the new memories superimposed on me. I sometimes find it hard to remember which events and conversations actually happened.

The lines of reality and these parallel universes have to blur to the point that Jake gets confused when speaking to these women about their shared history. While it doesn't seem like he is on good terms with many, he's remained friends with Ashley. Has he ever slipped and brought up something that never happened? Or is it just me who struggles to keep it all straight?

Jake takes my hand in his own, holding it close to his chest before bringing it to his mouth to kiss it softly, sending me into a complete tailspin mentally. I can't separate the feelings that are organic from those I've been given.

Staying up long past my expiration with Jake invigorated me. I spent all day hoping that Jake would come by again. His call came as I lay in bed, just as I started drifting off to sleep.

"Hey, you." He calls from the hammock.

"Hey you," I return, the slightest smile bathing the words in affection. We're back. It really feels like we're back.

"You're a disaster!" Jake exclaims as I get close enough that he can see me.

"What? No, I'm not." My top knot isn't exactly neat, but it's not like it's anything Jake isn't used to seeing. I'm still wearing my white T-shirt and sweats I donned earlier in the afternoon.

"Is that blood on your shirt?" Jake touches the spots in question as I climb onto the hammock next to him.

The spots are, in fact, spaghetti sauce. Sauce I didn't realize I splattered as I slurped the noodles until just now.

"It's sauce."

Jake shakes his head, silently judging me.

"So who did you meet up with today?" I brace myself for hearing about his life with another woman.

"No one."

"Oh." Relief and disappointment move through me simultaneously. While I'm dreading hearing about him maybe falling in love with someone, I'm also worried we'll have nothing to talk about without the pretense of exploring a vision. And I don't want him to quit coming over. I _miss_ our hammock talks. They are some of my favorite memories as a teenager.

"I was going through my notebook where I write down a summary of each encounter, and I thought maybe you could help me like process them." He holds up a little book and taps it.

"I'd love to read your diary."

"Not a diary. more of a ledger."

"Hmm... sounds like a diary. Hand it over Larsen."

We dig right in and no two visions are alike in any way. I guess I expected to find a string of similarities, yet the only common thread is that they all end on a bad note. Deception, cheating, anger, and resentment color the stories he outlines with each woman he revisited. Every single other vision is the opposite of what we saw.

He got punched in the face with each encounter and still returned for more, each time hopeful that it would be something better than he'd seen before. Seeing _that_ much of your own darkest moments must have changed him in ways I'll never fully understand.

"I thought it was me," he confesses. "that because I'd been raised by Dave, I was somehow incapable of having a functioning relationship. I've never hit a woman, not even in my visions, but there have been some where they've given me the look I used to see my mom give my dad. A terrified adoration. That look scares me more than anything I've seen."

"You are not your dad, Jake."

"No. No, I know that." He says he knows, yet after minutes of silence he leaves for the night.

As if we never stopped meeting on the hammock, we pick up exactly where we left off, if only a little more damaged than we had been back then. We lie side by side, Jake swinging us softly. Some nights are light, while others are heavy, dealing with Jake's falling out with his parents or the parts of my marriage that in hindsight I can see were unnecessarily hard.

"Is it weird being with someone and expecting to spend your entire life with that one person?" Jake asks.

"No, not weird. It's comforting. The feeling of not having to impress someone. I mean, isn't it exhausting going from girl to girl, constantly trying to put yourself on parade?"

"Exciting, but yeah, I guess a little exhausting."

"I mean, I think the hardest thing was Scott wanting to slow us down, move back here, and raise Noah outside of the city. It felt ridiculous to fight over _not_ moving back to my hometown."

"Why didn't he want to move back to _his_ hometown?"

"He didn't really have one. His parents did humanitarian work, so he lived all over the globe. They died right before he and I met."

"I can see why he'd want to experience small-town life."

Scott never had childhood friends for more than a year or so; his stories consisted of him joining a group and following in the antics before picking up and moving again. He'd never been in a place long enough to know its secrets.

I know all the shortcuts across town to several houses where I would always find something to do. I know the details of the generations-old Harrison and Miller family feud. I'm greeted warmly in the drugstore, no matter how long it's been since my last visit, and offered a butterscotch candy because they were my favorite when I was young.

"Yeah, so can I." I'd denounced small-town life, yet looking back my memories were almost entirely good. Had I taken it all for granted? Was Scott right all along?

Our meetings remain a secret, safe from expectations of where our relationship should be heading. There is also the hope that in <u>not</u> having to justify our friendship, Jake will realize on his own that we're meant to be together. It'd be great if it doesn't take him too long to figure it out.

"Have you ever gotten married in any of these other lifetimes? I mean, other than to me?" I want to be the only one.

"No. I was engaged in a few, but I've only been married the one time." His shoulder pushes against mine. I'm his only.

It's becoming harder and harder to imagine Jake finishing his list and <u>not</u> choosing me. Nothing in his notebook even seems like a threat. Heather, however, is notably missing from the pages.

"You know, my dad told me once that I didn't deserve you." He holds my hand under the quilt. Jake's other hand traces the seams connecting the different fabrics as he speaks, giving me something to focus on other than the electricity between us.

"That's ridiculous. I hope you didn't believe him."

"Oh, I did. He was especially effective at bringing me down." His voice is detached and far away. Noah's voice does the same thing when he recounts a nightmare before falling back asleep in my arms. Too bad Dave wasn't just a bad dream.

"When was the last time you talked to them?" I ask tentatively.

"Couple years ago. In court." He adds 'in court' almost as an afterthought.

"Court?"

"After Gramma June died, they showed up for the first time in years. I honestly don't even know how they found out she died. Small town, I guess."

There are no secrets in a town of only a thousand. Even it if _is_ a suburb of the bigger city. Busybodies can't help but spread the latest gossip. It's a miracle that Jake didn't know I was back in town until we ran into each other. Not to mention the fact that Ben hadn't known Scott died. The gossip seems to mostly circulate through our parents' generation and older. I'm sure a younger gossip circle is biding their time, waiting for the baton to be passed to them.

"They were pissed when they found out that she and Grandpa left _everything_ to me. So they sued me."

"Seriously?" My cheeks warm at the pure audacity and entitlement his parents continue to display. Jake's grandparents took him in when his parents lost custody, and they _still_ felt entitled to an inheritance. They are the absolute worst.

"The judge seemed confused as to why they thought they had a case in the first place. We were in there for like ten minutes before he told them to move on and dismissed their claim."

"Good!" At least one thing went his way. "That was the last time?"

"Oh, well my dad found me in the parking lot. My mom must have been in the car already. He stormed up to me, yelling. I think he expected me to cower, but I'm a lot bigger than him you know. So when he got close enough, he realized he no longer held the upper hand. There was just a _moment,_ this split second when I saw something like fear in his eyes. I was no longer a punching bag, and that pissed him off. He got right up into my face and told me he didn't have a son, that I was dead to him." He takes a deep breath. "But the thing is, they were dead to me the second I left their house for the last time. So he couldn't even hurt me with his words."

Watching teenage Jake work so hard for the approval of his parents, and knowing he would never find it, was hard. The most he could hope for was a bruise somewhere no one would notice or a full night's sleep without waking up to his mom crying or his dad screaming. The false memory of dinner at his parents' house still haunts me. The frozen look on Jake's face as I took his dad on single-handedly. This was one way his life was better _without_ me. He found the strength to stand up to him all on his own.

"I'm really proud of you." I squeeze his hand tightly. "I've thought about your parents over the years. I can't imagine letting _anyone_ hurt Noah, either physically _or_ mentally. I know it's not my place to judge, but I just don't understand how your mom could have allowed it. I <u>know</u> she was ... well probably still <u>is</u> a victim, but I don't think I could just stand by and see someone do the things he did to you."

"That's because you're an incredible mom."

"Thanks, Jake." Nestling my head onto his shoulder, I allow his reassurance to settle us both.

It's hard to sleep on the nights Jake doesn't call to meet him on the hammock. I check my phone every few minutes hoping for a text. Worried that if I fall asleep I'll miss a notification.

Each night we spend together, I fall even harder for Jake than I previously thought possible. Without any romantic expectations, we share the intimacy of friendship in the way we did as a couple of kids. Snuggled up on the hammock pouring our deepest desires and thoughts into the security of each other.

My mom told me that we needed to rediscover our friendship before anything more could follow, and now I see the wisdom in the advice. My evenings are a giant internal pep talk, working up the courage to tell Jake I'm <u>helplessly</u> in love with him. But I'm a coward.

As Jake kisses me goodnight gently on the forehead and our fingertips meet to fold the quilt, I curse myself for being too weak to tell him. He needs to finish his list. I <u>promised</u> to help him finish his list. I can't make him choose again.

"You good?" he asks as I fold my half of the quilt towards the corners which he holds in his fingertips.

"Oh, yeah, yeah I'm good." A complete lie. I'm not okay, I'm conflicted. I'm in love, I'm grieving, and there is nothing about me that is okay. "I uh, found Zoey."

Zoey is one of the names on the list he's so far been unable to locate. A woman I've never met yet somehow managed to track down. What can I say, I know my way around a good ol' fashioned internet stalking.

"Oh, no way!" The sleepiness leaves his face, replacing it with surprised excitement. "Where?"

"She's in Bend." Only two and a half hours away.

I haven't seen the list, but I know that after Zoey there are only two left. In a matter of weeks, this can all be behind him. Behind <u>us</u>.

Twenty One

The comic book store still smells like body odor and cheap plastic. While it never bothered Jake or Ben, I learned to breathe through my sleeve to minimize the smell every trip.

"Mom!" Noah calls from behind the figurine display. "Mom, they have a graphic novel about Plants versus Zombies!"

Comics were a gateway to the world of graphic novels, much to Jake and Ben's dismay. He loves borrowing from their collection but has started his own collection of a more modern nature. Finding a graphic novel about one of his favorite video games is something I never even thought to look for.

"Looks like there are a bunch of them." Turning the corner, I come face-to-face with the entire display.

"Did they have these when you used to come here?"

"No. We only had a handful of video games, and there definitely weren't books based on them."

"What books did you used to get when you came here?"

I choke as the laugh threatens to rise up and out of me. I push it right back down. If it comes out, Noah will second guess his love of books. I'm not about to have that be _my_ fault.

"Oh, well I usually just checked out the board games."

"This one has Dr. Zomboss!" he continues, unfazed by my comment.

"Hey..." I've tried to broach the subject of my beginning to date again for weeks. With Jake nearing the end of his journey I'm running out of time. "What would you think if I started going on dates?"

"With who?"

"I don't know. The who isn't important. I just don't want to do something that might make you uncomfortable."

Noah sets the book down on his lap as he sits crisscross against the shelf. I crouch and sit next to him on the carpet that is somehow dry _and_ moistly sticky at the same time, like an old blockbuster video. Gag.

"I think you're happier when you are around friends than when you're alone. So I think it's probably a good idea. I like it when you're happy."

"I'm happy when I'm with you."

"That's different. That's _mom_ happy."

Mom happy. It's true that in the year that had taken so much from me, I've never leaned more into my role as a mom as I have since Scott passed. It's the one constant. Noah is the one person that didn't and still doesn't tiptoe around me. He needs me more than he ever has.

"Maybe Jake would take you on a date so you could practice not being so weird."

"I don't think there is _any_ hope for that." I fold my lips under my teeth so they completely disappear, making a creepy, lipless smile.

"Mom! Don't!" Noah pushes the palm of his hand against my shoulder. Shoppers step over us like we aren't even there.

"Don't what? I'm just trying to be normal."

"Please," he whispers as a group not much older than him turns the corner. Feeling merciful, I swipe my tongue between my lips and teeth, releasing them to their normal position. I receive a raised eyebrow rather than any real gratitude.

"You're always the most important guy in my life. You know that, right?" I'm a mom before everything else. There is nothing I wouldn't give up if it put Noah's safety or happiness in jeopardy.

"Yeah, I know. Just don't be so weird in public. Or no one is going to want to take you on a date."

We sit for a long time, side by side, as Noah flips through the pages, shaking softly with laughter while I read silently over his shoulder.

"Do you think Dad liked comic books?" The question is more to the universe than me in particular.

"I don't know, buddy. He never had a collection, but he did the Batman movies quite a bit."

"Do you still love him?"

Woah. I wasn't expecting that. Have I done anything to make him think I don't?

"Dad? Of course I do."

"You don't cry as much anymore." It's an observation that feels more than a little accusatory.

"I don't, do I? But you don't cry as much either. That doesn't mean we don't love him or don't miss him. It just means we're starting to heal. Dad wouldn't want us to cry every day for the rest of forever, would he?"

Noah shakes his head. The kid behind the sales counter sniffs loudly, reminding me that we're not alone.

"I'll tell you what I think, though. I think Dad would've <u>loved</u> these graphic novels. He loved reading with you more than almost anything." I flick my finger across his nose.

"He was a good dad." Noah's fingers run over the edge of the pages.

Twenty Two

The fall festival is all Noah has talked about for weeks. He's watched so many movies featuring small-town fall festivals, and his standards are set much higher than where mine lie. Our idea of a fall festival growing up was a gymnasium with stations set up, a cake walk, face painting, and if we were really lucky maybe a coloring station with pages that once finished could be brought to our local grocer to exchange for a Tootsie pop.

"First things first, I have to bob for apples," Noah insists from the seat next to me. He's sitting on the nail polish stain in the backseat of Jake's Jeep.

"That's not a thing people actually do. That's a movie thing, and also it's how you get herpes," Ben corrects him over his shoulder, breaking the news that I've tried to explain more than once over the previous weeks. Maybe, if it doesn't come from Mom, it will be worth listening to.

"What's herpes?" Noah asks, latching on to the word.

"Thanks, Ben." I lean forward, smacking him on the shoulder with the back of my hand.

"Uh, you know cold sores?" Ben wades into dangerous water tentatively.

"Yeah."

"That's <u>one</u> type of herpes. You get it from kissing."

"No, you can get it from a bunch of things. Almost everyone has it, but not everyone gets the sores," Jake chimes in from the driver's seat. If Noah continues his line of questioning, how in-depth are they planning to go with their answers?

"That's another reason I don't ever want to kiss anybody. Ever." Noah pulls a face and sticks out his tongue.

"Oh don't say that, little man." Ben's taken this as a personal affront to him. "Kissing is fun."

"One day you'll meet a girl <u>or boy</u>..." Jake turns, his arm over Ben's headrest as he backs his Jeep into the parking spot on the west end of the gravel lot "...and they will make your heart race and your whole insides feel like Jell-O, and then you'll think of nothing but wanting to kiss them."

"Nope." Noah rejects the notion in its entirety. There's still time before I have to start worrying about Noah having a love life. I lean into the knowledge that cooties are still very much a part of his core belief system. Clicks replace our voices as we all move to unbuckle and pull door handles.

Gravel crunches beneath our feet as the four of us make our way across the lot toward the path, still hidden by trees. The path winds around one large tree before the entrance is visible. Large lanterns sit at the base of a cornstalk and sunflower archway. I brush my hand lightly on a sunflower as we walk through it. It was baby's breath and irises when I'd last seen it in our shared vision.

The dense forest before us is dark, though the sun is only just beginning to set. Lanterns hang from branches above, and line the dirt path leading us through a forest maze. Jake walks slightly ahead with Noah as they search the lights for the hidden jack-o-lanterns that are scattered along the trail.

"The trail goes just up ahead before—" Ben begins.

"Before we cross the footbridge," I finish for him. "Then we reach the clearing."

Ben turns to me, eyes narrowed. "There is no way you have been here before."

I give a quick smile, challenging his assertion.

"It's a perfect wedding venue."

The moment we were within sight of the archway, I knew exactly where we were.

"You know, I didn't believe Jake at first." Ben muses as we wind around a small cluster of trees, finding Jake and Noah once again. "I figured it was some manifestation of his childhood trauma. Almost, like he was wishing his life could have gone differently so hard that he was able to craft these stories. I figured it was harmless, and hoped it would bring him some sort of peace to what his life <u>was</u>."

"Do you think he knew you didn't believe him?" I ask, remembering that Jake has been confiding in me rather than Ben.

"I don't think so. But I became less and less supportive of him obsessing over it all. So he quit talking about it, and I figured it was over. Till he told me you had seen it all too."

"I mean, I don't even know that I believe it, and I lived it," I admit as we round the last turn, revealing the clearing ahead. "I just wish it had been enough, you know?"

"Enough for what?"

"For him to decide he didn't need to keep looking for happiness. Enough for me to embrace that happiness was an option so soon after everything with Scott. Just enough." The articulation of all I'm wrestling with comes without hesitation. My feelings are safe with Ben.

"What do you want, Liv?" Ben's question echoes my own I posed to Jake. Though I know what I want, it's Jake who never had an answer.

"It doesn't matter. We're suppressing all that for the sake of our friendship." My tone is light by force as I fight the urge to fall apart and tell Ben just how badly I need Jake.

"You two were never meant to be friends. Anyone who has ever seen you two together knows that."

"We were friends for years!" It's the argument I keep having to make.

"His feelings for you from the get-go made lifelong friends an impossibility. It was always going to be all or nothing."

The sentiment is similar to the one my mom shared.

"We're friends now, though."

"Nah," Ben quips. "You only think you are. Everyone on the outside can still see it's going to be all or nothing."

"I hope you're wrong. Jake has no interest in the all, and I don't want to go back to nothing."

"All I know ..." Ben starts.

"Liv!" Jake's voice interrupts us. Ben shakes the thought away, and I know that he's not going to continue what he almost revealed.

"All you know is what?" I come across as desperate, which definitely won't get him to reveal anything.

"All I know..." he moves in a different direction with his thoughts "...is that you convincing Jake to dress up as Dorothy is the greatest thing ever."

"It's freezing. I wasn't about to be bare-legged out here. Plus, he's got the legs for it." I grin, feeling my face paint stretch.

The air burns my lungs as I gently jog to where Jake and Noah stand. The blue and white checkered dress stops mid-thigh on Jake. I'd stupidly left the package on the front porch forgetting the doorbell even rang. I went to meet Jake on the hammock, completely unaware that I would find him zipped into the dress I ordered for myself.

I managed to put together a scarecrow costume with some flannel and overalls already in my closet, allowing Jake to commandeer the role of Dorothy.

Noah's lion tail dangles from his hand.

"I can't help. One, because I can't bend over in this dress or I'll hulk out of it. And two, because I'm not going to have my hands down where it's necessary to attach this. It's a mom job." He winks at Noah with this last thought.

"I told you Gramma should have sewed it on. She's a better sewer," Noah whines.

"Well, Gramma was busy." Pulling a safety pin out of my pocket, I reattach the tail to where the thread is still visible from the tear. I suspected my handiwork wouldn't hold up for the entire evening, but I hadn't expected it to last less than five minutes. "There. Now go find Lincoln and Grayson."

A light swat on his tail sends him bounding across the clearing, where he seems to already spot his friends playing tic tac toe with white and orange mini pumpkins. The festival is closer to Noah's vision than my own, and I'm not mad to be wrong. It's all a little magical.

"You look cute." Jake looks me up and down, really seeing me maybe for the first time in weeks. "The freckles are a nice touch."

His finger brushes the side of my nose so lightly and lingers on my cheek so I can't help but lean into his touch. I know the compliment is directed at my costume more than me, but it's enough for me to hold on to for now.

"People are gonna get the wrong impression about us, Larson." Don't correct me, just tell me that the impression people might get is closer to reality than I think. The way he holds my gaze, his finger still tracing the face paint freckles makes me think that I might not be too far off base.

"Nah, they all know we're just friends." He keeps my eyes locked in his, and with a wink, challenges his own words. This man is playing with me at this point, and I don't know how much longer I can play the will-he-or-won't-he game. Maybe he just isn't that into me.

"Liv!" A thudding follows as the voice jogs towards us.

Jake's hand falls to his side as I'm lifted into a swirling bear hug. Arms pinned to my sides, I struggle to identify the body behind the force of strength. Once returned to the ground, I take in the face. Devin.

The friendly face when I had no one in New York City. I've picked up my phone to send him a text or call him so many times over the years, never quite able to follow through. Seeing him here is like seeing a teacher at the grocery store. You know they live in town, but it's weird to see them out of their environment. To me, Devin will always belong in the city.

"Dev!" I don't mean for it to sound so swoony, but it does and I catch the hint of jealousy in Jake's eyes as I squeal, propelling my arms around Devin's neck. I'm overdoing it, but if Jake wants to play games, I can play too. I plant my lips on his cheek. Jake was driven mad by the mere idea of me and Devin having a history. Maybe this is what he needs to light a fire in him. "It's so good to see you. You look fantastic."

Jake scoffs so softly that I know Devin couldn't have heard it. Devin's never been the prettiest boy. Friend zoned by nearly every girl we grew up with, mostly because he's the type of guy you want to keep around long-term. The kind of guy who makes you laugh in any situation but can then turn around and give the kind of advice worthy of an after-school special—even if he doesn't have the body built by a Bowflex commercial. He's the kind of man I hope Noah will grow up to be. Humble and good.

While the compliment is given without <u>entirely</u> pure motives, it's genuine. Devin lost the gauntness of his youth, filling out to a softer man. One a woman would feel comfortable indulging around without fear of judgement. It's been years since we'd last gotten together for lunch in D.C.

"I look fantastic? Look at you!" Devin's eyes lower to my hands which are still clasped around his own. "You're single?" My engagement ring had been impossible to ignore the last time we got together.

The indentation from my wedding ring is still visible. I haven't actually stopped wearing it, I just didn't want to lose it in the renovation.

"Devin." Jake slides his arm around my shoulders in a show of possession that makes my stomach leap while also pissing me off. Wasn't it him who just said that we were just friends? Is he sending me a signal that he's all in or only that he doesn't want anyone else to have me? "How are you, my man? Still up in Seattle?"

Devin's eyes focus on Jake's hand fiddling with the strap of my overalls. His face mimics my thoughts. Does this mean something?

"Jake." His voice matches Jake's in the lowered tones of chest-beating. "I am. I just accepted an attending position at Seattle Children's Hospital."

This <u>can't</u> be going the way Jake intended. I knew Devin intended on working toward medical school, but I'm curious about what Jake thought he was doing in Seattle.

If ever there had been a person I would have liked to have a glimpse of what could have been, it would have been Devin. Though we'd spent nearly a month making out, I always thought that there had been potential. His hug had, for the briefest of moments, made me realize what Jake's been chasing. It's not all about finding someone to spend his life with. It's a curiosity about how different life could turn out if only for one different choice. The rush of getting to live these lives without <u>any</u> of the risk.

If we'd stayed in contact, or gone to the same school, there was a real possibility that we could have ended up together. Maybe we'd have lived in Seattle during his residency while I took a job in state politics—the two of us living on a sleepy street, overgrown with ivy and filled with gossip from our elderly neighbors.

"I'm so proud of you." I'd be lying to myself if I tried to deny the enjoyment I feel at the shade of green Jake is taking on in his state of envy. "I <u>am</u> single."

"Widowed," Jake adds unnecessarily. "And she's got a kid."

What the hell? Does he want to mention my stretch marks and student loans while he's at it? I reach up and brush his hand off of my shoulder.

I've been the faithful friend, tracking down his exes so he can mark them off, pushing aside my own feelings. I have no intention of running off into the sunset with Devin, but with Jake acting possessive, it's making me rethink that. Jake hasn't even promised that once his list is done we'll be together. Perhaps opening myself to the idea of dating Devin, or anyone else, could be a win-win. Either I'm happy with Devin or Jake realizes the chance to lose me is a real possibility.

"Do you want to go get some wassail?" Devin motions with his head to the small wooden booth, ignoring Jake's attempt to make me undesirable.

"Let's do it," Jake accepts the offer obviously meant for me. And here we go.

The evening progresses with Jake and Devin flanking me around the festivities. Devin asks questions about my life, I pick his brain about medical school and all he's done, and Jake jumps at every opportunity to answer. Like some sort of boast that he knows me better than Devin does.

"I mean, didn't you like date her mortal enemy? What are you even doing here?" Devin lowers himself to where Jake has decided the bar is set for the night. I watch their back and forth. Apparently, I'm some prize to be won in their pissing contest.

I attempt to rein it in, bringing the conversation back to the chili we are supposed to be judging, but it's no use. They don't hear me. I step backward slowly, leaving them to one-up each other to the moon.

Anger floods in me as I move further back without either one noticing. I've spent nearly two months cuddling Jake and helping him in his search for happiness, yet the moment another man looks in my direction, he's possessive. Right now I don't have to push any feelings for Jake aside. They are almost nonexistent.

"Mom!" Noah runs full speed before jumping onto my back, his arms hanging around my neck and catching me off guard. "Let's go on the haunted hayride!"

My arm is pulled desperately towards where Ben waits. The wagon is nearly at capacity by the time Ben, Noah, and I are loaded into the back. Noah quickly moves toward the front of the wagon to watch the horses with the rest of the kids on board as the adults pull the flannel blankets provided around themselves. Ben pulls a blanket up over our lap before reaching into the silver leather jacket he wears as part of his Tin Man costume, producing a small metal flask. Oh thank God, finally a man who has my best interests at heart.

The wagon jerks into motion, causing the occupants all to bump together. I glance across the clearing to see Jake and Devin still standing at the chili table, scanning the festivities, searching for me.

Ben and I exchange the flask, taking sips of whiskey. The heat moving from my throat down to where it coats my insides does more for the cold than the thin threadbare blanket.

"So what's the deal with Devin? Jake finally getting answers about you two from him, since you've purposely been avoiding the subject?" Ben reaches for the flask.

"We dated. Well, I wouldn't even call it dating. There was really nothing to tell. Which is the only reason I haven't told Jake. I wasn't ready for a relationship. I didn't realize Devin was waiting for me, and then I was seriously dating Scott when he finally asked if we could go out again. Things just never quite lined up."

"It seems to be enough to get Jake jealous. See, I told you there was more to his feelings than you thought."

"He doesn't get to be jealous. It's his game and his rules we're playing by. Except he doesn't even really want me to play. I just get to sit and wait for him to come tell me all about his adventures. It's some bullshit, Ben." Dirty looks from parents make me sit back.

The horses trot slowly through the now pitch-black forest, only lanterns lining the path give any depth and shape to the darkness. The group of children that gathered near the front all now return to their parents. Noah nestles into me in a way he hasn't done in so long.

We ride in relative silence, parents whispering to their young and each other without the loud chatter that accompanied the beginning of the journey. Despite what Noah thought, the hayride isn't haunted, just dark. Lanterns scattered deep in the trees give it a magical and mysterious ambiance. The bounce of the wagon is enough to distract me from my irritation as I brace myself so I won't drop Noah or fall over.

As the clearing and festival come back into view, the noise in the wagon picks back up. I shift, expecting Noah to stand in response. My legs are numb but his body remains heavy on my chest.

"He's asleep," Ben whispers, crinkling his nose in a smile as he relays this.

I have to take a deep breath and readjust my body so I can stand, holding my now eight-year-old against my chest. It's been years since I've had to carry his limp with sleep body. His fifty-five pounds is both heavy and comforting. There's also no chance I can carry him across the clearing through the forest and back to Jake's Jeep.

"Let me carry him to the car. You go find Jake." Ben pulls Noah from my arms, reading my mind. Noah's arms hang limp down Ben's back, his head resting on his shoulder. It's a mirror image of the countless memories throughout Noah's life, only he'd been asleep on Scott in every instance before.

In the short time we were in the forest, the crowd shifted from young families to young adults, prepared to stay out as late as the music plays. The DJ, who played "Monster Mash" and "Baby Shark" only an hour ago is now blasting some artist I couldn't name if there was money on the line.

I half expect to find Jake and Devin in some sort of toxic masculinity dance-off and am equally disappointed and relieved that this isn't the case. Instead, they are both sulking on hay bales around the bonfire. Men are children, I swear to God.

"Noah's asleep. Ben's taking him to the car." Hopefully, he catches my irritation, because I'm doing nothing to hide it. "It was good to see you, Dev. Let's get together before you leave and <u>really</u> catch up." I'm less upset with Devin, but I'm not super happy with him either. Jake sucked him into this petty bullshit.

"Where'd you go?" Jake asks as we shoulder our way through the crowded entrance of the forest. I don't want to be swimming upstream the entire way to the parking lot. This is the place to be for anyone under twenty-five.

"I went on the haunted forest wagon ride with Ben and my son. You seemed occupied enough with your little measuring contest, I didn't think you'd notice or care."

"Measuring contest?" He sounds authentically confused.

Irritation grows as we walk and Jake fails to understand why I could possibly be angry. The path is too crowded to openly argue with Jake.

"I think you're being a little dramatic." Jake throws the accusation the moment we reach the parking lot. His boots crunch on the gravel just behind me. Ben's leaning against the Jeep, Noah's arms still slack over his shoulder.

"Dramatic?" I'm tempted to turn around and <u>show</u> him dramatic. Make a big ol' dramatic scene in front of everyone present.

"Liv!" An out of breath Devin shouts from the direction of the trees behind us. I lock eyes with Jake who gives me a "don't" look, and it takes everything in me not to lose it.

"I'll be right there." I nod, sending him on to the car. Once he continues walking, I turn my attention to Devin. "What's up?" I'm exhausted mentally and physically. I have very little left in the tank. But I know Jake is watching.

"I just wanted to check and make sure your number is the same so maybe we could grab dinner. Or coffee," he adds as an option.

I want to tell him I'm not ready to date. Repeat the same excuse I gave him years ago. That I'm still mourning the death of my husband on top of being completely in love with a guy who's still a little hung up on <u>his</u> exes.

"I'd really like that." The Jeep roars to life behind me. It's just the "low maintenance" engine knocking, but it feels like it comes from the depths of Jake's soul. Headlights shine directly onto me and Devin as I nod, telling Devin that it's the same. Jake's probably fuming in the car as he watches me with a man he feels threatened by. It's this thought, and a bit of Ben's liquid courage, that fuels me as I launch at Devin. Pulling him into a kiss that's almost entirely for show. Some may even say it's a bit dramatic.

The drive is suspiciously quiet as Jake broods in the front seat, unwilling to answer any question Ben asks in his attempt to diffuse the situation and unable to break the scowl he's adopted.

I felt victorious at first. I managed to make him feel the slightest bit like I have each time I hear about the visions of lives he could have lived. But now that the whiskey seems to be wearing off, I feel like shit. I <u>offered</u> to be there for him as he searched through the visions. My own jealousy moved me to be spiteful, something I never meant to be. I kissed Devin out of pain and it hurt Jake.

Ben opens his door before the Jeep even stops in front of their house, leaving without so much as a glance in my direction. Dammit, it's worse than I expected if Jake decided to drop Ben off before taking me home. The pit in my stomach grows as I dread the confrontation we're headed straight for.

"Noah, hey, buddy." I rub Noah's back as we near my parents' house. "Hey, I just need you to walk for a minute. Go hop right in bed. You can brush your teeth in the morning." I coax him out of his seat and through the door of the Jeep, following him up the sidewalk without a word to Jake. I can't do anything but hope he'll stay in the Jeep. We can revisit the events of tonight when we're both sober and cooled off.

Noah closes the front door behind him in a sleepy daze as I hear the door of the Jeep slam shut behind me. Fuck, we're far too upset to have a rational conversation. I keep walking.

"Why?"

"Why what, Jake?" I turn, exhausted already by his indignation.

"You're really thinking about going out with dad-bod Devin? Are you serious?" Jake throws his arms out as if he is somehow superior.

"You're an asshole. You're going to stand there and talk about somebody else's body as if that makes you better than him in <u>any</u> way?" My eyes narrow like they do when I dare Noah to test me. It's a warning he'll be smart to heed. I'm not sure what's worse, that he is so incredibly shallow or that he thinks <u>I'm</u> shallow enough to dismiss Devin for his lack of abs, ignoring his intellect, humor, and compassion.

Jake looks sufficiently admonished; he stooped to a level realizing it might not be where he wants to be. I turn to leave before spinning again to continue. Everything in my head keeps spinning after I stop.

"And why do you think you get to have <u>any</u> opinion on who I do or do not go out with? You gave up that right when <u>you</u> broke up with <u>me</u>!"

"Liv."

"No." I turn my back to him, starting up the steps of the front porch. Holding the tears in, fearing they'll show a vulnerability I desperately need to keep to myself. The warnings from Ben, my mom, and somewhere deep in myself. Jake and I were destined from the start. Destined to love or destined to lose? I'm worried the answer is a hell of a lot closer than I'm ready to face.

He broke my heart. I've spent every day since the moment on the ridge looking for any sign that Jake feels as strongly as I do. He's tracking down women who may be enough. Enough to make him stop looking in the way that I'm clearly not. He told me to pretend my feelings weren't there and then continued to stand in front of me, making it impossible for me to do so.

"Liv." He tries again.

"What, Jake?" My braids flick as I spin on my heel. We stand, the sidewalk between us miles long and feet apart. "What? Are you going to stand there and tell me that you've changed your mind? That you're done searching out women who would have broken your heart a million times or killed you over milk? Because I can't do this anymore. It <u>hurts,</u> Jake." The tears break through as my voice cracks. "It hurts that you come back to me as though I'm some sort of safety net or consolation prize. Not good enough for you to want to be with. It <u>hurts</u> to love you. To love you and want nothing more than for you to be happy in whatever way you can be. And to realize you <u>don't</u> want that for me."

Destined to lose. It repeats over and over in my head as I leave Jake standing on the sidewalk, wearing the blue and white checkered dress.

Twenty Three

J ake hasn't called.

I hate that I'm awake, holding my phone in both hands tightly, unable to sleep. The TV hums almost inaudibly with the laugh track of *I Love Lucy*.

I hear nothing.

Why hasn't Jake called to calm my fears and tell me that I <u>am</u> enough? Is it because I'm not?

"Hey, kiddo." Clad in his bathrobe and socks, my dad shuffles in and takes his place in the armchair next to the side of the couch. "Oh, I like this one. You used to laugh so hard you would choke." A low chuckle rumbles through him.

I haven't paid attention and only as he speaks do I even realize which episode is on. The gigantic loaf of bread is being pulled from the oven.

"Dad, I messed up."

"I figured as much. You and Jake haven't been out on the hammock in a few nights, and I don't think it's just because it's getting colder." He smirks with a wink. He knows about the hammock?

"You knew we were out there?" It's an all-encompassing question; has he <u>always</u> known or is this a new discovery?

"Kids aren't ever as sneaky as they think they are." The wooden lever makes a snapping noise just as the footrest flings up meeting his waiting feet. "So what happened?"

I can't tell him about the experience in the coffee shop. At this point, I don't think it even matters. It had been the catalyst, but my feelings go far beyond that moment.

"He's fixated on how his old relationships ended. That somehow things could and should have gone differently. That if I hadn't broken up with him, we could have had the most wonderful life together. He's on some journey to revisit all his old relationships and make sure that there wasn't something he missed."

"Sounds like he missed the biggest thing."

"Which is?"

"You and Jake didn't end when you broke up. You ended when he made the mistake of believing a rumor."

"Why does that matter?"

"He's going around trying to tie up loose ends and make amends, right?"

"More or less."

"Then it's silly of him to think that your loose end is with your short-lived romance. Your friendship was always more important."

From the moment I sat across from Jake at the coffee shop, neither of us have addressed where our relationship had <u>actually</u> ended, beyond me telling him it wasn't me. We'd been shown a parallel timeline stemming from when we'd broken up in high school and hadn't questioned it. Now that my dad brings it up, I can't unsee it.

Jake's visions are flawed.

After breaking up with Jake in the hallway things were good with us. Almost better than before we started dating. He'd promised me that if things didn't work we could say we gave it a try. If I am completely honest, I didn't give it a real try, but it seemed to be enough for him. We went back to late nights on the hammock, holding hands as friends and I trusted him <u>more</u> because he respected my boundaries. I found myself starting to fall for him.

Maybe it was that for the first time he wasn't actively pursuing me. That him not wanting me made me realize that I sort of liked it when he did. It took months of Jake just being there without expectations but I'd fallen for him. I was about to admit it to him, to tell him we should try again, when he accused me of turning him in to CPS.

The parallel timeline would have been more accurate if it had stemmed from that moment in the parking lot when Jake chose to believe Heather without a second thought. How do I explain this to Jake though? To him, this whole system is fate guided by Grandma June.

"But you can't go back," Dad muses from his seat. "And rehashing the past can only get you so far. He needs to do the work now, if he wants any relationship to work now."

"What if he digs up some old relationship that he thinks will make him happier?"

"He's slow sometimes, but he always arrives where he's supposed to."

Snatching the remote, he turns the volume up. This is all the advice he'll be bestowing.

It took Jake nearly two decades to come around last time. How long am I expected to wait? Sitting and waiting for him is going to do me no good. I need a distraction.

"Mom?" Noah's voice is panicked in the hallway.

"I'm out here buddy."

"Mom, there's a bug stuck in me."

"I'll get the lighter." My dad stands, making his way to the kitchen.

I see the fear on Noah's face. I endured my dad's torturous tick extractions more than a few times as a kid and landed in the pediatrician's office every time after his efforts failed, leaving the tick burrowed deep under the skin. I don't feel like subjecting Noah to the same treatment. I pull my phone out, knowing there is someone I can call.

Devin arrives only a few minutes after I call, small kit in hand.

"Alright, buddy, let's see if we can get this little guy out."

"Are you going to burn me?" Noah asks, glancing back at his grandpa over Devin's shoulder.

"Oh, no no no. I have this cool little sucker tool. I just put it on like this." He presses the open end onto his own arm before pulling up on the plunger, suctioning his skin into the tube. "And then he'll pop right out. You'll feel it, but it won't hurt, okay?"

Noah nods apprehensively. Devin takes Noah's leg in his hands and rubs his thumbs gently around the area before positioning the sucker. With one pull the tick pops out. Devin removes the device and grabs the tick with the tissue I offer.

"There ya go. Good as new." Devin smears a small dab of cream onto the spot and pats Noah's leg.

Noah examines his leg before standing and walking back toward his room without a word.

"I think I'll follow after Noah. Night, kiddo. Night, Doc."

"Night, Mr. Turner."

"Thank you again for coming by. I'm sorry it's so late." I stand from where I'd knelt, brushing my pajamas back down and wiggling my legs back to life.

"Of course. I'm glad you called." He stands so uncomfortably close to me that I can feel the heat from his skin radiating. Ducking my head down and to the side, I break the connection. Devin gathers his kit. "I have to leave in a couple days but do you think you could sneak away for dinner, maybe tomorrow night?"

"I'm sure I could make that work. Are you staying at your parents' place?" It's not that I think I owe him for this. It's more like a sign. Like maybe I'm supposed to allow myself Devin as a distraction.

"Nah, I got a room in town. Less prying eyes."

If he's mentioning his hotel as an offer, he's gonna be disappointed when I decline. There is no way I'm ready for <u>that</u>.

"I'll pick you up around six if that works for you?" He's trying to play it cool, but the excitement in his voice bubbles over.

"I'll scc you at six."

TWENTY FOUR

Dinner with Devin starts on a high note. He takes me to a Thai restaurant that while completely different from the one we frequented in New York, it gives off some of the same vibes. An expensive bottle of champagne had been ordered before we were even sat down at our table.

"Their tacos blow the New York ones out of the water," Devin says over his menu.

"Oh, those were incredible!" My mouth waters at the mention of tacos. "Do you remember that guy who came by our table and asked to try yours? He ate the whole thing. Who does that?" A chuckle escapes as I remember the stunned look on Devin's face as he just leaned back and gestured toward his plate.

"I didn't know how to say no back then."

Conversation comes easy as we order and wait for our food. It isn't until we nearly clean our plates that I begin to really scrutinize the possibility of being <u>with</u> Devin. A long-distance relationship might be the perfect opportunity to jump back into dating without the seriousness of someone close by at all times. Only seeing him once or twice a month could take the pressure off and keep everything light and casual.

"Man time sure got away from us."

"It has a habit of doing that." I agree with a halfhearted smile.

"I'm sorry about Scott. He always seemed like a good guy."

"<u>You</u> knew Scott?" Scott never mentioned Devin.

"I met him a few times at parties, so not <u>well,</u> but yeah." Devin's eyes narrow in the same way Scott's would when he was waiting for me to show a certain reaction. I don't know what he's looking for. This is supposed to be a distraction, and now it's not really feeling like one.

I never noticed the similarities between Scott and Devin before, but now they're impossible to ignore. Scott was always aware of when something was bothering me and had a way of making me know that he empathized with me. Devin has spent dinner doing precisely the same thing.

Being with Devin has the same easy nature Scott and I shared. Nothing past an intensity level of around a five. This means fewer arguments like the type Jake and I seem to constantly engage in, but it also means that the passion never passes a five either.

It hadn't bothered me when I was with Scott, but that was all before I'd seen what a life filled with passion at a nine was like. I don't know if I can choose comfort and ease again knowing an alternative is available. I can't live a life like my parents.

Paying the check, Devin stands and pulls my chair out from the table, offering his hand as I wobble to my feet.

"Wanna grab our jackets from the car and go for a little walk?"

"Sure." It's cold, raining, and windy, the exact kind of night I would generally avoid such an activity. While my jacket might protect my shoulders and arms, I dressed to impress tonight, and that means my bare legs will be exposed. I'm glad I chose boots over heels—even if my mom said I looked a little hookerish; she's said literally the same thing when I wore tennis shoes and shorts once. Sex work is valid, unlike her opinion.

As we make our way down the road I hold my arms tightly around myself to keep warm, but also to avoid an opportunity for Devin to take my hand. Because I <u>know</u> he'll take it, and I haven't decided if that's something I want.

I should want it. Maybe it's the thing I need to let Jake go or at least let him finish his quest. Then he can choose who he wants to be with instead of feeling any obligation to be with me when all is said and done. I don't want to be his pity choice.

"Do you think we would have worked out if you <u>had</u> been ready for a relationship?" Devin asks.

"I don't know. Maybe."

"I was heartbroken when you showed up to lunch with an engagement ring on. I thought I was doing the right thing by stepping back and giving you time."

"It <u>was</u> the right thing. I <u>did</u> need time."

"You just sorta forgot about me when you <u>were</u> ready, I guess."

"I wasn't looking for anything with Scott. I just kinda fell into it. It had nothing to do with you, I swear. Plus, you were <u>super</u> busy in med school." Smirking, I bump my shoulder into his arm as we walk.

"I <u>was</u> in med school!" Devin attempts to justify.

"You were a freshman. Is that even considered pre-med?" I'm teasing.

He was <u>that</u> guy, the one to tell <u>every</u> person he met that he was going to be a doctor. From the time we'd been in middle school, it had been one of Devin's defining traits. The kind of irritating thing that kept most girls from being interested in him rather than the turn-on he assumed it to be.

"I head back to Seattle tomorrow but I'm planning on being back in a few weeks. My mom is doing her big Thanksgiving thing." He talks like this Thanksgiving thing is something I should know about, but I'm not even entirely sure I've <u>met</u> his mom.

"Oh! I'm finishing the renovations on Crane House, and if it's done, you should stop by and see it."

The breeze picks up as we exit the park, and I'm so glad I can see his car.

"I'd really love that. I always thought that house had potential. I thought about buying it and fixing it up as a rental unit, but you beat me to it. Can't wait to see it."

The horn beeps as the lights flash. Devin reaches across me, pulling the handle and opening the door for me. The new leather groans as I lower myself into the seat. The car is so low I'm practically sitting on the ground. My dress moves higher, exposing most of my thigh, and <u>now</u> my mom's assessment doesn't seem so off. It's been years since I've gotten dressed up and gone out to dinner. Scott and I were a takeout couple, opting for living room picnics with Noah rather than securing a sitter.

This dress is from an event I attended at the White House almost exactly a year ago. I was worried about it being too revealing for the occasion, but Scott talked me into wearing it. He'd also cornered me in a room, for a few minutes alone, where he talked me into <u>not</u> wearing it, at least not pulled all the way down. My cheeks warm at the memory as Devin opens his own door and lowers himself next to me.

"I'm really glad we did this. You're even more beautiful than I remember." His finger moves from the edge of my dress on my collar to the thin chain resting against my collarbone. His hand is soft on my skin, and it sends chills down my arm. He's sweet, complimentary, I need to talk myself into this. It would be good for me.

"This was <u>really</u> nice," I repeat the sentiment. His touch reminds me of the comfort I found in his company in New York. After a year of grieving and loss, I have to admit that the touch of a man, without any of the complications, is intoxicating and fucking tempting.

"It's still early, and I'm staying at the Inn at the 5th, if you want to check it out."

I choke back the impulse to say no. But Jake, I know, is out looking for Lexi. Chasing down the serotonin high I know all too well accompanies each vision. And there isn't a shot in hell that they don't sleep together in whatever life they didn't actually have. Is it terrible of me to want just one thing in my life to be easy?

"I'd like that."

Devin reaches across the center console and takes my hand from where it lies on my bare thigh. It it feels so good and only a little wrong.

"I actually ran into Jake like a year ago near Seattle. I was out interviewing at the hospital. I went out for drinks with some friends, and he was there. I thought he was alone, but then he approached the bartender and spoke to her. It looked like they were old friends or something. It was weird. He reached out like he was going to touch her, and she slapped him away."

"She what?" I turn in alarm, somehow forgetting that this had been long before we'd reconnected.

"She knocked his hand right out of the air, like a ninja." Devin whooshes his hand from the steering wheel through the air before returning it. "The weird thing though, was that he looked almost smug afterwards, like he'd already gotten what he wanted."

He got <u>exactly</u> what he wanted. Closure.

The hotel is far more luxe than any place I've stayed since my wedding. It's like fluffy robes in the bathroom level fancy. I imagine collapsing on a chaise lounge in a bamboo robe, eating from a bowl of fresh fruit I neither have to buy nor prepare.

The elephant statue near the elevator sends off alarm bells in my head, the kind that are reserved for things a child can reach and ruin. As the doors open, nerves shoot through me. I'm nauseous.

Going to Devin's room is something I won't be able to take back once done. Jake isn't sleeping with the women he's been tracking down. He only needs the smallest, quickest touch to see the entirety of their life together. Even if Jake sees intimate details with these women, he's not actually engaging in the acts he's witnessing. Driving here with Devin, knowing what we're going to his room to do, is worse.

But I lived through one of Jake's visions, and the sex felt more real than many nights in my actual life. One night with Devin is hardly anything in comparison.

The more I think about it all, the more nervous I become. If I wait until we reach his floor, I'm for sure chickening out.

"Dev." I turn towards him. His back against the railing, he watches the numbers move higher and higher.

"Yeah?"

I leap across the small space and into his arms. Moving from the elevator to his door is a blur. I don't pull away as he fumbles in his pocket for the keycard. He uses my back to push the door open.

Devin seizes the opportunity that my four or so glasses of champagne have provided. His hands clumsily work the zipper until it's clear he isn't going to make progress with it. He abandons it and moves his hands to the bottom of my dress.

"Are you on the pill?" He asks breathlessly while patting his own pocket. I can only assume he's looking for the condom he put in there for precisely this reason. It shouldn't, but it bothers me. Did he count on the night going this way? And why would I be on the pill? Jake didn't ask that because he already knew the truth. I'm an infertile widow. But how would Devin know that? Is that something I should tell him before I let him think about getting involved with me? But this isn't supposed to be anything long-term. I don't want to be with Devin, I <u>want</u> to be with Jake. And sleeping with Devin isn't a one-night stand. That isn't the kind of guy he is. He'll expect more, and it's not fair of me to think that I can realistically offer anything more. Just a selfish night for me to feel something other than the all-consuming loneliness.

Before I even have a chance to step back Devin lays me down on the bed, which is the most comfortable bed I've ever touched. Silky cool sheets and a pile of down feathers. We are in vastly different tax brackets. His belt jingles as he moves between my legs and over me.

I have to stop this now.

"Dev, wait." Scooting back from under him, I find my way to a sitting position, where I can pull my dress down to cover myself. As much as it covers at least. "I'm sorry. I don't think I can do this."

Devin's head hangs in defeat. He expected this.

"It's Jake isn't it?" Looking up, his eyes draw together. The lines on his forehead deepen.

I can only nod. Tears begin to well. I never intended to lead Devin on, though that's exactly what I did.

"God, I should have known. It's <u>always</u> been Jake."

"Everyone keeps saying that, but we were just friends." I mean, aside from the time that we weren't. The mountain of pillows provides a soft backrest for me to lean into.

Devin climbs up and over, finding a place next to me, and leans back with a large exhale, resting his hand on my thigh. There is nothing sexual about his touch now. It's not charged with tension and lust, it's the touch of a friend who, despite everything, really just wants the best for me.

"There was always something between you two, like you knew all of the other's secrets. Most people never find a friendship like that. Add in the absolute adoration he had for you, and I think we all knew it was just a matter of time." He squeezes lightly. We sit catching our breath. The taste of his gum still lingers on my lips. "So what's the problem? Why are you <u>here</u> with me instead of off with him?"

"He just wants to be friends." The words are flat, final.

"Yeah, no. That's bullshit. I don't buy that for a second." More silence. More breathing. "Let me find my keys from wherever I tossed them, and I'll drive you home."

"No. I'll get an Uber. I feel bad enough."

"Liv, that's ridiculous, let me just take you home." Devin moves to stand. I can't let him take me home. I don't want to make the guy I just friend-zoned—hard, take me home. That would be humiliating for him and fucking awkward for me. Plus something with the tacos must not be sitting right, the last thing he needs is for me to finalize his rejection by vomiting all over his ridiculously clean car.

"No. Thank you, but no. I'll call an Uber."

The drive is dark and quiet. Thankfully my driver is too occupied with his podcast on animal migration in the southern hemisphere to chat. I only have my thoughts to fill the drive. There's only Jake. I've known this all along. It's the reason losing him as a friend all those years before felt like losing part of myself. Because I did.

There is only Jake. Every moment since we stood in the school parking lot led me back to Oregon, to Coburg, to Jake. Goddammit, I'm gonna puke.

TWENTY FIVE

Every tile I place has to be pulled off and adjusted a half dozen times. Ben showed me how to do this, making a big deal about every tile needing to be perfect for the backsplash to all line up in the end. My mind isn't present enough to line them up as effortlessly as he had.

It doesn't help that my nerves are making it impossible for my hands to remain steady. I'd chalked the nausea I felt with Devin up to guilt at betraying Jake. It didn't pass, and by the next morning, I found myself hunched over the pink padded toilet seat in my parents' house. Feeling better throughout the day, I was surprised when I found myself in a similar position after just the briefest smell of pancakes coming from the kitchen.

On my way to Crane House, I grabbed a test from the store, not wanting to take it somewhere my parents or Noah could find it. I knew that by bringing the test to Crane House, I could take the test and toss it into the construction dumpster, never to be seen by another person. I didn't need the test to tell me what I already knew though. I'm fucked.

"Damnit!" The tile slips for the fourth time, smearing adhesive across the already installed clean tiles. Throwing it against the wall to my side, the broken pieces scatter on the concrete countertops.

"Want some help?"

I haven't seen Jake since our argument last Friday. It feels so much longer than four days. So much has happened. I'm never the one to reach out first after an argument, regardless of how badly I know I should. This time is different, though. I had, aided by more than half of Ben's flask, confessed my love and Jake said nothing in return. After my date on Sunday, I wanted to find him to talk about it, but he hadn't been home. And since I was still upset and embarrassed, I opted to just ignore him until one of us died; it seemed easier than revisiting all we've said and done.

Things have changed though. That's no longer a possibility. We will forever be linked by the small plastic stick in the pocket of my coat.

Jake leans against the counter next to where I sit, cross-legged.

"I called you," he says after placing a tile perfectly in the spot I've been fighting, with as little effort as Ben had.

"I know." I want so badly to still be angry with Jake over our argument. Anger is a thoughtless emotion. It requires little effort or self-reflection in the moment.

"HGTV called. They picked your house." He knows that Ben had already passed on this bit of news to me, but I have to give him credit. He's trying.

"I heard. Looks like you'll get the funding for the lake development after all." I <u>am</u> grateful for his effort to move on and recover some bit of normalcy. "They actually just emailed me the filming information, I'll forward it to you. They are airing it over the holidays, so we have to decorate for Christmas, which is not my strong suit."

A memory of our accidental Charlie Brown-style tree from our could've been life comes to mind. Jake walking in after his journeyman's test to see Scarlett and me attempting to decorate a tree that was shedding needles faster than we could put on ornaments.

"Hmm." I don't know if he's remembering the same tree that I am, but he doesn't do that thing when people tell you that you're actually good at things you <u>know</u> you are awful at. "Okay, well Jenn does an incredible job. She did the lake house for me last year. We can have her bring those decorations over here."

"That would be amazing. Thank you." The anger has melted. I don't want to fight anymore. I hold the tile in my hand against the wall longer than necessary, trying to garner the guts to ask him. "I'm going to have a housewarming party the evening of filming since it'll all be fancy already. I'd love for you to be there. I mean, you <u>did</u> have a hand in this whole thing. This house is practically as much yours as mine." Well, that came out more awkward than I intended.

I twist to take in all we've accomplished since first sitting on the patio only two months before. I wanted something dark, but warm and inviting, to contrast the all-white pallet Scott planned on. The home is unrecognizable from the old Crane House that generations of kids have avoided. It's almost offensive to the house to keep referring to it as the old Crane House.

"Of course I'll be there. Wouldn't miss it for the world."

We tile the backsplash without speaking more than a few words to each other. Instead, we anticipate the other's moves like a dance we've practiced over a lifetime. It takes a fraction of the time it would have taken me to finish it on my own and we move on to the only thing left in the house to finish, a final paint coat on the upstairs bedrooms.

"So how was your date with <u>Doctor</u> Devin?" Jake calls from Noah's room. It bounces off the walls before reaching me in the guest room, where I'm gathering my roller and the step stool.

"It was good. We went to this Thai place in Eugene." I think I hear a scoff, but I'm going to be the bigger person, and ignore it in the name of civility. "It was nice to get dressed up all fancy for a night on the town. It was nice to catch up."

"Oh ... well, I'm glad you had fun." His tone tells me he's anything <u>but</u> happy with the thought of me having fun if it involves Devin. "You think you'll go out again?"

"Probably not." More like out of the question. Desperate to keep things light, I switch to a subject I know can't be weighed down. "Noah finished the latest batch of comics you lent him."

"He hasn't even had those two days!" He shoots me a look of incredulity as I join him in Noah's room with my brush and bucket.

"I'm just glad you and Ben have a never-ending supply. It's saving me from dipping into his college fund."

"College is overrated."

"Says who? Just because <u>you</u> make a decent living without a degree, doesn't mean I want that for my kid."

"I <u>have</u> a degree."

Have I really never asked about his education, assuming because he never pursued a formal education in his life as an electrician, that the same would also be true of real life Jake?

"I have a master's in architecture and was in the PHD program, but stepped back to focus on the lake house project."

"Doctor Larson," I try the name.

"Sounds a hell of a lot better than Doctor Devin."

"Eh. A little pompous if you ask me." I smirk, knowing I've struck a nerve, but more so I've returned us to the place where we thrive, this back-and-forth banter fueled us for years. Nothing feels better than friends being able to poke fun at each other. Fight over.

As we paint the rooms, we talk mostly about all the movies that have been released since high school. Jake lists every zombie, apocalypse, and spy thriller I've heard of, as well as many that I haven't. In return, I name the movies that are significant for either the style they were shot or the story they told.

"It was just a kid and a tiger in a boat for the entire movie!"

"Exactly!" I'll argue this one. "They have to learn to trust and respect each other in order to survive. It was gorgeous and made me want to read the book."

"So how _was_ the book?" He knows damn well I never picked up the book.

"I ... okay well I haven't read it yet." I continue to roll the same section of wall, long after the paint has run out, to avoid his gaze.

"Uh huh." Jake congratulates himself on his point being made. "There has to be at least one movie we both loved."

"Oh, that's easy. Inglorious Bastards." The fact that I got there before he did is surprising. Honestly, I can't believe it didn't make his initial list.

"Oh my God! Yes!" Jake shouts, his echo carrying through the entire house. Our taste in movies on the surface seems fundamentally different. They aren't. We both live for the quippy one-liners we can tuck into our pockets and recall whenever the occasion arises. "It's a bingo!" Jake pulls one out. We used to have entire conversations in nothing but movie quotes. Back and forth until the other showed any sign of weakness, of not knowing where the line in question originated from.

I mourned the loss of _this_ Jake for years. The way we can go from angry to laughing without either of us feeling like we lost whatever fight we were having. I was never _as_ angry with Scott about any part of our life as I can get with Jake over the smallest things. Every emotion is dialed up.

And then, just like that. The last corner of the last room is painted. The house is done. Our excuse to spend time with each other is gone. Well... this excuse at least. I slide my arms into my peacoat, the plastic pregnancy test a weight in my pocket. Do I tell him now? No. I'll wait until after this weekend. Once the stress of all the house stuff is behind us, and once the doctor confirms whether this is viable or not. I'm trying not to get my hopes up, knowing it could very well end in another miscarriage, but fuck. I want this. A lot.

"Alright, so I'll see you on Saturday then?" I can tell him about the pregnancy once everyone goes home after the party. Maybe I'll wrap up the test and give it to him? Well, that's probably not the best idea. He'd probably make a joke about me giving him a covid test. Without actually realizing what it was.

"Saturday?"

"Yeah, HGTV will be here at four, so they can get the house just before sunset and then also some night shots. I told everyone the party will be at seven. The producer said to have you wear something identifiable with J&B Designs but to still look sharp. Which just sort of comes naturally to you, so I don't think you need to worry—"

"Liv, I <u>can't</u> be here on Saturday." And the air that just seconds ago was lifting me towards cloud 9 is sucked out of my lungs.

"What do you mean you can't <u>be</u> here? This is what we've worked on for months. This is what is going to fund your lake development. They're coming to interview J&B designs ... That's you, Jake. You're the J." I leave myself out of it.

"Ben's going to have to do the interview. I'll talk to him about it. He'll look sharp. He's far more charming in front of a camera anyway."

Jake pulls his coat on in an act of finality, denying any further explanation. This is <u>huge</u> and he's blowing it off like it's nothing.

"I don't understand. What could possibly be more important than <u>this</u>?"

Jake moves to the wall, flipping the light switch off, before brushing past me to the hallway.

"Jake!" My voice bounces off the rafters, hitting us both a second time. "Talk to me."

I can feel him slipping away, back to where I can't reach him<u>.</u>

"Talk to me." I hate how the words struggle to escape. "Please." It's quiet and desperate.

"I don't want to hurt you, Liv."

The words he spoke on the mountain ridge ring through my ears like tinnitus. "That's what we do. We say we're friends, but then we hurt each other."

I sit on the bottom step of the new staircase. A chill moves through my shoulders as Jake sighs, taking the space beside me. This is it. The end.

I brace myself, jaw clenched. What he's about to tell me must have something to do with to do with his visions and the list. What else is there? What if he's seen something worth putting it all behind him? Fuck, I'm going to be sick.

"I never asked for any of this." His hand moves in an encompassing motion. "I never asked for my life to be tossed into a fucking spin cycle. I thought I did something to piss off the universe when this curse first started. You don't know what it's like to know that every time you touch someone you might be assaulted with a barrage of memories that make you feel like everything you know is a lie, that who you are, is a lie. You know what it felt like to have it happen one time but to have it looming over your head forever, never knowing if or when it will ever stop, it's torture. But then we saw what our life could have been and for a minute, it didn't feel like a curse, it felt like all the suffering was for something."

Our life. Two words that are impossible to explain what they mean to anyone who isn't us. The life that includes a daughter and a love that rivals that of any story I've ever heard.

Jake reaches over, taking my hand in his. I lean my head on his shoulder moving my thumb over his hand methodically. Is this how Jake felt all those years ago when I held <u>his</u> hand as a friend? Did he want me as badly as I need him now? Did he let me go, giving me time without a second thought, knowing that he might die of heartache? My chest is tight.

"So why are you still out there tormenting yourself?" I've been stuck on this for months. What is it about <u>me</u> that makes him want to go back out there and hurt?

"Because it's looming. It will loom over me, over us." His free hand traces the spaces where our fingers intertwine. "Liv, I'm <u>almost</u> done. I only have one name left and I'll be free from this. Free to move on, to whatever is next for me." Free to be with you is the unspoken sentiment that turns the churning into butterflies. He's almost free to be with me. I can cling to this smallest bit of hope.

But what if this last one is something he wants more than what we have? I could tell him now. Two words that once spoken would make it impossible for him to make a choice that isn't me. The plastic is warm in my hand. Opening my mouth, I begin to pull it out. But Jake speaks first, so I push the words back down and return the test to the bottom of my pocket.

"I'm driving up to Vancouver this weekend."

The silence sits without the weight he seems to be expecting.

"Okay?" Is Vancouver supposed to mean <u>something</u> to me? He seems to think so.

"I'm going to see Heather."

Jake's hand grips mine tighter in an attempt to what? Keep me from bolting? Or reassure me? He's pulled the hope out from under me. His words finally sink in; he said free to move on with whatever was next for him, without specifically mentioning me.

I knew at some point he would come to me with tales of a life he never shared with Heather, yet some part of me thought it had already come and gone without him feeling any need to tell me, knowing my history with her.

"Don't," I plead, knowing full well I'm asking him to do something I swore to myself I wouldn't. It's his turn to flinch, but the ask is already out there and I can't take it back now. "Jake, we've spent months repairing damage, and if you go, I worry that it has all been for nothing. What can you possibly see that will be better than what <u>we</u> saw? What could you see that would be worth it?"

"I don't have a choice Liv." So it's not the curse that would be looming over us forever, it's Heather that would be looming. God, she's the worst.

"You do though! All of this has been about choices we've made and how different everything <u>could</u> have been. But this. Doing this. This is a choice and don't pretend it isn't. What are you really looking to find out? If Heather is better than me? I'm better for you, and you know it. You don't find this ..." I gesture between us with my hands; I don't need to use a pregnancy to get him to stay. He knows how special what we have is. "More than once in a lifetime. Stay with <u>me</u>."

"I can't."

It hadn't been meant as an ultimatum, but once he spoke we both understood that he answered it as if it had been. When Jake returns from Vancouver, it will be with the knowledge of whether a life with Heather is or is not more appealing than a life with me. That kind of knowledge taints any decision he makes, and I don't think I can move past it. I could have stopped him from going if I told him about the test. But I don't deserve to be a consolation prize, and this baby sure as hell won't be resented as the reason he never finished what he started.

Twenty Six

Saturday morning is exactly the scramble I've spent days preparing for. With Jake noticeably absent, Ben plans to step in to ensure everything is picture-perfect. But he's not here when the decorations from Jake's lake house are brought on the truck, along with the staging furniture Jenn keeps in storage for Jake's model homes. Some friend I am; I didn't even know she had a whole house staging business on the side, but I'm grateful for the help. Questions on furniture placement are directed at me. I try my best to answer despite the vague directions Ben gave me.

It takes a team of four men nearly an hour to construct and decorate the fifteen-foot Christmas tree against the large windows. White lights illuminate translucent dried orange slices, each holding a star anise hand sewn into the center. The glowing orange and red give a warmer glow than the coldness usually associated with white lights. Cranberries are strung around cinnamon sticks and pine cones. This tree is mountainous and cozy.

Live garland winds around the banister and hangs from the mantle, adding the smell of pine to the hints of citrus and cinnamon.

This may be my home, yet nothing in it reflects me or Noah in any way. Not my style—more like lack thereof. This is a home designed for a magazine, not for a mother and son who care more about practicality than aesthetics. It's going to feel dull and empty once the staging furniture is taken and I'm left with my mismatched couches, ragged quilts, and a stark lack of knickknacks to fill shelves that I'll probably clutter with books, Noah's growing comic book collection, and a few picture frames.

Ben arrives in time to take over the final touches, moving nearly everything I placed, so I can sneak away to get Noah for the reveal. I don't care about film crews or people watching and judging from home. I only care what Noah thinks.

"Is this our house?" Noah gasps as we pull up to the curb leaving the driveway clear for filming, just as the e-mail instructed.

"Looks a little different, huh?"

The home, at some point in its history, was white. The siding and roof were the first thing I insisted on updating before even moving in. Things hadn't gone to plan with the wrong siding being ordered, followed by a series of summer storms and Tom Sweet refusing to hire the crew necessary to complete the siding. Noah and I moved into Crane House with the chipped white paint on the old boards flaking like architectural dandruff each time we closed a door.

Ben being a true magician, not only managed to save the original siding but by opting to burn the boards rather than paint them, he was able to give the wood a natural treatment against moisture while also giving me the dark look I requested. The whole process had a fancy Japanese name that I'll never remember, despite it being repeated to me multiple times during the process.

Noah stands on the grass, speechless, for the first time in his life. Crane House no longer looks like it's on the verge of falling down if he sneezes. It looks brand new. The black of the siding sitting against the background of evergreens gives it a real mountain retreat vibe. That has to be one of the main reasons it was picked for the HGTV special.

We cross the lawn in the exact way we did only three months before, hand in hand, ready to embark on the next chapter of our lives with only each other by our side.

Inside is bustling. Ben stands in the center of the living room, conducting the orchestra of movers and decorators. Noah moves toward him, being pulled into his orbit. Looking up at the last moment his mouth falls open in amazement.

Scooping his hand in the air, he beckons me to join him in admiring the beams overhead. Only once I'm next to him and look up do I realize he's not looking at the beams.

"Mission accomplished." Noah congratulates himself.

When I arrived at my parents' house to pick up Noah, I was irritated that he was still in his pajamas, hair a complete disaster. It took me the better part of an hour to clean him up so he would be presentable enough to be filmed. I grumbled the entire time, while Noah apologized over and over, without any real feeling behind the words. I now see that this was the plan. Noah kept me away longer so they could install the super secret project my dad and Noah have been working on for months.

The chandelier hangs low into the space, the curled wood branching out from the center and stretching in every direction. How they transported this, let alone built it in the small workshop, given its gargantuan size is by itself amazing even if it wasn't gorgeous in its complexity.

"You made this?" It's my turn for disbelief. Noah nods, no words necessary. "Buddy, that's incredible. It's beautiful."

"Grandpa let me do most of it." He beams.

"Honestly, I was expecting candlesticks for the mantle."

I pull Noah into a side hug as I follow the curves of the chandelier, only breaking when Ben steps backward out of the way of a couch being brought in, nearly knocking us over. We are in the way. I take Noah to continue our tour of our home, doing my best to stay out of the pathways everyone follows so closely. They are ants and I am the fallen leaf, disrupting their marching. We go through my room, the primary bath, hallway, his bathroom, his bedroom, and finally the little slanted room affectionately known as "Dad's office." Originally planned as an office for Scott, it's now a game room complete with giant bean bag chairs.

"It's too fancy." Noah sits at the island, sipping on a large glass of eggnog.

"All the fancy stuff will be gone tomorrow. Then our old stuff will be moved in and it will really be home."

His assessment is more than fair. It feels like a lie to stage the house in a way that it will never look like again. It gives people that unattainable expectation. I've fallen victim many a time.

I have zero idea what to expect from the entire filming process and as a result, find myself shaking with nerves when the HGTV crew arrives. The producer, Lynn, a stout woman only a few years older than me, brought a pack of cookies and frosting. She quickly sets me and Noah to work decorating the newly built island—presumably to dispel any nerves, but also to keep us out of the way of the film crew. I really hate feeling like I need to apologize for taking up space in my own damn house. But today, the house isn't mine, not really. It's Jake and Ben's.

One camera crew sets off with Ben, who greets them like old friends, exploring the renovations, while the other cameraman remains with us and Lynn decorating cookies. Lynn talks to us so warmly it doesn't feel like she's a stranger conducting an interview.

"How did you come to find Jake and Ben for the renovations?" Lynn's midwestern accent adds to her personable demeanor.

"Oh, I mean we've been friends since middle school."

"Was it always the plan to have them renovate then? Having lifelong friends in the business certainly makes it an easy choice, right?"

"We hadn't spoken in a long time, but when we reconnected it just sort of happened really fast. Especially when they found out I was trying to YouTube my way through making this place livable. Once I saw their lake house development, it was a no-brainer." I slip it in so smoothly that I hope she doesn't think I practiced that line in the shower, because I did.

Lynn leads us through several rooms, coaching Noah and me on activities to do while they're filming for what she calls B-roll and taking pictures for the accompanying blog. I lift Noah as he pretends to hang ornaments on the tree. We then moved to Noah's room, where he empties the backpack filled with comics onto the rug Jenn laid over the new carpet. We lie on our stomachs as Noah excitedly explains to me why Hawk and Dove are his favorite duo. I do my best to look as interested as possible. The <u>last</u> thing I want is to look like a bad mom on national television.

Just as I start to feel comfortable in the process, nearly forgetting I'm being filmed at all, Lynn claps her hands.

"Okay, I think we've got everything. It was so nice to meet you, Liv. And you Noah..." she leans forward "...you enjoy your new house!"

The HGTV crew packs up and leaves in the same flurry they arrived in. Ben follows them out to the driveway. And it's just Noah and I, for the first time. We're both buzzing with excitement. This house has been nothing but a dream of Scott's for years, and now it's done. And it's perfect. It feels like the best way to honor his memory. To make the memories in the house, and town, he wanted for us.

"When's the party? Is Lincoln on his way yet?" Kids are always ready to move on to the next activity. I check my watch, doing the math.

"We have like an hour or so. Why don't you go hang out in the game room? All that stuff is staying. Get all set up for when everyone gets here." I don't have to tell him twice. He's up the stairs before I finish.

Leaving the house to retrieve our overnight bags from my car, I find Ben surrounded by the entire HGTV crew on the front lawn. He's talking about the lake house development. I want to find a minute to talk to Ben before the rest of our friends arrive, but It'll have to wait. The entire point of Jake and Ben taking on my renovation is that it held the possibility of steering attention towards not only their construction company but the lake house development as well.

While it has a full booking for the grand opening in the spring, there are still retail vacancies in the shops of the little town square. Judging by the look on their faces as Ben scrolls through pictures on his phone, it's going well. Good.

I only invited a few friends to this housewarming slash Christmas party, mostly those who were at the Labor Day campout. I should have known word would get out. Now I honestly have no idea how many people to expect. I <u>want</u> to show off the incredible job Ben and Jake did, but the idea of so many people in my house gives me flutters of anxiety.

Friends arrive in droves. Kate and Brendon, with their three kids in tow, are among the first to arrive. Lincoln and Leah bound up the stairs, eager to find Noah and escape the boring grown-up festivities. I can hardly blame them. Every time I bring a coat up to my room, I hide long enough to take a few deep breaths. Ashley and Michelle have matching khaki trench coats that I lay next to each other on the bed as the doorbell rings. Someone thankfully answers in my absence and relief washes over me. I get just one more moment alone. I still need to find Ben, but for all I know, he's securing his own HGTV show.

The screen on my phone lights up for the fifteenth time as I unlock it before stopping myself. I want to call Jake. I want desperately to tell him how everything went. How Noah's chandelier surprise took my breath away, how Ben has been charming the pants off of the entire crew, how Jenn transformed the entire space just like he said she would. But then I also want to tell him about the pregnancy test still sitting in my glovebox along with the fuzzy black and white ultrasound from yesterday. I want to tell him how that one afternoon in our little green house was more magical than either of us could have known. But Jake is with Heather, or almost to Heather. I didn't exactly ask about a full itinerary. I only know he's supposed to be back tomorrow night. And I don't know what I'm going to do or how I'm going to tell him.

The top dresser drawer sits empty. It's the perfect place to stash my phone to prevent further temptation. Returning to the party, I find Devin standing in the doorway of my bedroom, coat in hand.

"Hey, I texted you this week," Devin says, his voice hopeful as he moves from the door to the window, leaning against the sill.

"It's been crazy over here." I smile politely if not dismissively, hoping that he won't press me. Devin steps closer, clearly planning to press. Okay.

"Can we talk? I haven't stopped thinking about our date."

Thoughts of pretending to be needed elsewhere are tempting. I didn't leave Devin without an explanation, so I'm not sure what else there could possibly be to talk about.

"Dev, I'm sorry. I just don't think that's a good idea." It's all I have to offer. I can't come right out with the real reason. Oh hey, remember how I almost puked in your hotel room? Well, there's a reason for that.

"Don't be sorry. I just can't get you out of my mind. I was thinking if maybe we—"

"I'm pregnant." I haven't said the words out loud other than to my doctor, and Devin isn't the first person I want to share the news with.

"Wait, what?" Ben's voice comes from behind me and it's full of hurt.

"I'm just gonna—" and Devin disappears before even thinking about finishing his sentence leaving me and Ben still staring at each other. Nothing's gone the way I planned, and now I have to worry that Devin is downstairs spreading the gossip through the house. By the time I return to the party, word will have probably gotten back to Jake.

"Does Jake know?" I can't read his expression, is it concern? Excitement?

"Not yet. I found out the other day, but then he told me he needed to go see Heather, and I didn't want this to be the only reason for him to stay. I didn't even think I could get pregnant. Scott and I tried for years after Noah."

"Liv, he would have stayed."

"It doesn't matter. If what he sees with Heather is happy, he'll want to do everything in his power to build on what's possible with her, but then he'd feel trapped with me and a baby. But if what he sees is unhappy. I'm always going to feel like a backup plan. Someone he's only with because I got knocked up. There wasn't a way to tell him before without forcing his hand. It's fine, we can co-parent. All the cool kids are doing it." I have to brush it off with a joke or else I will have to be honest. I've never felt more inadequate and unwanted and lonely and absolutely terrified.

"I didn't know you guys had even slept together." Ben sits on the coats, pulling his hand over his face in disbelief.

"That little green house he bought? It was ours. Well, the one we saw the one from our other life. He found it and bought it. We spent an afternoon there, and well ..."

"Well ..." he repeats, a grin spreading across his face. "I'm gonna be an uncle."

Twenty Seven

B en's the last one at the party, staying to help clean, though somehow we're unable to restore the house to the condition it was in only hours before. Noah went home with my parents around nine, exhausted but unable to sleep with the noise. So much for the overnight bag.

The movers are scheduled for tomorrow morning to remove the staging furniture and unload the pod where Jake, Ben, and I packed up the house. Tomorrow, I'll have to unpack the entire house... again. I've been dreading it since we started this adventure.

"Come lie down." Ben pats the carpet at the base of the Christmas tree next to where he's lying.

"There are couches. Why would I want to lie on the carpet?"

"It's brand-new carpet, Liv. Trust me."

I adjust my shirt as I move to lower myself onto the carpet next to him. It's like laying on the grass for the first time after a long winter, it's warm and inviting.

"It's soft, huh?"

We lie in silence, watching as the light twinkles through the citrus on the tree. I don't spend enough time with Ben alone. It's always been Jake and me or Jake, Ben and me, or even Jake and Ben. There should be more Liv and Ben time. It's nice. No expectations, just friendship.

"You're gonna be a mom. Again." Wonder fills his voice

"Am I too old to have a baby?"

"Yeah, probably."

"Ow!" Did he just pull my hair?

"Gray hairs and everything."

The hair he plucked has a decent probability of being gray. I quit dyeing my hair just after I quit having to go into the office, not seeing the point and instead deciding to embrace the grays that continue to pop up. Plus, I've had my hair done in Coburg, and it didn't end well. The incident resulting in an accidental pixie cut is still painful. I'll just grow it long and gray rather than take another chance. Embrace my witchy-ness living in the old haunted house.

"Thank you." I throw my body to the side, knocking my shoulder into his.

"For what?"

"This incredible house, being here today, being so great to Noah ... take your pick." <u>My</u> shoulder moves as Ben knocks his own into mine. He's the brother I never had. "Love you, Ben."

"Love you too, Liv."

The worry that Jake and I would grow apart was amplified by the fear that if we did find a distance between us, Ben would be on the other side... again.

"You haven't lost Jake." He's reading my mind. "Give him time. He'll come back to you. He <u>always</u> does. And I think you have a little something that might give him the push he really needs. I don't know what it is that you two saw that day in the coffee shop, but since then he—"

The ringtone in his pocket brings us out of the dreamlike state we've been in. Since then he what? Great, now I'll never know.

"Hello?" He sits up as he answers. "Yeah, this is he."

The voice on the other line is far away and muffled. I'm trying not to eavesdrop, but it's late, and the concerned look on Ben's face has me sitting up. I study his face, looking for answers to questions I don't know.

Ben's eyes dart to mine with a look I haven't seen in his eyes before but know on a cellular level inside me. Something is wrong. Really wrong.

"I am getting in the car now. I will be there in less than two hours. Will you please call me here with any updates?" The muffled voice responds as Ben bobs his head. "No, Yeah, I understand that. If anything changes please can you ... yeah, okay. Thank you." Tears well on his bottom lids as he ends the phone call and holds the phone in both his hands. "We gotta go."

"What's going on?" I'm frozen in place.

He doesn't say anything but the speed at which Ben stands and moves to flip light switches confuses me while I sit on the rug still waiting for an answer, any answer. Something happened, and we need to go. What happened? Where do we need to go? I can't ask the question again because he'll give me an answer that I don't want.

"Liv!" Ben shouts from the hallway keys jingling through a closed fist. I look up, his eyes don't meet mine but the look of dread on his face matches the pit swirling through my middle.

"What happened?" I ask, slowly pushing on my hands to balance myself as I get up. Steadying myself, I repeat the question with authority. "Ben, what happened?"

"Jake's in the hospital. We gotta go." He moves from stunned to frantic. His words are out so fast, I can't move I can't speak, fuck I can't even breath. I just keep staring at him, trying to process those words. Jake's in the hospital. It's déjà vu and not the fun kind like seeing the place where I never actually got married. This is Scott all over again. "Liv! Now!"

Ben's out the door before I ever make it to the staircase, finally meeting his speed and panic level as I race up the stairs to retrieve my phone from the dresser drawer. The phone glows as I move it, alerting me to four text messages, six missed calls, and two voicemails, Jake's name is attached to each notification.

The truck is already in drive when I climb in, sliding into the seat beside Ben.

"Why the fuck is he in Portland? He should've been in Canada hours ago." Ben stomps on the gas. The truck is flying around the corner so fast it feels like the tires on my side are lifting off the pavement. We're going to be joining Jake in the hospital if Ben doesn't settle down.

"Maybe he got there and then decided to drive home tonight rather than wait the night. Maybe it went worse than he expected ..." I try to offer as an explanation.

Holding a button on the steering wheel, he waits until the beep sounds through the speakers. "Call Heather."

"Calling Heather Jones."

I shrink into my seat as if Heather will know I'm here even if I don't say a word.

"Benny! What do I owe the pleasure?" Her words are slightly slurred but peppy as the trill of her voice fills the cab. Is she drunk?

"Hey, Heather. Have you seen Jake?"

"Nope. I got a call from him last week. We were set to meet for dinner tonight, but he never showed. Big surprise there." She continues to slur through her rant. "When you see him, tell him don't bother rescheduling. I'm busy and not interested in more of his excuses."

"He's in the hospital, Heather."

"Oh shit. Is he okay?" Her tone changes from that of a disgruntled ex to one of genuine concern. It's the first thing she's ever done that makes me think she might have a shred of decency in her. Like maybe a <u>single</u> shred.

"I don't know yet. I'm on my way to Kaiser in Portland right now. I'm just trying to figure out what happened and why he's in the middle of you and me."

Their voices fade as I fall into the déjà vu of the situation. I'm going to lose Jake in the exact same way I lost Scott and there's nothing I can do. My breathing becomes erratic, and I can feel the panic attack building. I need to focus on one thing, squeezing my hands around <u>my phone.</u> The messages and missed calls!

<u>Hey, is the film crew still there?</u> The first text reads. Followed only a few minutes later with: <u>I'm on my way back. Can I come by tonight?</u>

I stare at the screen, regretting that I left my phone in the drawer as long as I did.

Another text: <u>Liv, I know you're still mad, but please pick up the phone. I need to talk to you.</u> And finally: <u>Sorrrr.</u>

The shadows on the side of the road give the illusion that we're moving incredibly fast, on a race track that repeats every few feet like in an old movie. At some point it must have started raining because the wipers are moving at full speed. I swipe my finger down, showing the notifications, and touch the one for voicemail. Lifting it to my ear, I close my eyes.

"Hey, I don't know if you just don't have your phone or if you're still mad. I was wrong. Tonight was a big deal, and I should have been there. I'm on my way back. I turned around near Seattle I should be back in like four hours. I hope you're still awake. If not, I'll come by tomorrow to help you unpack. I'm sorry, Liv. Really." He changed his mind. He was coming back to me, just like Ben said he would.

I hold the phone out from me as the message ends. I can't bring myself to listen to the last one. Ben ends his call with Heather, I can feel his attention on me, his eyes sharing time with the road and the only light in the cab, my phone. Jake.

I want to hear this in private. But I know if it was reversed that Ben would let me in, so I click the more recent message, putting it on speakerphone. The static of rainfall is as good as silence.

Our bodies both shift towards the phone, straining to hear something, anything. Then a beeping, no it's more like a chime. maybe the dinging of the seat belt reminder ... followed by crackled breathing. Jake's breathing.

"They left me here, Liv" he says as if he expects a response rather than leaving a message. "They said they had to get help, but I don't think they're coming back." He gasps for breath and I feel my own breath leave my body. "I told them I would wait here." Laughter follows a gurgling sound. "It was a joke, cause I'm stuck ... Like really stuck. but they didn't laugh. Did you laugh? I bet you did. You think I'm funny." A smile betrays my fear, moving across my face before I can stop it. But It doesn't last long. Now is not the time for Jake's gallows humor.

"Liv, I need to tell you something, and since I might be stuck here forever, this might be my only chance." Rain, no sound but rain and his breathing, which is so slow I almost miss it. Whether he's preparing his thoughts or passed out, I'm not sure. His voice clears as he begins again. "When I was thirteen, I fell in love with you without even knowing your name. Then we became friends and I knew I'd never love anyone the way I loved you. Even if I had to love you from afar, I loved you for the potential I saw in you, in us." He pauses, gasping for breath. "You left but I never stopped loving you Liv. I gotta come clean. I knew you were living in DC. I lied that day in the coffee shop when I acted like I didn't know. I almost came out to try and find you a couple of times. Then when I saw what our life could have been, I fell in love with a you that never existed. I have been caught up, in love with versions of you I wished were real rather than accepting the incredible woman you actually are."

Tears stream down my face as I hold the phone between Ben and me. Neither of us makes a sound, worried we'll miss any of this last confession.

"Liv, there has never been a version of you that has failed to amaze and enrapture me. I love that you wear white when you eat spaghetti as if there is not a chance in hell you are not going to make a mess. I love that you can't tell the difference between two shades of gray, yet you can design a house worthy of being on TV. I love how you talk to Noah like he's your best friend in the entire universe. He's so much cooler than you, though, so you'd be smart to keep him around." A sound trying to be laughter barks before being stifled by gasping. "I know I can't expect the life we saw. I don't want that life. I don't need kids of my own. I want any life I can have with you and Noah. I love you, Liv, I've always loved you, and I'm always going to love you." His breathing takes over as he keeps the line open after his declaration. "Help!" His voice breaks the silence again in a call to a faraway voice in the background. The agony and weakness in his voice breaks me.

"Oh and, Liv ..." Jake starts again as if I was on the other line. "Tell Ben I'm sorry I didn't call him. He's my brother, though. He already knows how much I love him I didn't want you to not know, you know? Okay, I'm gonna let you go now." The line goes dead.

Now I'm gasping, sitting with what he just said to me. He's felt the same way for me as I have for him this whole time. Only now it's too late. I already lived this nightmare. Following the call from the hospital informing me that Scott had been in an accident, I drove there on autopilot, possessed by the need to be there. And it was too late. There was no voicemail, nothing after the goodbye kiss he'd planted on mine then Noah's forehead before leaving the house.

"I can't lose him Liv. He's all I have left in the world." Tears fall from Ben's eyes, soaking the collar of the work polo he wore while on camera. He lost both his parents and is now facing losing the closest thing to a brother he's ever known. I have no words to comfort him. The only thing I can do is be here as we face our world falling apart.

The roads are devoid of any cars, leaving open lanes for Ben to take advantage of. Not that there are any lanes at this point. The rain has erased any and all guidance. I just have to have faith that Ben can stay far enough away from the ditches. I want desperately to distract us both.

"It was Jake, you know." I offer before realizing I was thinking to myself and Ben would have no idea what I was talking about. "Your bike wheel, I mean."

"What?" Brows furrow I watch Ben as he tries to find the memory in the sea of a lifetime. "The broken one?"

"Yeah. You guys were in that fight and his dad had taken his bike, so he grabbed yours on his way to my house, there was a rock in the road and it bent your wheel. But you were still mad at him so I took the blame."

"Liv, I didn't talk to you for a week after that. Why would you take the blame for that?"

"Because he always had it hard enough with his dad."

We share stories of a young Jake as we drive. The Jake that convinced us to do terribly stupid things and then suddenly forget it had been his idea alone when we were caught. We keep the conversation light but are still unable to separate from the idea that we're talking about him like he's already gone.

Arriving at the hospital just before one in the morning, we find parking easily and race in through the front doors. I take four steps for every one of Ben's just so I can keep up with him. The woman at the check-in desk for the emergency room gives us directions to the surgical waiting room, with the name of the nurse to ask for any new information.

The surgical nurse brings us into a room where Jake lies, the beeping of the monitors the only indication he is, in fact, alive.

"They are prepping the OR so you only have a few minutes with him," she whispers as Ben moves closer to the bed. I can't bring myself to get closer, not yet.

"How long do you think he'll be in surgery?" I ask, switching into mom mode, the person who knows what questions to ask in a crisis. I'm trying to distract myself. If I focus on the fact that I've already lived this, I'll break.

"Could be as short as four hours, but I wouldn't plan on anything less than seven or eight. He suffered a spinal injury in addition to his collapsed lung, which was punctured by at least one of his broken ribs. His leg's in pretty rough shape, it was trapped for a long time. Once they get in there, they will see if repair is even possible. It will take a little less time if it turns out to be an amputation, not to mention the damage to his face. It's going to be a long day, and a long road before he's out of the woods. We're trying to get in touch with his next of kin, in the event that—"

"That's me." Ben offers before I have to try and make excuses for his parents. "I have the documents on my phone I can get you when he's in surgery."

A mangled Jake lies on the bed. His face is unrecognizable, coated in blood. His left eye socket appears to be broken, not quite lining up with his cheekbone. Wires and tubes connect him to a series of monitors. The beeping of the heart monitor catches my eye as it reads a hundred and twenty-six beats per minute, contradicting the motionless body in front of me.

"Ben?" The name is a painful wheeze.

"God, you look terrible. While you're in surgery, see if they can recreate my bone structure for you," Ben jokes, attempting to lighten the mood.

Too weak to laugh or even smile, Jake's eye opens, releasing a small stream of blood from a cut near the scar by his eye. Never a stranger to physical trauma—though this is far above what he's experienced before—I have to pray that his body can endure just a little more.

"I love you, man." Jake pushes out the words directed at Ben, who tries to shake them off. Tears continue to roll down Ben's cheek.

"Don't. You're going to be fine. They are going to fix you up so you are just as ugly as ever. And don't think this is going to get you any leniency in Ping-Pong."

"Will you tell, Liv ..." Jake starts.

"Tell her yourself."

Do I say goodbye? Do I tell him everything is going to be okay? Either one could be true but just as easily a lie. This is the moment I never got with Scott, and I don't know what to do with it.

"Liv." His eye lifts and I shatter, clumsily shuffling across the squeaky floor to him.

"Hey, you." His hand in mine, I try to slow my breathing. I can't cry when he needs me. Ben slides the stool from the computer under me so we are at eye level.

"I blamed you for wasting time, and here I wasted everything. We could have had the last two months. We could have had forever if I'd only—" He gasps for air, the crackling in his lungs audible to the room. "I shouldn't have gone looking when you were right there. I'm sorry, I ..."

"Stop. These last two months have reminded me why I loved you as a friend first and foremost. It showed me the incredible man you grew to be, and I wouldn't trade a minute of it for the world." His eye closes, and I'm not ready. "You're my best friend, Jake."

Jake's eye closes again and the crackling stills. The heart monitor continues to beep, so at least there's that.

"I love you, Liv. I've <u>always</u> loved you." His words fade along with him. No. He can't just be fine with leaving. I need him to fight.

"Jake, we're gonna have a baby."

"A baby?" He's confused. Hell, I'm confused.

"Yeah. You're gonna be a dad," my voice is an eager whisper, giving him something to fight for. He doesn't respond. "Jake, you're gonna be a dad." I'm desperate.

The transport team rushes in, ushering me and Ben against the wall, as they wheel Jake away without a word to those he's leaving.

We're brought to a waiting room with plastic-covered chairs without enough padding and seascape art that I want to rip off the walls and smash over my knee.

Ben sits down. He's sitting and doing nothing. Nothing. I, on the other hand, am being far more productive by carving a path into the carpet with my pacing.

"This is bullshit," I yell after hours of pacing. "Why hasn't anyone told us anything yet?" I shove the closest chair to me with my foot, barely shifting it.

"Calm down, Mighty Mouse. It's only been forty-five minutes." He pats the chair next to him. I narrow my eyes, before deciding against continuing my tirade. I collapse into the chair, and the gravity of the situation is somehow greater when I'm forced to sit with it.

"How are you staying so calm?" I ask, still huffing through my words.

"It's not my first rodeo." His dad. His mom. He sat and had to wait for them to die. I never had that moment with Scott. I've never had to sit and wait, coming to terms with the feeling of utter helplessness.

"You know whose fault this is right?" I ask like I'm trying to rally him to join me in a street fight. "Fuckin Heather."

If she never pulled the shit she did, Jake and I would have stayed friends and he wouldn't have dated her to get back at me. They wouldn't have history and he wouldn't have been driving to Vancouver in the first place. Once again, Heather pops up to ruin everything. Jake might die, and it's on her.

Ben laughs softly through his nose. "We both know this isn't Heather's fault. This isn't anyone's fault."

"Maybe it's your fault?" I'm not willing to let everyone off the hook. "You are the one person he trusts most in the world. You could have stopped him from going." It's out of line and unfair. I want to take the words back and beg for forgiveness.

"What about you, Liv?"

Me?

"How am I to blame?" But it's right there in front of us. Once again, I held the key to him staying, and I didn't use it. I let my inferiority complex get the best of me. I sent him off because I couldn't go on without knowing that he truly thought I was better than Heather. I was willing to lose him over having a conversation about my insecurities. He was on the road because of me, and he turned around because of me.

"Oh." It's a breath, not a fully formed word.

"Liv, this isn't your fault. It was an accident." He can make that argument as long as he wants. I can't unsee how my own issues have brought us to where we are.

What was the point of this all? How was any of this worth it if I just wind up with me being alone ... again? What was the point of seeing how our lives could've been different if we don't have the power to change them?

If I could just go back, I'd do better. I'd speak up, I'd fight. It wouldn't have to end like this. With Scott dead, with Jake probably dying, with me...alone.

"So do it right this time." Ben answers me. Except I didn't actually speak. How did he—?

"What?" I turn in my chair but Ben is gone. The sickly sterile smell of the hospital is gone. The room is gone.

TWENTY EIGHT

Locker doors slam in chorus bringing me abruptly into my new surroundings. School. How the hell? Did Ben do this? Was he behind it all the whole time? Where am I, time-wise? Where is Jake? And where is Ben?

"The girl's soccer practice has been moved to the gym today due to the ongoing geese incident." The loudspeaker crackles through the hallway. Oh. My God. I know exactly when I am. Is this another fake life though, or is this for real? This doesn't feel the same as before. I need to find Jake.

A bony shoulder slams into my own as I move towards the front door nearly knocking me to the ground. I don't need to look to know who is behind the assault, but I do. Heather.

"Oops. Didn't see you there." The sarcasm betrays her words.

"What is your problem?" The pettiness behind her every action is just as baffling now as they were the first time I lived through them.

"Not you for much longer." Eyes narrowed and her nose sucked in on both sides, she looks down at me before rolling her eyes, her head following the motion back and around.

"Hey Heather!" I call out for her. She whips back around poised for a fight. She's not going to get one though. If this is real, I'm not letting Heather ruin it for me. "I'm sorry about Aaron. You were right, I went after him to get to you, and it backfired." Her face softens before she realizes and covers it back with a glare. "And if he treated you in any way like he treated me that night at the beach. You don't deserve that. No one does. He's a fuckin tool."

This was not what she expected in the slightest, and she's obviously not sure what to do with what I just said. I don't wait for her to thaw from where she's frozen. I have somewhere to be.

The parking lot is emptying quickly, making it easy for me to spot Jake's Jeep. Jake and Ben stand near the front wheel, concern visible long before I can make out the words in their hushed voices. But he's here, alive and whole.

I don't know how to change the course of what's about to happen. I know what I did the first time I was here. It was the day Jake accused me of calling CPS. The day Heather told him I betrayed him. I said nothing. I let him believe the lie.

"Hey, what's wrong?" I move to complete the triangle, looking up into both of their faces, and attempting to read what they aren't saying.

"Liv, you should probably get a ride home with someone else," Ben suggests.

Turning to gesture to the now barren parking lot, I return his stare with one of my own.

"Oh? And who would you suggest?" I question, laughing.

"Maybe someone you're *not* willing to sell out like a fucking rat." Jake's words knock me back more than Heather's shoulder.

"I don't know what Heather told you. But it's not true." What if he doesn't believe me? What then?

"No?" Jake shouts, "You didn't go to Miss Grownski and tell her about my dad? Then who did?" He's trying to hold onto the anger, but I can see what I couldn't before. Tears are filling his eyes to the point that I don't think he can keep them at bay for much longer.

"I would kill your dad myself before I betrayed your trust Jake. My question is, how did Heather even know about your dad, or enough about the situation, to accuse me of saying something?"

"Heather said she overheard you in the counseling office yesterday."

"Heather says a lot of things. I don't know why you'd believe her, especially about something like this." He knows all the things Heather has done to me. He's the one that's had to piece me back together.

"They're taking me away." His eyes close as his breathing becomes slow and broken. A tear falls onto the ground between us.

"They're not taking you away. We'll figure it out, Jake." The options are already racing through my head; we can talk to Ben's mom, call Jake's grandparents ... I'll see if *my* parents will take him. I mean we're sixteen. Can't he get emancipated or something? I step closer and look up, already forgetting that Ben is still beside us. "Hey." I wipe the corner of his eye with my thumb before letting my hand cradle his cheek. "Hey."

I take his hands in mine, in the way I did the first night we spent together on the hammock when he needed me to anchor him, to be his safe place to land. My fingers stretch to intertwine through his.

Stretching up onto my tiptoes I pull his hand down. There's a silent question in his eyes. I answer by closing my own and pressing my lips to his. They're salty with tears and softer than I remember. My entire body is spinning and buzzing.

"What was that?" The question is dreamy and dazed.

"Jake Larson. I love you." The emotion moves into my throat and it's going to be him wiping my own tears in a second here.

"You what?"

"I love you. I've always loved you. I will love you for the rest of my life."

It's stronger than anything I've ever felt. Our eyes meet and *this* moment is the jumping-off point for the rest of our lives.

Epilogue

Hosting Thanksgiving is the furthest thing from relaxing. It's a week of cleaning and yelling at everyone in the house trying to get them to pitch in, followed by doing all the work yourself before shopping for more food than any family has any business consuming in a week let alone a single evening. But hey, as long as we sit around and say we're thankful, right?

"What time is everyone coming?" Jake asks with a kiss planted on my temple. He's asked the question no less than a dozen times, but I think he asks more as a conversation than because he truly doesn't remember.

"In twenty minutes. The kids should probably start getting ready."

"Noah, Scar, you heard her, let's turn off the games and get moving. Can we run a brush through your hair and put something on other than pajamas?" Jake clicks off the TV, a sure way to set off tempers. Not the way I would have approached it, but they haven't listened to me all week, so why would they start now?

"Dad! Why? It's just Uncle Ben and Caleb. They don't care if we wear P-jays."

"Well, I care, and Mom cares. So let's move, c'mon!" He claps behind them, attempting and failing to drown out their groans. By the sound of their protests, you'd think I was dressing them up in pinafores and suspenders like the holidays of mine and Jake's youth.

Doors close harder than necessary down the hallway, and I know I could go lend a hand, but he doesn't need my help. Their outfits are already laid out and ready to slide into.

"Happy Thanksgiving!" Two voices call from the front door.

"Hey!" I holler, giving away my location. As if you don't go to someone's house on Thanksgiving and expect to find them slaving over a stove.

Ben finds me first, leaving a kiss in the same place Jake had just moments before. I turn into him, the scent of Grace's cooking hits me hard as he wraps his arm around me in a hug. I really hope he brought enough egg rolls so I can start pregaming dinner now. I'm starving.

"Happy Thanksgiving boys." Releasing Ben I pull Caleb in for a hug. I hold on a little tighter than normal, he doesn't know, but Ben is planning on popping the question after dinner and while he already feels like family, I'm bouncing at the idea of them making it official. Ben deserves all the happiness in the world and Caleb makes him happy.

"And because I love you." Ben teases an egg roll just out of reach above my head. Caleb pulls it out of Ben's hand and deposits it in my own. I give him the nod and smile that says "Thank you."

"I think you mean because your mom loves me." It was me, not Ben who was given the family egg roll recipe when Grace's diagnosis made her future uncertain. We spent the month after her surgery with her splayed out on the couch, coaching me through each meticulous step. It was in those days I connected with her woman to woman. She was no longer the neighborhood mom to me, she became my dearest friend and confidant. Since her recovery, she's made sure to send over batches often enough that I never have to ask.

"To-may-to, to-mah-to." Ben quips. "Where's Jake?"

"Getting the kids dressed." I motion with my head, permitting him to make his exit. I'm sure they still have a proposal planning to finish. I'm not allowed in on the details since it was determined that I would ruin the surprise.

Caleb and I stand in relative silence, watching as the cranberries pop and bubble.

"Did you see that TikTok I sent you?" He asks, already pulling out his phone.

"Not yet." I'm not even sure where my phone is.

He holds his phone out between us so we can both watch, his hand cupped around the speaker end to amplify the sound. "It's that guy I was telling you about. I think he's gonna make a run for president and I really like him. He's cute too."

The 'guy' in question is quite cute as he sits in front of a large bookcase. He's in a button-down shirt but doesn't look presumptuous. His sleeves are rolled up and he looks approachable. The name on the bottom of the screen says Scott Faucette and while I know I've never heard the name, looking at him gives me the feeling that I know him, which is impossible unless he's from Oregon. Before he starts talking I can hear his voice in my head. I've heard it in dreams, dreams long forgotten.

"It's time that the wealthy know that they are no more elite than you or I. They are not above the law. No more luxury prisons for those responsible for the death and suffering of mass amounts of people. If someone does something wrong, the punishment should be the same no matter who your parents are."

"This guy almost died when a senator's son or someone hit him on New Year's Eve. The other driver was high out of his mind, and it was brushed under the rug until he came out and made sure the whole incident went viral on TikTok." Caleb reminds me of the history.

"He seems like a good guy. One to watch, for sure." I agree with Caleb. I don't tell him how my heart aches at the thought that he was almost killed in such a horrific way. I also don't tell him that watching Scott is deja vu to a magnitude I can't explain.

"Who's a good guy?" Jake asks, followed closely by Noah, Scarlet, and Ben.

"Oh this Scott guy, he's a politician in DC, but seems like a real contender if he throws his hat in for president." I don't need to say this much, Jake has probably already tuned out.

There was a time when I had my sights set on DC. Hopes for my own seat in Congress. Maybe if life had turned out differently, this Scott Faucette and I might have run in similar circles.

Maybe in another life I might have known Scott and the bustle of D.C. but not this one.

Life has taken me down a sweet path. It's hard to dream as big as making it in D.C. when you have everything you need right next to you.

A husband who has seen me in every stage from an awkward kid to a confident woman. Best friends who are there when you ask, but also show up without even having to ask. A village to help raise the twins Jake and I weren't expecting. Noah and Scarlett are the sweetest reflection of Jake and I. The chance to parent them allows us to reparent ourselves. To give the love we desperately craved in our own childhood. Every day we fall, pick each other up, and learn from our mistakes to keep going.

Life is propelled by a million choices, that throw us in a million directions. But I don't think there is a single thing I would change about where *this* life has landed me.

About the Author

Savannah Gardiner, BBQ boss mama extraordinaire, juggles spatulas and stitches with equal finesse. When she's not slaying the grill at her and her husband's up-and-coming joint on the Oregon Coast, she's weaving tales and threads alike. With a sassy fusion of political savvy and culinary genius, Savannah earned her stripes at Utah Valley University before trading textbooks for tongs. Her short story "The Guest Book" turned heads, earning accolades from the formidable Kirkus. Married to her high school sweetheart and wrangling four mini-mes, Savannah's life is a delicious blend of smoke, spice, and storytelling.